THE OWL HOOT TRAIL

You're one of us now, kid!

The kid had no choice. Join the outlaws or swing—for crime he didn't commit.

Ride hard!

They were on the run, day and night. Every man's han against them.

Shoot first—shoot to kill!

The law of the Owl Hoot Trail. Outlaws don't get a secon chance . . .

THE OWL HOOT TRAIL

Bennett Foster

GUNSMOKE

First published by Robert Hale, Ltd.

This hardback edition 2002
by Chivers Press
by arrangement with
Golden West Literary Agency

ISBN 0 7540 8180 X

British Library Cataloguing in Publication Data available.

Printed and bound in Great Britain by
BOOKCRAFT, Midsomer Norton, Somerset

CONTENTS

CAST OF CHARACTERS

THAD BREATHEA was young—but he could be pushed just so far.

TEN HIGH CROATES always had an ace in his sleeve —and a derringer too.

DALE KRESPIN didn't take chances. He liked his murders legal.

CHARLIE FARREL had enough guts to change his mind —the hard way.

BRICK MAHONEY knew the trail would end at Boot Hill. But he liked the kid.

SILK GERALD thought he could play it both ways.

CURLY WINTER was a killer who tried to make a deal.

MORGAN VERMILLION guessed who the kid was. He was tough—but he was square.

CHILDRESS VERMILLION was good looking—and Thad thought she was too good for a kid on the run.

BEN PRINCE did little jobs for Krespin.

LULU BLACK ran a saloon. She could tell some strange stories if she wanted to.

THE OWL HOOT TRAIL

CHAPTER ONE

The Man Across the Aisle

AFTER the long wait in the depot at Denver, the rhythmic clicking of the wheels crossing rail joints was a reassuring sound. Thad Breathea, his broad young shoulders pushing back against the red plush of the chair car's seat, his booted feet resting on the red plush of the opposite seat, let himself relax a little, only now and then casting an apprehensive glance at the bulging telescope grip that rested in the brass rack overhead. One day's travel had somewhat inured Thad to this utterly new mode of transportation and now that daylight had come he tried to appear nonchalant and at ease. He was weary, tired with a fatigue that hard work had never given him. The constant tension of the hours of waiting in the depot at Denver, staying awake and guarding the telescope grip, afraid to venture from the station into the turmoil of the town, had worn him down; and now, despite his will to vigilance, his head drooped and his chin rested on his chest. In all his twenty years Thad Breathea had never ridden on a train, never been any further from the Valley Ranch than the little cow-town of Fort Blocker, and while he did not wish to sleep, the clack of the wheels and the rolling motion of the car were very soothing.

The trainboy, coming through the car, stopped and looked down at Thad. The trainboy had sold this drowsing youngster a sack of candy, a sack of peanuts, and a dry and tasteless ham sandwich, the ham shaved to paper thinness between unbuttered slices of bread. Momentarily the trainboy toyed with the idea of wakening Thad. Then, an amateur psychologist because of his trade, the trainboy shrugged and went on. Greenhorn! the trainboy thought scornfully. Never been on a train before. He went on to the seats at the end of the car where he kept his stock and, sitting down, began methodically to rearrange his baskets. Cinders poured into the car through an open window, a whiff of smoke followed the cinders, and from the engine the long wail of the whistle announced an approaching station.

"Trinity!" the brakeman bawled at the door of the coach. "Trinity!"

The jolting of the stop awakened Thad. He sat up, looked above him to see that his grip was still in place, and rubbed his eyes with the big knuckles of his hand.

Outside the sun beat down from a blue and merciless sky, and on the platform beside the now motionless car, a voice drawled: "Don't come back, Ten High. You won't be welcome in Trinity."

There was no answering voice and Thad, looking out the window, could see the red brick of the station platform, a dray drawn up beside it, the horses hitched to the dray drowsing in the sun. A tall booted man, black hat pushed back on his head, stepped into Thad's range of vision and turned, exposing a star on the pocket of his open vest, and at the rear door of the day coach there was a small commotion and then the bump of a grip as it struck against the side of a seat. Thad, looking warily toward the aisle, saw a man in a checked suit come along the length of the car. There were hearty voices at the car door. Out on the platform someone wailed: "All a . . . booo . . . ard . . ." and with a jerk that snapped Thad's head against the plush, the train started.

Across the aisle from Thad the man in the checked suit was settling himself. With the ease of the accomplished traveler he swung his grip to the rack over the seat, sat down and removing the narrow-brimmed, brown derby that he wore, blew a cinder from its brim and placed the hat beside him. Thad, watching from the corner of his eyes, saw the new passenger stand again, pull off the modish checked coat and, folding it meticulously, place it over the back of the seat. With that done the newcomer rolled back his shirt cuffs, sat down once more and carefully pulling up each trouser leg a trifle, rested his feet on the seat opposite him. Thad envied the man his nonchalance. The rhythm of the wheels was coming in slower cadence and the engine snorted and cinders rattled on the car roof.

"Hot, ain't it?" said the man across the aisle.

Thad turned. The new passenger was looking at him, a grin on his small pointed face.

"Yeah," Thad agreed. "Mighty hot."

It was a relief to talk, a relief to say something. From Denver on, only the trainboy and the conductor had spoken to him. Thad twisted around a trifle in his seat.

The man in the checked suit waved a hand. There was a big signet ring on that hand, and a heavy fob-bedecked watch chain crossed the checked vest. "We go up quite a little here," the man said. "They've got a tunnel built up on top. You want to close your window when we get to the tunnel."

Turning, Thad reached toward his opened window.

"Not now," his fellow traveler counseled. "I'll tell you before we reach the tunnel."

Thad turned back.

"Travel much?" the man in the checked suit asked.

"Not much," Thad answered. "I don't travel a great deal."

"Where you headed?" The questioner stood up, swaying with the motion of the car.

"I'm going to Redondo," Thad answered.

The trainboy, coming along the aisle, surveyed the new passenger with shrewd eyes, passed between the occupants of the two seats and went on. No use of trying to sell that fellow anything, the trainboy thought. When he had passed, the man in the checked suit stepped across the aisle and settled himself comfortably beside Thad.

"Redondo," he said. "I don't know the town. I thought I knew every town along this line."

"It's not much of a place, I guess," Thad said apologetically. "It's close to Las Flores."

"I'm headed to Las Flores." The pointed face smiled and the small brown eyes studied Thad. "My name's Croates." The man in the checked suit held out his hand.

"I'm Thad Breathea." Thad took the extended hand and shook it. "I'm glad to meet you, Mr. Croates."

The conductor, coming along the aisle, paused beside the seat. Croates brought a ticket from his vest pocket, passed it to the trainman who took it, punched a slip and scrawled a cabalistic figure thereon. "Las Flores?" asked the conductor.

"That's right," Croates answered.

The conductor put the punched slip in a clip above the seat, eyed Croates narrowly, looked at Thad, seemed about to speak, and then, evidently thinking better of it, went on toward the head of the train.

"Cowboy, ain't you?" Croates said. "Where you from, Mr. Breathea?"

"I'm from Wyoming," Thad replied.

"That's a good country," Croates announced. "Not so hot up there as down here. You travelin' on business?"

"Kind of," Thad answered. "You see my father died up there and he left me a letter to deliver to a man down in Las Flores. We had a hard winter and the bank had to close us out after father died, and there wasn't anything to keep me there so I . . ."

Croates nodded. "You thought you'd see some new country," he suggested. "I don't blame you. Travel is broadenin', I always claim."

"That's what I think too," Thad agreed. "I never . . ." He broke off abruptly. He had been about to admit the inadequacy of his experience with that broadening influence.

"You'll do a lot of it," Croates prophesied. "That is, if you got money enough. It takes money to travel."

Thad grinned ruefully. "I had the price of a ticket to Redondo," he announced. "That was about all the bank left me."

Croates was still smiling. Now, at Thad's announcement, the smile remained but the interest in the brown eyes died away. "Well," said Mr. Croates, "if I can help you any let me know. I'm right across the aisle." He stood up, grinned briskly at Thad,

and went back to his seat. The train toiled on, up and up. Once
more Thad rested his head against the red plush.

Enough money to get to Redondo, he had said. That was
essentially true. There was a little more than that, but not a
great deal, and Judge Althen had warned Thad not to tell anyone that he was carrying money. In the pocket of Thad's coat
the envelope holding the one hundred and four dollars, and the
other envelope containing his letter, crinkled as he moved, and
Thad, after a glance across the aisle, put his hand on the envelopes to reassure himself that they were both there. Satisfied,
he lowered the hand. A brakeman, coming through the car,
paused beside his seat, scowled at him when he looked up, and
reaching over Thad, closed the window.

"Coming to the tunnel," the brakeman announced.

Thad sat erect. He had never seen a tunnel. There were many
things he had never seen. The beat of the engine was a muffled
roar; gray walls began to slide past. The gray was supplanted by
darkness and Thad put his hand on his envelopes again. They
were in the tunnel.

When daylight once more entered the car, Thad relaxed.
Across the aisle Croates was asleep. Mountains were on either
side, moving slowly by, and Thad let his head droop once more.
Weariness encompassed him but the brief exchange of words
with the man in the checked suit had stirred his mind, recalled
him from his anxiety and alertness and started his thoughts back
over the chain of events that had brought him so far. One by one
those events marched across his mind, his father's death from
pneumonia early in the spring, the request that that strange,
silent man had made of Thad; Judge Althen's office and the
talk that had gone on there, all the events, large and small, that
had pulled Thad Breathea from the lonely ranch in Blocker
Valley and brought him thus far along the way. Judge Althen
had not wanted Thad to make this trip alone, had protested
against it, but Thad had persisted.

"Gato!" the brakeman bawled. "Gato!"

Across the aisle Croates was putting on his coat. He smiled at Thad. "Stretch my legs," he announced. "You comin'?"

"No," Thad said. "I don't think I will."

There was a commotion at the rear door of the car. Passengers were getting on at Gato. Thad Breathea broke off his introspection and looked back at the door. Men were filing into the car, three of them. Behind the third man came Croates, a broad grin on his face. The train jerked as it started, causing the newcomers to stagger in their stride. Thad, watching, saw the new passengers sit down. Croates sat down with them.

The train moved again and Thad, having roused temporarily, gradually settled into his thoughts again. Ahead of him in the car, voices drawled indistinctly. Under him the wheels beat swift rhythm. The sun slipped westward, struck into the car hotly and Thad Breathea perspired and thought back over the years. And through the thoughts one thing struck home: he knew but little of himself, but little of his father. All he knew was the years he had spent in Blocker Valley, the ranch, the horses, the cattle, the work, the books that he had read, the stern face of his father, his father's voice setting tasks for him to do, the few men that came to the ranch, the little town of Fort Blocker. Those things he knew and now with strange and exciting new knowledge he was on his way to prospect into the past.

"You want some peanuts?" the trainboy said. "Nice fresh roasted peanuts?"

Thad Breathea looked up at the trainboy. "I don't want any," he answered. "And I don't want any candy and I don't want another sandwich."

"There ain't any use gettin' tough about it," the trainboy snapped. "I just asked you."

"I don't want any," Thad said again. The trainboy went on.

Thad's tongue touched his dry lips. He was conscious now of the heat, of the perspiration on his body and the thirst that burned his throat. Rising he went to the water cooler at the end of the car. There was no water in the cooler. Looking back toward the rear of the train Thad saw that the car was empty.

Croates and the other passengers had disappeared. With a glance at the telescope grip, Thad turned from the cooler, paused indecisively and then went on forward, across the two rocking platforms and into the smoker.

As in the day coach, the water cooler in the smoker was at the far end of the car. Thad, steadying himself with the seat backs, walked forward. Croates and the three men who had got on at Gato were playing cards, seated about the center of the car. As Thad passed, Croates looked up at him and grinned. Two other passengers were leaning on the seat backs looking over the card players' shoulders. Thad reached the end of the car, took the chained tin cup and filled it from the cooler.

He drank two cupfuls, let the cup dangle from the end of the chain and started back. As he reached the card players, hot voices rose and one of the onlookers stepped out into the aisle. Perforce Thad stopped.

"You can't get away with that!" One of the players had both his hands spread on the table and glared hotly at Croates. "There's not enough cards in this deck. I had that ace of diamands . . ."

"Now wait!" Croates interrupted smoothly. "You can count the cards if you want to." Thad felt something brush against his leg. There was a foreign substance in the leg of his boot. He glanced down. Croates' hand was resting on the seat arm, just beside Thad.

"You bet I'll count 'em!" The man with his hands on the table suddenly began to sweep the cards together. There was money on the table, Thad saw, a pile of it in front of Ten High Croates, smaller piles before the other players. "You're damned right I'll count 'em, an' if I'm right . . ." He broke off, glaring at Croates, the cards gathered in his hand.

"Count them then," Croates said. "I thought this was a friendly game to pass the time. If that's the way you feel about it though . . ." He made a little gesture with his hands. The man holding the cards wet one thick thumb and began to count.

"Forty-nine," he announced when he finished. "I knew you'd been holdin' out, you little skunk! Damn you . . ."

"Search him, Joe!" The onlooker who had stepped into the aisle made the suggestion. "See if he's got the holdout on him."

Croates' pointed face was pale. "Gentlemen . . ." he said.

"He won't have it on him," the man beside Joe spoke up. "He was holdin' out all right but he won't have his holdout on him. This fellow here was sittin' across the aisle from him when we come in. Mebbe he's got the holdout. Mebbe he's workin' with Ten High." The speaker was looking at Thad. All the others looked at Thad.

"How about it?" Joe snapped. "You workin' with Ten High?"

"I never saw this young man before," Croates announced, his voice reedy. "I never . . ."

"We'll search 'em both," said the man in the aisle. "Here, you . . ." He reached out a hand toward Thad Breathea.

Thad, remembering the envelopes in his coat pocket, recoiled from that reaching hand. Joe snarled: "He's got it," and came struggling up from behind the table, bumping against it, his hand reaching back toward his hip pocket.

"Stand still," the man in the aisle commanded.

"Keep your hands off me!" snapped Thad.

"The hell I will!" the man in the aisle growled, and took a step forward.

Thad Breathea was twenty years old. There were sloping muscles under his coat, rounded and firm, toughened by work, rawhide in their strength. Long smooth muscles they were, capable of explosive power. The reaching hands touched Thad's coat and those muscles leaped into action. Thad's hard right hand, clenched into a fist, moved up from his side in looping, devastating swiftness. The fist crashed against the jaw of the man in the aisle and that man sagged like a bundle of old clothes and dropped limp.

Joe, behind the table, held a gun in his hand. Thad saw that weapon and leaped toward it. Straight across the table he went, lengthening out, long lithe body stretched like the body of a mountain lion in motion. His right hand clamped on Joe's hand holding the gun. Joe's breath, heavy with liquor, struck Thad's face. Then, left hand pumping, Thad struck again and again and yet again. In his bearded face Joe's eyes glazed and went blank and Thad released his hold on the hand and weapon.

Croates had come out of the seat as Thad leaped in. Somehow he had cleared the tangle of bodies over the table and was in the aisle. As Thad straightened, preparing to strike again, ready to run when the chance offered, Croates' voice came shrilly.

"Now gentlemen. Now gentlemen. This is a peaceful game but if you . . ."

"He's got a derringer!" One of the others shrilled the words. "Look out! He's . . ."

Thad was clear now. He went over the man who lay in the aisle, tripping in his haste and regaining his feet by catching the seat backs. Blindly he fled toward the door of the smoker, reached it, jerked it open and gained the platform. Behind him, as the door swung shut, he could hear shouting voices. He did not pause. Crossing the platforms, stepping over the coupling, he pulled open the door of the day coach and went in. There, beside his seat, the brakeman stood, swaying in the aisle.

"You're gettin' off at the next station," the brakeman announced. "We're comin' in to Redondo. Say . . . what's the matter?"

"In the smoker," Thad panted. "There's trouble . . ."

The brakeman brushed by him, running toward the front of the car. Under Thad's feet the speed of the train began to lessen. The brakeman was gone, disappearing through the door. Thad reached up for his telescope grip, pulled it down and hurrying, carried the grip toward the rear door of the chair car. As he reached the door, the train slowed further and when he had gained the steps a yellow box car, resting on the ground, slipped past and the train halted. Thad, gripping the telescope, went down the steps. Further down the train the conductor, standing on the ground, lifted his hand and waved it. The engine barked explosively and the couplings clanked and the cars jerked. Still grasping the telescope Thad hurried around the end of the box-car station, stopped and looked indecisively to right and left. Behind him the train was in motion. Tentatively Thad looked toward the train. There were the moving red painted wooden cars. There was the conductor on the step, waving again to the engineer. From the engine came a sharp *boot . . . boot . . .* as the signal was answered. Just those things and nothing more. Thad put the telescope on the ground. On the track the last red car rolled past and Thad could see the iron railing that surrounded the rear platform. He wiped the sweat away with the back of his hand and watched the platform grow small. Then, as it disappeared, he reached up to make sure that the letters were in his coat pocket. His eyes grew blank and he brought out his hand—empty. The two envelopes were gone!

CHAPTER TWO

Lazy 5

WITH the discovery, Thad took two steps after the departed train and then stopped. There was no use in chasing the train, no use in doing anything. His letter and his money were gone and he could not get them back. He picked up the telescope grip and went around to the front of the box car. The sun was hot and there was no shade. The box-car station was deserted. It sat beside the tracks, the steel reaching away to north and south, mountains lying smokily to the west, plains stretching endlessly to the east. Thad called. He pounded on the door, he peered through the single dirty window. He heard nothing; saw nothing.

Presently, desperate in his predicament and yet helpless, he sat down on the telescope grip and stared at the mountains. There was no one at the Redondo siding, no soul except himself. And there was nothing he could do. He felt the strange presence in his bootleg and mechanically reached down into the boot top and brought out what he found. There were three cards in his hand: an ace of clubs, a king of diamonds, a king of spades. Thad looked at the cards, not heeding their significance, hardly noticing them. Listlessly, he opened his hand and the cards fluttered down.

He was still sitting on the grip, heedless of sun and heat, when the cart came. Thad heard the sound of hoofs on the ground, the rattle of wheels on stone, and getting up from the telescope grip he went to the end of the box car. There was a two-wheeled cart stopping behind the station, a single horse hitched into the shafts, a single occupant on the seat. Thad stared at the man on the seat and the man on the seat stared at Thad. Presently the silence between the two was broken.

"You're Thad Breathea?" said the man on the cart.

"I'm Thad Breathea," Thad answered. "Are you Mr. Krespin?"

The man on the cart nodded and dismounted slowly. "I got your letter," he said advancing. "I wrote for you to get off at Redondo. It's closer to the ranch than Las Flores. You might as well get in."

"I'll get my grip," Thad said.

When he returned, carrying the telescope bag, Krespin had climbed back to the seat. He gestured toward the rear of the cart and Thad lifted up the telescope and put it in the box. When he climbed to the seat, Krespin clucked to the horse and, staring straight ahead, turned the animal in a long curve and drove toward the east.

"So you're Carl Breathea's boy," he said, after the curve had straightened out and the horse was trotting steadily eastward.

"Carl Breathea was my father," Thad agreed.

"You wrote you had a letter for me from Carl," Krespin said.

Thad looked at the man beside him. Krespin was not a small man but rather medium in size; still he gave an impression of smallness. His face was pinched down narrowly and a narrow goatee decorated his chin. His shoulders slumped forward and his chest was hollow. The gray hair at Krespin's temples was thin and his hands were thin, and the veins stood out prominently across their backs.

"I had a letter but I lost it on the train," Thad answered. "Dad gave me a letter to you before he died, and made me promise I'd deliver it. I was going to do that."

"You lost it?" Krespin's voice was sharp.

"And my money," Thad answered. "There was some trouble on the train. I don't know whether the letter fell out of my pocket or if my pocket was picked."

Krespin made a little clucking sound with his tongue against his teeth. "You got any way of identifyin' yourself?" he demanded. "Any way so that I'll know you're Carl Breathea's boy?"

"I lost the letter," Thad said again. "It was all I had."

Again Krespin clicked his tongue against his teeth. "That's bad," he said, and then after a little pause, "It 'ud be mighty bad if it was anybody but me. You'd have trouble."

Thad made no comment. Krespin eyed the boy narrowly, looked at the road and spoke once more. "You see," Krespin said, "yore grandfather is dead. There's his estate to settle up. You've got a little money comin' from the estate."

"I didn't know," Thad said slowly.

"Yore father never told you nothin' about how things were down here?" Krespin asked. He was looking at Thad now, searching the boy's face.

"No," Thad said, "he didn't. It wasn't until just before he died that I knew where he'd come from."

Krespin said: "Umm," the sound whining through his nostrils.

"He gave me that letter he'd written and he told me to bring it to you," Thad said sturdily. "He said that his father lived close by Las Flores. He said that I was to come to you or to his father and that one of you would look after me. I didn't need looking after." There was pride in Thad's voice. "I could have got a job in Wyoming, but Dad asked me to come."

"So you wrote to me an' I wrote back," Krespin said. "An' now you're here."

"I'm here," Thad agreed. "I wish you'd tell me about my father, Mr. Krespin. And about my grandfather."

"You don't know a thing?" Krespin persisted, looking at Thad again. "Nothin'?"

"Not a thing." Thad shook his head. "Dad died of pneumonia. I think he wanted to tell me at the last, but he couldn't. He gave me the letter and I promised to bring it to you, and after that . . . " Thad's voice trailed away. His eyes were hard with the thing that he was remembering.

"Well," Krespin said, watching Thad's eyes, "your father and your grandfather had trouble. They had a quarrel. Your mother died and your father got into a fight and killed a man. Right after that he took you and left this place. I'd never heard of him till I got your letter."

Thad nodded wordlessly. Krespin flicked the loose lines against the rump of the trotting horse. "You see," Krespin said, "your grandfather, Jake Breathea, married again after your grandmother died. He married my mother. I've been with him ever since then. Up until he died."

"Then you're my uncle," Thad said.

"Step-uncle," Krespin corrected.

"And my grandfather's dead?"

"He died pretty near a year ago."

The horse trotted steadily. Krespin kept his eyes on the horse and on the road. "Yore grandfather," he said suddenly, "left the ranch to me. I'd been with him, you see, an' him an' your father had had this fallin' out. He left me the property." Krespin's eyes flicked from the road to Thad's face. Thad was not looking at his companion. Thad's face was blank of expression.

"Of course you got a little legacy," Krespin continued. "You got . . . two hundred dollars!" He got out the last words hurriedly.

"I wish you'd tell me about my father and mother," Thad said. "Is my mother buried here?"

"Yeah," Krespin answered. "In Las Flores. She . . . Whoa!"

The horse stopped. Krespin was reaching under the seat. He brought out a short-barreled Winchester carbine and his eyes were fixed toward the right of the road. "Coyote!" he snapped. "He . . . Here! You shoot! Do you see him?"

Thad too was staring toward the right. He saw the brownish-gray, doglike animal loping off toward a rise perhaps a hundred yards from the road. Automatically he held out his hand for the carbine.

"I see him," Thad answered.

Krespin put the gun in the boy's hand. Thad moved to leave the cart and Krespin spoke sharply. "Don't get down! Shoot from the cart!"

Thad stood up.

All his life Thad Breathea had handled weapons. The Winchester cuddled familiarly to his shoulder and his cheek pressed against the stock. The hammer clicked sharply as he cocked the weapon and then there came the flat, whiplike report. Under the running coyote the dust spurted, and the bullet whined as it ricocheted. The horse stood up in the shafts, rearing high and leaping ahead, almost upsetting Thad. Krespin brought the horse down.

"Missed!" he snapped. "Here, give me . . ."

The coyote was running now, really settling down to business. Thad's hand raced on the lever of the Winchester. Once more the gun's report sounded, sharp and authoritative, and the running coyote, caught in mid-leap, came down, a limp bundle of fur. Once more Krespin quieted the horse.

"I wasn't used to the gun," Thad said quietly, reseating himself. "I held too fine the first shot."

Krespin took the gun from his passenger, replacing it under the seat. Starting the horse he circled out from the road toward the coyote. When they reached the limp body he stopped the horse and giving Thad the lines, got down and lifted the coyote by the tail. "Hide's no good in the summer time," he remarked.

"You hit him in the shoulder anyway. That spoils a pelt. You want to shoot for the head."

Thad made no answer. He considered that he had done well to hit the coyote at all. The animal had been running, was a good hundred and twenty yards away, and Thad had been shooting from the shaky platform of the cart. Krespin dropped the dead coyote and climbed back into the cart. Taking the lines from Thad's hand, he drove back toward the road.

"You said my mother was buried in Las Flores," Thad reminded him after they had reached the road.

"Yeah," Krespin agreed. "She's buried there. I'll show you her grave. Likely you'll want to see it."

"I do," Thad said.

The cart rolled along, the silence broken only by the sound of wheels and the *clop* . . . *clop* . . . *clop* . . . of the horse's hoofs striking dust.

"I'll take you in an' get you that money tomorrow," Krespin said suddenly. "Two hundred dollars."

Still Thad said nothing. Krespin's voice was sharp when he spoke again. "Likely you thought you had a fortune comin'," he snapped. "Let me tell you, young fellow, you're lucky. Anybody but me would tell you to get the hell out of here. You haven't a thing to prove you're Carl Breathea's boy."

"It isn't the money," Thad said. "I was just thinking about my dad and my mother."

"Oh," Krespin grunted.

The bay horse kept a steady pace. Krespin, his eyes narrow, watched his passenger, dividing his attention between the boy and the road. The road broke sharply, turning a little north and diving sharply down. Lifting his eyes, Thad saw that they were going off a cap rock, dropping over a sheer escarpment, down and down. Beyond the cap rock lay a flat country broken by buttes and hazy with the distance and the sun. Never before had Thad Breathea seen a rimrock country such as this, and he drew in his breath with a sharp gasp.

"A big country," Krespin said, voicing Thad's thoughts. "Mighty big."

The road went on down, twisting and turning. The bay horse held back against the cart, pushing against gravity, following the road. Then the descent ceased and they were at the bottom of the hill. Krespin turned toward the south and presently the horse stopped at a fence. Thad, dismounting, opened a gate, closed it, and got back into the cart after Krespin had driven through. The cart rolled on.

"This is the Lazy 5," Krespin announced. "Here we are."

They were going up a canyon now, an indentation in the gigantic wall of the rim. Before them was a cluster of buildings: a house, sheds, corrals, a barn and a low lying bunkhouse. Krespin stopped the cart in the yard.

"Here we are," he said once more.

Thad watched while Krespin unhitched and unharnessed the horse and turned the animal loose, then the two walked toward the big dwelling house, Krespin talking as they moved.

"We're brandin'," he said. "I've got a crew out with the wagon. There's nobody at the ranch but the cook."

As though to corroborate that statement the door of the house opened and a Mexican, brown-skinned and gray-haired, came out on the porch. Thad and Krespin had reached the porch steps and the native spoke swiftly to Krespin, his Spanish sibilant and swift. Thad, with no word of that language, looked at the man blankly. Krespin answered and the native went back into the house.

"If it's all right with you," Krespin said, turning to Thad, "I'll put you in the bunkhouse. There's beds down there. I'll take you down now. You'll want to clean up before supper."

Thad nodded. He was preoccupied, staring about him, looking at the buildings, at the corrals and above all at the great rock wall that towered above the place, dwarfing it.

"Come on, then," Krespin said.

There was water in the bunkhouse, and soap and a towel. Thad used these and ran a comb through his stubborn brown hair. When he had completed his toilet, he left the bunkhouse just in time to see a man ride into the yard, dismount and turn his horse into the corral. The newcomer walked stiffly toward the bunkhouse. He paused when he saw Thad in the doorway and then came on. He was a slight-bodied man, narrow shouldered, hawk-faced. As he reached the bunkhouse he nodded to Thad, who stepped aside, said: "Howdy," and went on in.

Thad said: "Hello," and waited beside the bunkhouse door. Krespin came hurrying down from the big house. As he reached Thad he said: "That's my foreman, Prince," and he too went into the bunkhouse. Thad seated himself on a bench that stood against the bunkhouse wall. Voices floated out to him as he waited. Presently Prince and Krespin reappeared and introductions were made. Prince had a pleasant, drawling voice and his black eyes were alert and keen. He looked competent, well worn and useful. A cowman, Thad decided; a good hand on any man's ranch. Prince had that thing that Krespin lacked: the ability to put a man at ease, and as the three walked toward the big house together Thad felt a release from tension. He liked Ben Prince, felt a growing consideration for the man. But as they reached the house that consideration died. A cat followed by two small kittens came from the house and walked sedately toward them. She passed by, clearing the approaching men, but the kittens, little and clumsy, did not get out of the path. Prince, still drawling pleasantly to Thad, kicked a kitten from his way, not picking it up on the toe of his boot and lifting it away, but kicking viciously, sending the furry little figure flying. And Prince's voice did not break its even tenor.

In the kitchen of the house, supper was ready. Pedro moved from stove to table, setting out the meal, and both Prince and Krespin spoke to the man in Spanish. Thad could not tell what was said nor anything of the import of the conversation. He noted that Pedro eyed him curiously, but the boy thought nothing of that.

When the meal was finished Krespin spoke to Thad. "I've got to talk to Prince before he goes back to the wagon," he announced. "There's a lamp in the bunkhouse an' you'll find a bed there. I'll see you before you turn in."

So, summarily dismissed, Thad left the two men together in the kitchen, and made his way to the bunkhouse. Lighting the lamp he sat down beside it, and idly picked up a dog-eared book he found on the rough plank table. He did not read the book that lay on his knees, but rather stared at the wall, thinking, revolving in his mind the events of the day. He was sitting there, motionless, when Prince and Krespin came in. Prince was returning to the branding camp. He bade Thad good-by pleasantly, spoke briefly to Krespin concerning the work, and departed. Krespin sat down opposite Thad. Silence reigned between the two and about the ranch, broken only by the sound of Prince's horse trotting off into the darkness.

"I wish you would tell me some more about my father," Thad said, breaking the silence.

Krespin sat down in the doorway, hands drooping over his knees, eyes fixed on the outer blackness. "There ain't much to tell," he said. "Like I told you, your father an' your grandfather quarreled. They quarreled over your mother an' your dad pulled out of here. He had a little place close to Las Flores. Your mother died. It seemed like your father blamed that on your grandfather. Anyhow they never spoke to each other after that. I had all the work around here to do. Everything. Your father never helped. Then he got into trouble with the Parkeses. They had some difficulty over water an' there was a fight an' your father killed Tom Parkes. It was self-defense an' he was turned loose, but there was a lot of feelin' in the country an' finally Carl sold out his place an' took you an' left. We never heard from him."

"And that's the story?" Thad said, his voice choked.

"That's it," Krespin answered. "When your grandfather died he left me the ranch. I'd earned it. Tomorrow I'll take you in to Las Flores an' give you what money you got comin'."

Krespin got up abruptly. With no further word he walked off into the darkness. Thad Breathea sat in the bunkhouse beside the table that held the lamp. The lamp, its wick uneven, began to smoke. Automatically Thad reached out and lowered the wick.

CHAPTER THREE

Las Flores

DESPITE Thad's weariness, despite the long trip and the wakeful night spent in Denver, the boy had not slept much the night of his arrival at the Lazy 5. All night long he dozed fitfully, at each awakening his thoughts reverting to the story that Dale Krespin had told him. He believed the story. What else was there for him to believe? With the coming of daylight Thad dressed and joined Krespin in the kitchen of the big house, and they ate breakfast. Krespin talked but little during the meal but when they had finished, he made an announcement.

"We'll ride in to Las Flores this mornin'," Krespin said. "We can cut across an' save time. I've got some horses up."

That was so. Thad had been awakened by the horses coming in, and before he dressed he had looked out to see Krespin penning them. The two left the table together and walked down across the yard toward the corrals. Krespin opened the gate and went into the pen and Thad stood outside. There were two bridles on the fence and a rope hung from a post. Krespin took the rope.

"You can use that split-eared bridle," he called to Thad. "I'll get you your horse."

Thad took the bridle from the fence and watched while Krespin roped out a big bay from the milling horses. When the bay was roped Thad went in and put on the bridle. Krespin pulled his rope down over the headstall and reins and Thad led the bay out of the corral while Krespin caught his own horse and bridled it.

They tied the horses to the fence and went to the saddle shed together. Krespin pointed out a saddle that Thad could use, an old A-forked affair, so ancient that the leather was cracked and curled. Drawing out the old blanket on which the saddle rested, Thad used it to rub off the bay's back, then putting the blanket in place, he tossed up the saddle. The bay stood quietly enough, rolling one glassy eye at Thad as he pulled the latigo tight, and swelling a little when the cinch bit in.

Krespin finished saddling before Thad was done and leading his horse out from the fence, mounted and waited for Thad to finish. Completing his saddling, Thad also led his horse away from the fence, twisted out a stirrup and mounted. The bay humped his back when Thad hit the saddle but stood quiet and Krespin said: "Come on. Let's go."

Thad pulled the bay around. The brute was surly and unwilling. Thad knew that the horse was mad; he could tell by the way the animal stood, the way his ears laid, everything told that. Thad might not know men but he did know horses. Krespin was moving toward the end of the corral. As he reached it his horse shied and bucked a jump and Krespin yelled shrilly. With no warning whatever, Thad's horse broke in two.

The bay's head went down between his knees and his back arched and he bucked viciously, pitching in a circle, throwing his sides as he pitched. Caught off-balance and unprepared, Thad was loose in the saddle. Still he made a ride. The first few jumps jolted him clear to the crown of his head and seemingly parted his belly from his backbone. Then, regaining equilibrium and watching the horse, Thad began to outguess the bay, began to move as the horse moved, shifting weight and balance with the automatic instinct of the real bronc rider.

The bay was squealing now, head still between his legs, back arched high, feet pounding as he came down. Thad was riding him. The bay, apparently, knew it. He redoubled his efforts and then, as Thad still stuck, the horse reared. Thad was expecting him to go up and come down. He knew that the horse was a hard bucker but he did not think that the bay was crazy. There he misjudged his mount. The bay went up, front legs pawing, head up, rearing to his full height, and then threw himself on over toward the back, willing to kill himself if only he could be rid of the clinging man on his back.

Thad went up with the horse. He expected the bay to come on down and keep on bucking. Then he felt that added surge and knew that the horse was going over. Thad kicked free of the stirrups and threw himself to the left and as the bay crashed down on his back, legs threshing, Thad Breathea too struck the ground, falling on arm and shoulder and rolling free. Only a horseman could have done it and only a horseman with luck riding his shoulders, would have been in the clear as the bay threshed over to his side and lay, momentarily quiet.

For a moment Thad lay on the ground, then scrambled to his feet. Krespin, his face white, was off his own horse, running toward the bay and Thad. As the boy gained his feet Krespin reached him and stopped. The man was panting, his eyes wide and his lips parted showing his yellow teeth.

"Are you hurt?" Krespin demanded. "My God! I thought he'd kill you."

Still dazed, Thad could not answer for the moment. Krespin reached out a hand and grasped Thad's arm. "Are you hurt?" he asked again.

"I'm shook up some," Thad answered, regaining his breath. "For a broke horse that's . . ."

"He never did that before," Krespin rasped. "He never bucked when we broke him. I don't . . ." He wheeled from Thad toward the bay.

The horse was getting up. The bay got his forefeet under him and sat on his haunches like a big dog. Krespin took a step toward the animal. Thad, a little to one side, saw that the man's face was livid, his eyes black with fury. Krespin reached a hand under his coat, jerked out a gun and before Thad could intervene, the gun crashed and the bay dropped like a steer that has been poleaxed.

"That'll teach you, damn you!" Krespin shrilled.

He wheeled to Thad then, the gun still in his hand, the livid color still flooding his face. For a moment Thad was frightened at the madness that shone in the man's eyes. Then, his hand trembling and the color slowly draining from his face, Krespin restored the gun to its hidden holster and taking a step or two, reached the corral fence and leaned against it, trembling violently.

"I thought he'd got you when he threw himself back," Krespin said. "I thought he had."

Thad felt a little sick. He walked over to the bay and looked down at the horse. Krespin's shot had struck the animal behind the ear and there was a little stream of blood issuing from the hole. Mechanically Thad noted that there was a brand on the bay's neck: a Diamond Bar. The boy turned away from the horse and looked at Krespin.

"There wasn't any need to kill him," Thad said quietly.

"I'll not have a horse like that about the place!" Krespin rasped. "My Lord, man! Don't you know he almost got you?"

"I got clear," Thad said, and turning so that he would not look at Krespin, bent down and loosened the cinch on the bay. He felt the need for something to employ his hands.

Presently Krespin joined Thad. The cinch was loose now and the little ranchman pulled off the saddle while Thad eased the weight of the dead horse from the cinch. When the saddle was clear, Krespin put it against the fence, got the bridle from the bay and put it on the saddle, and then walked over to where his own horse stood some little distance away. He had no trouble catching the animal and when he had led the horse to the fence, he began to unsaddle.

"We'll drive the cart into town," Krespin announced. "I don't think I could ride in after that."

Thad made no answer. When Krespin had freed his horse, Thad picked up the old saddle and the split-eared bridle, put the blanket over his arm and followed Krespin to the saddle shed. Emerging from the shed he looked toward the house. Pedro was standing on the porch watching the men and the corrals. Idly Thad wondered how long Pedro had been there.

Krespin made short work of catching another horse and harnessing the animal. He hitched the horse to the cart, wrapped the lines around the whipstock and spoke briefly to Thad.

"I've got to go to the house a minute," he announced briefly, and strode away, leaving Thad beside the cart. When Krespin returned, he climbed to the seat of the cart and gestured for Thad to get in. Thad, coming over the wheel and settling himself, knew why Krespin had gone to the house: the odor of liquor was heavy on the man's breath. Krespin lifted the lines and the cart started. Thad looked down at the dead bay as they rolled past, but he said nothing.

The two rode out of the ranch yard and along the winding road that had been traversed the previous evening. Thad opened the outside gate, let the cart through and climbed back in. No word had been spoken. It was not until they had begun to climb the great hill that led to the top of the cap rock, that Krespin spoke.

"I wouldn't have had that happen for anything," he said. "Not anything."

"It was an accident," Thad agreed.

"That horse never bucked before," Krespin repeated. "I never knew him to buck."

"Well," Thad said, "he won't do it again."

"No, he won't, the devil!" Anger shown on Krespin's face. "I killed him . . . and good riddance!"

No more was said concerning the horse or the almost fatal accident. Thad wished to avoid the subject and apparently Krespin was satisfied. Silence fell between the two on the cart. Twice during the long ride Thad tried to break that silence, tried to get Krespin to talk about Carl Breathea. Krespin's answers were so short, so abrupt, that the boy finally lapsed into silence.

It was eleven o'clock by Carl Breathea's watch that Thad pulled from his pocket, when they reached Las Flores. Instead of driving to a livery barn, Dale Krespin turned the cart toward the plaza of the little town. There, in the square, he tied the horse to a hitchrail and looked up at Thad who had not as yet climbed down from the seat.

"I got to see a man," Krespin announced. "You wait here for me. I'll be right back."

"I want . . ." Thad began.

"Yeah," Krespin interrupted. "You wait for me an' I'll go with you. I'll drive you to the cemetery." He did not stop to see that Thad waited, but turned and went off across the street. Thad blinked at Krespin's back and then slowly climbed down from the cart seat and going to the hitchrail leaned against it, standing in the shade of a great cottonwood that grew from the little plot of ground in the center of the plaza. Krespin went into a brick building that bore on its glass windows the sign: "First State Bank," and Thad, pushing back his hat, relaxed against the hitchrail.

He wanted, he wanted desperately, to begin his search. Here he was in Las Flores and in this town there were men—there must be men—who had known his father. The trouble was that Thad did not know where to begin. All the way down from Wyoming he had been bewildered. He was still bewildered. Thad Breathea had read books, he knew horses and cattle and he knew a few men. He was a man in body and a child in experience. He would wait for Krespin, he decided. That was the thing to do.

Krespin came out of the bank and, not looking at Thad, went on down the street. Thad started from the hitchrail as Krespin appeared and then, as the ranchman walked on, relaxed once more against the rail. Krespin turned a corner and went out of sight. He would be back in a few minutes, Thad told himself. He could afford to wait a few minutes.

Leaning against the rail he watched the pattern of the little town. Las Flores was built around the plaza. There were adobe buildings, long, low, single-storied affairs, flanking the plaza on its four sides. Streets ran into the plaza on each corner so that their intersections made right angles. In the shade of the cottonwoods in the plaza a half dozen men loafed, men that moved slowly when they moved at all and were capable of long pauses when there was no motion whatever. In front of the buildings there were tin awnings shading the board sidewalks, and occasionally a man came from a doorway and passed along under the awnings, to enter another door. Horses drowsed at the hitch-racks that surrounded the grass plot, and flies buzzed, and from somewhere in the distance a woman's high pitched voice called indistinctly to a child. Thad Breathea spread his elbows on the rail behind him.

The pattern about the plaza began to break. A man, leading three horses and riding another, came from one of the streets to the south and rode slowly around the square. He stopped just beyond Krespin's cart, dismounted deliberately and holding all the horses, looked at Thad and then back toward the brick bank building. Thad eyed the horses critically. They were good, mighty good, he thought. There were yellow slickers rolled and tied behind the cantles of the saddles as though the owners of these horses were traveling, and in a saddle boot on one horse a carbine rested, its butt protruding.

From a store building close by the bank a man emerged and stopped to look into the store window, and another man coming up the street, stopped and joined him. A man walked into the bank, leaving the door open behind him, and down the square toward the south, two men appeared casually and stood, looking at the bank. The man holding the horses paid no attention to those on the sidewalk in front of the store but rather stared at the two further down the street. Thad, watching him incuriously, did not note the little stir in the plaza behind him, and the horse holder turned to Thad and spoke courteously.

"Brother," he said, his voice carrying a soft drawl, "I got to go get me some tobacco. Would you mind holdin' these horses a minute?" He tendered a handful of reins as he spoke and Thad, straightening from the hitchrail, accepted the leather.

"I'll be right back," the horse holder drawled, and stepping out from the shade, turned his horse and mounted in one easy, fluid motion. In the saddle he looked down at Thad and grinned, then turned his horse and trotted along the side of the square and turned a corner. Down the street two men sauntered casually along under the awnings, moving toward Thad. The men who had been looking in the store window had disappeared and a man came out of the saddle shop that stood beside the bank and looked to right and left and then went back into the shop. One of Thad's horses stamped impatiently and brushed at a fly on its belly with a foot, and a vagrant puff of wind stirred the cottonwoods so that all the leaves rustled.

The quiet was broken by an explosion within the brick bank building. The shot sounded, loud and yet with that curious ringing quality that confinement gives to sound. On the heels of that first explosion came two others, sharp and authoritative. From the saddle shop two men came scrambling out. A man burst from the door of the store on the bank's other side. Under the awnings the two loiterers were running and Thad caught a glint as sunlight struck metal when they crossed an open space. He was alert now, standing straight, looking to right and left. From the bank three men burst out, running across the dusty street toward him. One had red hair and a brick-red face. The running men caught the reins from Thad's surprised hand, snatched them away and whirled the horses. The man with the red hair and face shouted, "Let's go!" Then horses pounded in the plaza and Thad was hidden in a cloud of dust. Through that dust cloud something sang thinly and the plaza echoed to a burst of gunfire.

Thad came out of that cloud of dust. He broke from it, running, half blinded, unable to see. Guns were still roaring and something plucked sharply at Thad's leg and he felt a burning sensation and stumbled. As he came to his feet again his arm was grasped viciously and a voice, high and excited, yelled in his ear. "I've got you! Get your hands up!"

Thad whirled to meet that voice. Something smacked against his head, the world turned red and he reeled and went down. When he tried to get up again there were legs all about him. A boot shoved roughly into his chest sent him back to the ground and in that babble of voices, one rose, harsh and excited: "This is one of 'em. He held the horses!"

Another voice, deeper and slower, announced, "They shot Dan Oliver," and then hands grasped Thad and he was jerked to his feet.

There were angry faces all about him. Questions were shrilled. One high, angry voice kept yelling: "String him up! String him up!" Then a man pushed through the crowd, his smooth tanned face expressionless, reached Thad's side and put his hand on Thad's shoulder.

"This is one of 'em, Charlie," a man announced. "He held their horses. I got him before he could get away."

"I'll take him," the tanned man said, and the quietness of his voice stilled the cacophony of the others. "Come on, you." The hand on Thad's shoulder shoved him forward.

Thad pulled back. "There's a mistake," he begged, his voice so hoarse that he hardly recognized it. "I wasn't with them. A man asked me to hold the horses . . ." His expostulations were lost in a burst of derisive sound. Still he held back against the pushing hand.

"I'm Thad Breathea!" he shouted. "I wasn't with 'em. Find Dale Krespin! He knows me. I came in with him. I . . ." Thad stopped. The man holding him was facing those angry others, and in the center of those others, Dale Krespin stood.

"Is that right, Mr. Krespin?" the man holding Thad demanded. "Is that right? Did this fellow come to town with you?"

Dale Krespin took a step forward into the little cleared space before Thad and his captor. Krespin's face was a sallow white and his eyes would not meet Thad's.

"I never saw him before in my life," Krespin said flatly. "He didn't come to town with me. I never saw him before!"

CHAPTER FOUR

F.O.B. the Jail Door

MR. TEN HIGH CROATES was an opportunist as well as a tin-horn gambler. Confronted with a very ticklish situation in the smoking car of Number Nine, he had seized the opportunity that Thad Breathea's open boot top afforded him, and rid himself of the three cards he had filched from the deck. Further than that, when Thad went into action, so did Ten High. He had refrained from pulling his derringer before Thad leaped at Joe, due to the reputations of the card players. Joe Pierce was a very tough gentleman indeed and as for Walt Davis who had watched the game and who had occupied the aisle until Thad removed him, Mr. Ten High Croates shuddered every time he thought of Walt.

But Thad's frightened resistance had given Ten High an edge and he took it. He was still holding a gun on the bewildered card players when the brakeman came bursting through the rear door of the smoker. Ten High whispered: "Ditch it! The Con!" and scooping up his winnings with one hand, hid the derringer with the other.

The brakeman was wrathy. He used some curt and peculiar words from his trainman's vocabulary and because he was holding a brakeclub and was backed by authority, he was not corrected. When the train started after its brief pause at Redondo, the conductor came up to augment the brakeman and the card game was definitely postponed; not, however, without some promises on the part of Joe Pierce and Walt Davis.

Before leaving the smoker Ten High made a quick survey of his surroundings. Seeing a scrap of white protruding from beneath the seat of the smoker he stooped to retrieve it, thinking that he was picking up a card. In place of that he garnered two envelopes from the floor, stuck them into his pocket and went on back to the chair car, escorted by the fuming brakeman and stern conductor. When the train stopped at Las Flores, Ten High jauntily cocked his derby over an eyebrow, resumed his checked coat and, swinging his grip, left the car. His assurance was justified because Walt Davis and Joe Pierce were going to Albuquerque.

Las Flores was an old story to Mr. Croates. He had friends there and in great high spirits Ten High proceeded from the depot to the plaza, passed along one side of the square and on down the street.

Before a garishly painted frame building he paused, briefly inspected the street he had just traversed, and then went in the opened door. There was a bar opposite the door and to the left of the bar a cleared space surrounded by an ornately carved piano and a few tables placed close to the wall.

"Lulu here?" Croates asked the bartender.

The barman, surveying his visitor with eyes the color and complexion of a double-yolked egg, nodded briefly. "Out back," he said. "She ain't goin' to be glad to see you, Ten High."

Ten High grinned. "I'll take the chance," he announced, and passing the end of the bar went through a door and down a hall. Another door leading off the hall confronted him and he paused and knocked. From within a high-pitched voice demanded: "Who's there?" and then before Croates could answer, the door opened.

The woman who stood in the doorway was big. There was still a kind of blowsy prettiness about her face, but her body was flabby and swollen, and her eyes puffed with sleep.

"Oh," the big woman grunted, "it's you, is it?" She turned then and went back into the room, seating herself on the bed and brushing back disheveled hair with a plump white hand.

Ten High crossed to a chair, swept a tangle of clothing from it and sat down. "Hello, Lulu," he greeted affably. "How's things?"

"They're hell," Lulu answered succinctly. "We had a party

last night and I've got a head like a barrel. An' business is punk. I ain't hardly makin' a living."

"Well," Ten High said cheerfully, "I'll stay awhile anyhow, I guess. Want me to take my old room?"

"No," Lulu did not even lift her head. "I got Pearl in there. She's singin' for me now. You take the room at the end of the hall."

Grinning cheerfully, Ten High gathered up his grip and left the room. In the little cubbyhole at the end of the corridor he bestowed his grip on the bed, pulled off his coat and shirt, washed, and removing the grip from bed to floor, lay down on the bed and locked his hands behind his head. As he moved a crackling sound came from his coat. He sat up again, drew the coat to him and drew from its pocket the envelopes he had retrieved on the train. The first envelope he opened poured manna into Ten High's hand and he stared wide-eyed at his fortune.

"Well!" exclaimed Mr. Croates throatily. "Well, look at this now!"

Counting the money he found the sum to be one hundred and four dollars. The bills felt smooth and fine under his fingers and he counted them again, not doubting his accuracy but because he liked the feel. Then, having placed the money in a roll in his trousers pocket he thrust a finger under the flap of the other envelope and ripped it open. A folded piece of paper and a second envelope rewarded this effort and Mr. Croates fell to reading.

He finished the brief letter, ripped open the second envelope and perused its contents, stared awhile at the door and then getting to his feet, opened the door and yelled into the hall: "Hey! Lulu!"

Receiving no immediate answer, Ten High yelled again, continuing the clamor until presently Lulu issued from her room, bare feet padding on the floor. Her raucous voice bade Ten High shut up for the sake of Divinity, the while she made her wrathful progress down the hall. Ten High returned to his bed. When Lulu came in he was sitting on the bed, holding two pieces of paper, a pleased grin on his face.

"What the devil do you want, Ten High?" Lulu demanded angrily.

Ten High waved the papers. "Sit down," he ordered. "I've discovered a gold mine, Lulu."

"Huh?" said Lulu, and sat down beside Ten High.

"Do you know a man named Dale Krespin?" the gambler demanded.

"He never comes here," Lulu said. "He's a ranchman out east of town. Some of his boys come in sometimes."

"Do you know Jake Breathea?"

Lulu's profanity was heartfelt. "That old devil?" she completed. "Everybody knew him. He lived here four hundred years. He was sheriff when I came here. Was *I* glad when he died! Krespin was his step-son. Krespin inherited the Breathea place."

"Inherited it, huh?" Ten High grunted. "How much do you think it would be worth to Krespin to keep it?"

"What'll stop him from keepin' it?" Lulu demanded. "Krespin was Jake's only heir, wasn't he?"

Ten High shook his head. "Old Jake had a son," he said.

Lulu furrowed her brows in thought. "Yeah," she announced finally, "he did have a boy. They had some trouble. The boy got married an' Jake didn't want him to. I remember somethin' about it now. Carl was the boy's name. He married a girl out of a show company that played here. She died after they were married. Didn't Carl get into some sort of trouble?"

"I don't know about that," Ten High said, "but I know that I can find old Jake Breathea's grandson. Carl's dead."

"Well, what of it?" snapped Lulu.

Ten High flourished the letters. "I've got a letter here to Dale Krespin that was written by Carl Breathea," he announced. "Breathea said in the letter that it would be delivered by his son after Carl was dead. I've got it, so I guess Carl's dead all right. Breathea asked Krespin to look after the kid and give him a chance. There was another letter in with it that Carl wrote to old Jake. He said in it that he was sorry that he hadn't come back to see the old man and that this was his boy bringin' the letter. Now what do you think of that?"

"Where'd you get 'em?" Lulu asked practically.

"Never mind about that," Ten High retorted. "We can use these letters."

Lulu was skeptical. "How?" she demanded.

"Why, Krespin has inherited the Breathea ranch," Ten High said. "Natchully he'll want to keep it. It ought to be worth somethin' to him not to have to split it up with Carl's boy."

Once more Lulu grunted. "You tell me where you got them letters," she commanded.

"Well," Ten High explained, "I got 'em on the train." With that beginning he proceeded, completing the tale and looking questioningly at Lulu.

"He must have got off at Redondo," Lulu said, when Ten High had told his story. "You didn't see him at the depot here?"

"No."

"Then he did get off at Redondo. That means that Krespin or somebody from the ranch met him. Your scheme won't work, Ten High."

"Why not?"

Lulu looked witheringly at the little gambler. "Because by now," she grated, "your Thad Breathea boy is sittin' down with his step-uncle eatin' Lazy 5 beef, that's why not. You get up an' get your clothes on an' go out an' rustle some business. If you're goin' to stay here you got to earn your keep. An' don't go yellin' for me down the hall an' wakin' everybody up. Don't you think we got to sleep?"

With that parting shot Lulu majestically departed, leaving a crestfallen Ten High Croates sitting dejectedly on the bed. He was crestfallen for only a moment however. His gold mine had proved a gold brick, but he still had one hundred and four dollars profit.

Ten High played a little stud poker that night. He mentioned the attractions of Lulu's establishment to one or two strangers in Las Flores that he thought would be interested. He attracted the unwelcome attention of Charlie Farrel from the sheriff's office, and he re-established a former liaison with Lon Popples, the town marshal. In general, Ten High spent a useful and fairly profitable evening. About two o'clock he went to bed and he was still sleeping when, at noon, shots sounded in the plaza of Las Flores. It was not until late in the afternoon that Ten High issued forth once more.

When he reached the plaza men were still standing around in small groups, talking. Ten High, seeking out an acquaintance, asked the cause of the excitement.

"Bank was held up," the acquaintance answered. "Brick Mahoney an' two others got away. They caught the man that held the horses. He's in jail."

"Brick, huh?" Ten High queried. He knew Brick Mahoney, had seen him several times and had even played cards once with that redoubtable gentleman.

"Yeah," Ten High's friend drawled. "Funny about the one they caught. He claimed he wasn't with 'em. Said that he'd come to town with Dale Krespin. Krespin was in the crowd and he said that he'd never seen the fellow before. The guy's just a kid."

"Oh," said Ten High. "Good lookin' kid?"

"He's in the jail. You can go see."

"I'll just do that," Ten High agreed, and started toward the courthouse.

Ordinarily Ten High Croates, having occupied several jails, stayed as far away from them as he could. Now he wanted to get into one. The courthouse in Las Flores was off the plaza. Ten High pushed through the crowd which milled about the building, worming his way into the corridor. The corridor was filled and there was a good deal of talking. Ten High listened to the talk.

"He says that he come to town with Krespin," a man before Ten High stated. "He keeps insistin' on it. Krespin says that he never seen the kid before. I think the kid was with Brick all right. There's nothin' in it that would make Krespin lie about it."

Ten High squirmed back, stepped on some toes, was cursed, and finally cleared himself from the crowd. On the street he settled his hat at a jaunty angle, shrugged his shoulders into the disarranged checked coat, and strolled back to Lulu's. There, without ceremoney, he proceeded to waken that astute lady of business.

"So my idea's no good?" Ten High jeered when Lulu was fully awake. "So you don't think we can shake Krespin down, huh?"

"No," Lulu answered sturdily.

"Well listen to this," Ten High commanded. "Young Thad Breathea is in jail. He's there on a charge of bank robbery an' mebbe murder, an' he claims he came to town with Dale Krespin."

"Well?" Lulu questioned.

"Well," Ten High announced triumphantly, "Krespin says he never seen the kid before. Now mebbe you'll tell me that Dale Krespin don't want to get rid of that kid an' keep him out of sight."

Lulu, arising from her bed, padded to the door and opened it. "Hey," she yelled, "Buster! Bring two bottles of beer down here."

Thad Breathea spent a miserable afternoon. Hustled to jail, bumped, jostled, cursed, he was thrown into a cell. The smooth tanned Charlie Farrel had protected him as best he could but it was a thoroughly frightened youngster that got up from the floor after the cell door clanged shut, and crept over to the beddingless bunk and sat down. Bewildered, frightened, dumb from shock, even then he was not let alone. Charlie Farrel had already departed to organize a posse to follow the bank robbers, but there were plenty of lawmen left to question Thad, to slap him and knock him about and shout at him when he persisted in his story that he was Thad Breathea and that he had come to town with Dale Krespin and that a stranger had given him the horses to hold.

Dale Krespin was brought into the sheriff's office where the questioning took place. There, once more confronting Thad, he repeated that he had never set eyes on the boy before and knew nothing of him. The questioning went on and on and it was not until late in the evening when Farrel had returned from a fruitless chase, that Thad's torment ceased.

Farrel was not the sheriff—Gus Hoffman, fat and politic, held that sinecure—but Charlie Farrel ran the office. He walked in, looked at the men grouped around Thad, pushed through them and reached Thad's side.

"Come on, kid," Charlie Farrel commanded. "We'll get out of here an' they'll let you alone awhile." And with that he pulled Thad up out of the chair and escorted him out of the sheriff's office and back to the cell. When Thad was in the cell again, Farrel stood outside and looked through the bars.

"I'll get you somethin' to eat," Farrel announced, "an' when you've kind of got collected, we'll talk it over."

"I've told what I know," Thad answered desperately, sensing the kindness and the fairness in the man. "I came to town with Mr. Krespin. I . . ."

"If you're tellin' the truth you'll be all right," Farrel interrupted. "It don't look like you're tellin' it though. You think it over."

With that he walked away and Thad, for the first time that day, was left alone.

Thad ate a little of the food that Farrel sent in and drank part of the coffee. The turnkey took the tray out of the cell and peered through the dim light at Thad. "Farrel said that he'd be in the office if you wanted to talk to him," the turnkey announced, and walked off down the corridor, the dishes rattling. Thad sat on the bunk, his head in his hands. The head ached and thoughts were going around and around in endless procession. They were bitter thoughts and there was trouble in them. But uppermost in those thoughts was a question: Why had Dale Krespin lied? All Krespin had to do was tell the truth and Thad would be out of there. Desperately he cast about for a source that would prove his identity. There was none in Las Flores. He knew no one. One cheering idea came: He would send word back to Wyoming, back to plump little Judge Althen and Althen would come hurrying to his rescue. But aside from that, the whole thing was dark and gloomy. There were bad times ahead and Thad knew it.

The hours dragged by. The clock in the courthouse tower boomed eleven strokes. The jailer, coming down the corridor, peered curiously at Thad, and up in the bullpen a drunk began to cry, wailing lugubriously. It was almost more than Thad could bear.

The tower clock struck twelve . . . one . . . two . . . and then once more there were footsteps in the corridor and Thad looked up. The jailer, walking very stiffly, was coming toward the cell and behind the jailer was another man. The little procession paused outside the cell and a voice, utterly strange to Thad, said: "Unlock it, Jack."

The key rattled against the cell lock because the jailer's hand was shaking, and Thad saw a gun in the hand of the man behind the jailer, the weapon thrust into the jailer's fat and palsied back.

"Come on, kid," the man with the gun directed.

Thad got up from the bunk and took an uncertain step toward the door.

"Come on," the man with the gun urged. "We can't wait forever. Brick's outside."

Thad went through the cell door. As he started down the corridor he heard the sound of a blow and then the closing of the cell door. Footsteps thumped rapidly behind him and the stranger said: "I slapped him on the head an' threw him inside. I hope that bunk was lousy so he'll get 'em, the bastard!" A hand pushed against Thad's back and he hurried his step.

The drunk in the bullpen was still wailing as they passed. As they reached the courthouse corridor and started past the sheriff's office, the red-haired man with the brick-red face stepped through and closed the door softly.

"You have to hurt him, Brick?" Thad's conductor asked.

"Charlie Farrel?" the red-haired man scoffed. "No. Charlie's got sense. He put up his hands an' sat still. I tied him to his chair an' gagged him. You got the kid all right, Silk?"

"Sure," Thad's conductor grated.

Brick was pushing ahead along the corridor. Thad stopped short. "I . . ." he began.

"No time to argue, kid," Brick said cheerfully, catching Thad's arm. "You held our horses for us when that damned Lowell pulled out. We heard they'd got you an' we come back to get you out. Come on."

Once more Thad moved forward.

They passed through the big double doors of the courthouse and Brick whistled softly.

A man emerged from the shadows and said, "Right around here, Brick," and once more Thad was hustled along. In the darkness beside the courthouse a horse stamped and as they entered the gloom Thad could see four horses standing, their heads together. Brick took a horse. Silk took a horse. The man who had come from the shadows took a horse and said: "You have any trouble, Brick?"

"Not a bit, Curly," Brick answered and then, to Thad, "Grab those reins and come on, kid."

Thad took the trailing reins of the remaining horse.

The quartet moved stealthily away from the courthouse, Brick in the lead. He seemed to know the path for he twisted and turned corners and kept moving. Thad followed Brick and behind Thad came Silk and Curly. Presently Brick stopped.

"We can ride now." he said, and mounted. The others emulated him, Thad too climbing on his horse. The feel of the saddle under him was good. The stirrups were a little short but he settled his feet in them and gathered up the reins. Brick's horse was moving and Thad's horse joined the procession.

On they went, dark buildings on either side. Presently the

buildings thinned, became a scattered few, and Brick dropped back beside Thad.

"Now . . . " he began.

Behind them a bell began a mad clamor, booming out a tocsin of warning. A light flickered in a house, became steady and grew, sending a dull beam through a window. Brick began to laugh even as Silk cursed viciously.

"That damned Charlie Farrel," Brick chuckled, breaking his laughter. "I might of knowed he'd get loose. That's the firebell, boys, an' we're goin' to have 'em after us hot an' heavy. Let's do a piece of ridin'."

"Charlie Farrel!" Silk grated. "I told you, Brick. We should of killed him. He . . ."

"Oh hell!" Brick scoffed. "Come on, let's go!"

Hoofs ground against gravel. Thad felt his horse bunch under him, muscles gathering, then there came the full surge of power and, hoofs thundering, the four riders pounded away. And up ahead, clear in the night, ringing out even above the thunder of the ringing bell, came Brick's yell, high, clear, and taunting; wordless and yet expressing a world of meaning, flinging back a defiance at the law-abiding world.

CHAPTER FIVE

"He Asked For It"

AFTER that first wild yell the four settled into the business of covering country. Thad had made many a ride but never before one like this. The pace was punishing. Thad had no spurs but his horse kept up with the others. And still, with all their haste, with all their impetuosity, they were cautious. Brick broke their run when they came to rough ground, threading carefully through it, only to go on again at top speed when they were in smooth country once more. There was no conserving of the horses, no saving of the animals. Horses could not keep up this

pace indefinitely and Thad knew it. And yet there was an exhilaration about the flight, a rising of spirit, a swift pounding of
the heart so that the blood rang in Thad's ears and his cheeks
were warm with its flow.

The four rode west, making for the hills and the broken
country below the hills, and the stars told Thad their direction.

When morning broke, cold and gray behind them, they had
reached the foothills. The gray sky in the east was streaked with
pink and overhead the clouds clung, low and forbidding. Cedars
dotted the rock-strewn slopes they traversed and they wound
their way among them. And then they were going down a slope
and below them lay a rock shack, its roof broken in and a corral
close by. There were horses in the corral and Brick, reining in,
voiced his approval.

"Tony got here with the horses," Brick stated, and his horse,
moving once again, sent rocks rattling down the slope.

They changed horses in the corral and Thad gathered from
the talk that these fresh mounts had been moved here from a
previous hiding place. Brick expressed his satisfaction at finding
the animals waiting, but Silk growled: "He ought to have
moved 'em; we paid him enough," and went on with his saddle
changing.

Curly, the first to effect the change of saddles, hazed their
tired horses out of the corral and drove them down the little
canyon, disappearing from sight. When he returned his three
companions mounted and rode on. Neither Brick nor Silk spoke
to Curly concerning the disposition of the horses and Thad
gathered that all this was according to some prearranged plan
and that there was no need for orders or suggestions between
these three.

They went up now, moving more leisurely. The sun came
out briefly and then hid behind the clouds. They were out of
the foothills and in the mountains proper now and still they
climbed. Then Brick turned from the trackless canyon they
followed and entered a clump of trees, and Thad and the others,
following him, found that they were in a little rincon, the rocks

rising sheer around them. Brick had dismounted and he grinned up at Thad as the boy reined in.

"Light down, kid," Brick directed. "We'll stay here awhile."

Thad climbed down from his horse. He had no idea of how many miles they had covered. Silk was moodily moving off, leading his horse, and Curly was tying his mount to a tree.

"It's goin' to rain," Brick said with satisfaction. "That's what it's goin' to do."

"An' we'll get damned wet," Curly complained.

"We're going to stay here?" Thad demanded.

"Till night, kid," Brick answered cheerfully. He caught the question in Thad's eyes and went on to answer it.

"We haven't come far enough yet," he explained. "There'll be men out lookin' for us. If we move they stand a chance of seein' us but if we stay still . . ." Brick shrugged his broad shoulders. "It's a big country an' this is just one spot in it," he concluded.

That was Thad's first lesson. He stood still while he digested it. "They can trail us," he suggested.

Even the morose Silk who had come up to join them, grinned at that. "It 'ud take an Apache to trail us in the hills, kid," Silk said. "We rode east an' swung back. Where was you when we crossed the river? Wasn't you along?"

Thad remembered the stream they had splashed through, and kept silent. Here was another lesson.

"An' there's more than one way out of here an' either Curly or Silk or me will be watchin'," Brick completed the lesson. "Satisfied, kid?"

Thad had no answer.

Curly pulled a Winchester from his saddle boot and, carrying it cradled in his arm, went off among the trees. Silk was untying his slicker from the back of his saddle, and Brick, going to his own horse, also untied his slicker. "We didn't have time to get you a slicker, kid," he said. "We just picked the best horse we could find an' stole him for you."

Again Thad had nothing to say.

There was cold food in Silk's slicker. Thad ate some of it. Brick and Silk wolfed down the cold meat and the bread, and Silk took a portion of it out through the trees. He had gone to give the food to Curly, Thad knew. When Silk came back he stretched himself out beside his yellow oilskin. Brick sat with his back against the bole of a pine and eyed Thad.

"What was the trouble, kid?" he asked suddenly. "Why didn't you run?"

"I didn't know what was happening," Thad answered honestly.

Brick laughed. Silk sat up and stared at Thad. "How come you had the horses?" Silk asked.

"A man gave them to me to hold," Thad said. "I was standing by the hitchrail and he said he had to get some tobacco and asked me to hold them for a few minutes."

"Hoyt Lowell, damn him!" Silk growled. "He got cold feet an' pulled out on us. Somebody told them bastards at the bank, an' they were watchin' for us."

"But the kid held the horses an' we're all here," Brick said. "What's your name, kid?"

"Thad Breathea," Thad answered.

"Yo're in good company," Brick laughed. "I'm Brick Mahoney an' that's Silk Gerald, an' Curly Winter's watchin' the back trail."

"Why did you come back for me?" Thad asked.

"Ask Brick," Silk answered. There was something in his voice, some strange timbre that Thad could not explain.

Brick scowled at Silk. "We got connections in town," he said briefly. "We heard that the man who held our horses was in jail an' we come back an' got you out. That's all there is to it." He was still scowling at Silk.

Silk turned over so that his back was toward Brick and Thad. Presently the frown left Brick's face and he turned again to Thad. "The fellow that told us about you said that there was some kind of a jackpot," he announced. "What happened, kid?"

Thad answered briefly. "I came to town with Dale Krespin. When they arrested me I said that Krespin knew me an' that he could tell them who I was. He said he'd never seen me before."

"After you'd come to town with him?" Incredulity shone in Brick's blue eyes.

Thad nodded.

"He must of had it in for you," Brick said after a moment's reflection. "Well, you're out of jail now."

"Are you fellows goin' to talk all day?" Silk snarled from where he lay. "Damn it! I want some sleep."

Brick scowled at Silk's back and then after a moment he turned to Thad. "Might as well take a nap," he suggested and, moving away from the tree, stretched out on the ground.

Thad likewise lengthened himself on the ground. He knew that he was too excited to sleep. There were too many thoughts milling in his head, too many problems to solve. Why had Dale Krespin lied back there in Las Flores? Why had these men come back and taken him out of jail? Why . . . ?

Rain, a fine drizzle in his face, wakened Thad. Brick was under a pine, his slicker gathered about him. Curly was under another pine, covered by a slicker. Thad moved into the shelter of a tree. Neither Brick nor Curly offered to share his oilskin. Silk, Thad surmised, was out watching the back trail. Thad shivered. The rain was cold and the wind was throwing it with force under the pine. He moved around so that his back was against the bole of the tree, the trunk sheltering him from the rain. Water dripped soggily from the pine needles.

It was mid-afternoon when Silk came in, covered by his slicker and carrying a Winchester. Thad was soaked through by this time. Brick and Curly had been sitting together. Once in a while they spoke, so low-voiced that Thad could not hear them. Silk walked over to where Brick and Curly sat, and squatted down beside them.

"No need of waitin' any longer," Silk announced. "It's rainin' all over the world. If they'd picked up the trail they'd have showed up by now. We might as well move."

"We might as well," Brick agreed. "Let's go. Come on, kid."

"Now wait a minute!" Curly's voice was high with suppressed excitement. "The kid ain't goin' to go no further with us."

Brick turned so that he faced Curly. "I say that he is," Brick said levelly.

"Curly's right, Brick," Silk added his word. "I was fool enough to go with you last night when we got the kid out. I ain't a fool today."

Brick turned and scowled at Curly. "The kid done us a favor," he said. "We'd of been butchered in the plaza if it hadn't been for the kid. I say . . ."

"We got him out of the *juzgado* an' we brought him along so far," Curly growled. "It was damned foolishness in the first place, but I stuck with you. The kid don't go any further. Here's where we split up, Brick. You can stick with the kid if you want to."

"All right then!" Brick was very angry. "I stick with the kid. To hell with you two!"

Thad got up from his pine tree and walked over to the others. He stood, looking down at Brick and Silk and Curly. They looked up at him. There was defiance on the faces of Curly and Silk.

"You don't need to look after me," Thad said. "I can get along."

"You see, Brick?" Curly said.

Brick was looking intently at Thad. His broad red face was blank and there was a gleam in his blue eyes. "These two guys would turn you loose, kid," he said. "They'd let you ride down an' get throwed in jail again."

"But all I did was hold your horses," Thad protested. "I didn't know what was going on. I . . ."

"Kid," Brick's voice was grave, "we're on the dodge now. There was a man shot back there in that bank." He stopped and looked steadily at Curly. Curly averted his eyes. "Mebbe," Brick continued, looking once more at Thad, "we done the wrong thing when we took you out of jail. I don't know. But all hell couldn't make Charlie Farrel an' them others believe that you wasn't with us now. Not after we come back an' got you out, they wouldn't believe it."

"I don't give a damn," Curly said petulantly. "I ain't goin' to drag a green kid around over these hills. I won't do that."

He got up and walked over to his horse. Untying the animal from its tree he led the horse out into the little opening. "You comin', Silk?" Curly demanded.

Silk looked at Brick. He looked at Thad. Brick said nothing. Neither did Silk. Suddenly decision was written on his face. He turned and strode over to his own horse.

"I ain't that kind of skunk," Brick announced gruffly as though answering a question. "Go on, then!"

Silk and Curly mounted. Without looking back they rode out through the trees. When they were gone Brick Mahoney turned to Thad. "An' that leaves you an' me," he announced grimly, "an' we might as well move on, kid. We can get out of the wet anyhow."

"You can go with them," Thad said simply.

Brick Mahoney's hand clamped down on Thad's shoulder. "You'll do, kid," Brick announced. "I knew you'd do when I seen you. I wouldn't trade you for a half dozen like them two."

Dropping his hand from Thad's shoulder, he walked across the clearing to where his horse was tied. Untying the animal he moved him out from the tree, twisted out a stirrup and went half into the saddle. Then he put his right foot to the ground again, freed his left foot and letting the reins hang, began to fumble at one of the saddle-pockets that rode behind his cantle.

"I blame' near forgot this," Brick said, opening the saddle-pocket.

Thad, who had untied his own horse, stopped and watched his companion. Brick was pulling something from the saddle-pocket, a long length of leather. Thad saw that it was a gun belt and that there was a holster on it. Brick reached into the saddlebag again and brought out a gun. Placing the weapon in the holster he came over to Thad and held out the gun and belt.

"You don't want to go runnin' around these hills naked, kid," Brick admonished. "I picked this up in Charlie Farrel's office. Thought that you might use it."

Thad took the belt and looked at it. The gun in the holster was a Bisley Colt and there were shells in the belt loop. Thad could tell from the shells that the Bisley was a 32-20.

"Put it on, kid," Brick ordered. "It ought to be a good gun. It belonged to Charlie."

Thad latched the gun belt about his middle. Brick had gone back to his horse and was getting on. Thad likewise mounted. With Mahoney leading, the two set off out of the rincon, not following the path that Silk and Curly had taken, but angling off toward the north. When they were through the trees, Brick dropped back beside Thad.

"We'll hit for Branch Long's place," he announced. "We can hole up there tonight an' mebbe tomorrow. Anyhow we'll be out of the rain."

Thad, wet and cold and miserable, did not answer Brick's statement. Any place where there was a fire and hot food would suit Thad.

They rode on north, holding about even with the hills, dividing the distance between the mountains and the valley through which the railroad crawled. As the day waned Thad became colder, more miserable, more weary. His face, normally a ruddy tan, changed until its color approximated that of blue cornmeal. Brick, glancing at his companion, was alarmed.

"Cold, kid?" he asked. "Want my slicker?"

"There's no need of both of us getting wet," Thad answered dully. "I'm warm enough now anyhow."

It was true. The coldness which had engulfed him, had changed. Now, tempering the cold, burning flashes shot through the boy's body. Brick reached out and touched Thad's hand. It was hot as fire.

"Just a little further," Brick encouraged. "Stick it out, kid."

Thad made no reply. He held his saddle horn with both hands and looked straight ahead. Brick Mahoney's red face wrinkled in an anxious frown as he sent his horse along.

At dusk, with Thad still in the saddle, Brick followed a canyon into the hills. He was more cheerful now. He had been worried for he knew that he had a sick boy on his hands. But Thad had toughed it out and they were close to their destination. The big canyon forked into three tines and Brick, choosing the left-hand fork, forded the little stream that came down the canyon and, picking a dim trail, went on west. Within a mile after leaving the forks of the canyon he stopped his horse and said cheerfully: "Here we are, kid."

Thad opened his eyes. In the dusk and the rain he could see very little. Brick was pulling at Thad's hands, unlocking them from their grip on the saddle horn. He freed the hands and helped Thad down from his horse. Thad was conscious of a light that danced and jumped, seemingly in big distances, and then a man carrying a lantern was beside Brick and talking to him.

Utterly weary, Thad did not hear what was said. He stood, legs spread wide, head sunk forward, swaying on his feet. Then he felt Brick's thick arm under his shoulders and his reluctant legs were moving and Brick was saying, "Come on, kid. Come on."

Thad felt that his legs were not a part of him but some detached mechanism that carried him without any volition of his own. He stumbled over a step and was in a firelit room and Brick was lowering him to a bunk. Thad wanted to lie down on the bunk but Brick wouldn't let him. He became very annoyed with Brick, who pulled at his sodden clothing and at his boots, and jerked him around. Then Brick said, "All right; lie down," and the warm comfort of blankets engulfed Thad.

Brick said: "Plumb played out," the words a confused murmur to the boy on the bunk; then Thad heard no more, for he slept.

When he wakened there was daylight. Rain beat steadily on

a roof and dripped down from the eaves. Thad, by turning his head a trifle, could see a window through which the dim light came and the rain dripping outside the window. At the end of the bunk upon which Thad lay, his clothes were piled. There was his suit, the suit that with much pride he had bought in Fort Blocker only five days ago. Was it only five days? It seemed much longer. His hat lay on the suit, and the gun and belt that Brick had given him dangled from the end post of the bunk. There was a fireplace across the room from the bunk, black pots and a smoke-stained spider decorating the fireplace, and Brick Mahoney, a cigarette in his hand, crouched beside the fireplace and looked steadily toward the opposite side. Following that steady gaze, only his eyes moving, Thad saw a man standing, leaning against the log wall. This man, too, was smoking and staring intently at Brick.

"An that's the size of it, Kettleman," Brick was saying. "The kid played out an' I had to get him in."

Kettleman spoke smoothly. "So you ditched yore pals an' stuck with a dogie kid. That's kind of like you, Mahoney: ditchin' yore pals."

"I never went back on a man in my life," Brick snapped. The firelight, reflecting from his face, made it redder than ever. "You know I never did, Kettleman. Silk an' Curly rode off an' left us. If anybody did any ditchin' it was them."

"Silk will be glad to hear that," Kettleman drawled.

"I'd as soon tell them as I would you," Brick stated.

There was a noise further back in the room and moving his head a little more Thad saw another man seated on a box beside a table. He was small, dark, and with a pinched face. The man rocked on the box and watched Brick and Kettleman intently.

"You just about got a water haul at the bank," Kettleman mused. "You lost yore grip, Mahoney."

"Somebody tipped 'em off at Las Flores," Brick said. "They acted like they expected us. An' if it hadn't been for the kid, Lowell would of left us afoot. He seen what was comin' an' run."

Thad stirred. Kettleman's eyes were little and bright as he looked at the bunk. It seemed to Thad that there was a fire behind Kettleman's eyes.

"Yore friend's awake now," Kettleman announced. "There's nothin' to keep you here, Mahoney."

"There's nothin' to make me go," Brick stated defiantly. "We're welcome here, ain't we, Branch?"

"Why, Brick . . ." The small man got up from the box. "You know . . ."

"Don't try to shove it off on Branch!" Kettleman snapped. "Branch has got nothin' to say about it."

"An' it's his place too." Brick looked bright-eyed at Kettleman.

"Just the same you won't stay." Kettleman was definite.

Thad moved on the bunk. All his muscles protested as he sat up; and his eyes burned and his arms ached as he pushed back the bedding.

"Lie down, kid!" Brick was on his feet, moving toward the bunk. "You played out last night. Lie down."

"Get yore clothes on, kid," Kettleman's voice was cold. "Yo're leavin'."

Brick whirled to face Kettleman. Thad sat still on the bunk, the bedding across his naked knees. "I thought this was Branch's place," Brick said evenly. "Mebbe I was mistaken, Kettleman. Mebbe you own it!"

There was a tension in the room that Thad could feel, a tightening almost to the breaking point. Kettleman was glaring intently at Brick, and Brick had moved back until he was almost against the wall.

"I hold this place down," Kettleman said. "You knew I held it down. Yo're tryin' to rub it into me, Mahoney."

"I didn't know you claimed Branch's place or I'd not of come here," Brick flung back. "You wasn't here last night when we come in. Now you come along an' tell me that yo're the big bull in this pasture. You don't look too big, Kettleman."

"I'm big enough to tell you to leave," Kettleman grated.

"Nobody," Brick's voice was even, "tells me what I've got to do. Nobody, Kettleman. I'll back that any way you want."

The tension broke. Kettleman moved like a released spring, so swift that to Thad's watching eyes the movement was a blur. Thad heard Branch Long's box go over, and jerked his head around at the sound. Long was under the table, his mouth open. His yell was lost in the crash of sound and Thad pulled his eyes back to Brick.

Brick stood beside the fireplace, leaning against its rocks. He held a gun in his hand and his left arm dangled limp. In front of the fireplace Kettleman lay, face down, one arm thrown out before him. Just at the tip of his hand was a gun. As Thad watched, Kettleman's fingers closed as though he would grip the weapon, and then relaxed.

Brick took a step forward and stood, looking down at Kettleman. His voice was strange: hoarse and tight and hard.

"By damn!" Brick Mahoney rasped. "He asked for it!"

CHAPTER SIX

A Man Down!

BRANCH LONG scrambled out from beneath the table. He walked to Kettleman's body, half turned it with his foot, and then let it slump back. Turning to Brick he favored the red-haired man with a long, slow look.

"He's dead," Long said.

"I didn't think he was playin' 'possum," Brick answered. "What about it, Branch? Where do you stand? What do you aim to do?"

Long shrugged. "Nothin'," he answered. "But there's this thing sure: yo're goin' to have to move now, Brick."

"I'd like to know why." Brick's eyes were very bright and dangerous and his left arm swung limply as he stepped toward

Long. "Kettleman got killed because he said I had to move, Branch."

Again Long shrugged. "You know as well as I do that Kettleman's got friends," he said. "There's been boys droppin' in every day or two. Kettleman was out with some of his outfit last night."

"So you didn't tell me he was here." Still there was danger in Brick's eyes.

"You didn't ask," Long replied. "You wouldn't of gone on anyhow."

"No," Brick agreed, "I wouldn't. But it might of saved some trouble if I'd known he was at yore place."

Long did not answer that. "He hit you," he said.

"In the arm," Brick agreed. "I got to get it fixed." For the first time he seemed to see Thad, sitting naked on the bunk. "Git on yore clothes, kid," he ordered. "You look like a jaybird sittin' there."

"Let's see the arm," Long commanded.

Thad dressed while Brick's arm was bared. Kettleman's bullet had cut through the biceps. The wound bled profusely. Long washed out the arm wound, Brick sitting beside the table and resting his arm on its top. When Long brought a bottle of turpentine and applied it, Brick winced.

"I think the bone's nicked," Long said, and poured on more turpentine.

"Kettleman an' me had been on the outs for a long time," Brick said musingly, not speaking either to Thad or Long but voicing what was in his mind. "Him an' me had trouble down in Texas. We was on different sides of a grass fight an' our side got beat an' I had to run. Every time I seen him he rubbed that in. He bullied his way around an' got himself a reputation. Now he's got himself killed."

"Hold yore arm still," Long said grimly. "Kettleman had friends, you know. They'll be after you now. I can't figger it. Kettleman was supposed to be fast. He ought to of downed you."

"But I downed him!" Brick snapped. "Don't pull that band-age so damned tight, Branch."

"Mebbe you'd ruther do it," Long said.

"You don't need to pull off the arm."

Long finished his bandaging. "That'll do," he stated. "Now what, Brick?"

"I want a clean shirt," Brick ordered.

Without a word Long got up and walked to a dilapidated bureau. He rummaged in a drawer and pulled out a shirt. "One of Kettleman's," he commented.

"He won't need it," Brick said casually.

Long had to button the shirt, for Brick could not use his left hand. When the shirt was on and Brick had stuffed the tails down into his trousers, Long made a sling for the injured arm and stepped back.

"Now what?" he asked.

Brick looked at Thad. "Can you travel, kid?" he asked. "We've got to put miles behind us."

"I can go," Thad said.

"Then we'll go, Branch," Brick announced. "But we ain't runnin'. Nobody's drivin' us out, get that?"

"Sure," Branch Long agreed placatingly. "Sure, Brick."

"Be damned sure," Brick said.

"What about Kettleman?" Long waved a hand toward the body.

"He's in your place," Brick answered. "You'll have to 'tend to him."

Branch Long's sallow face settled into a scowl. "I suppose so," he agreed. "You know, Brick, I'm goin' to have to explain all this. I ain't goin' to take the blame for it. I'll have to tell Kettleman's boys."

"You can tell the whole damned world," Brick snapped.

"Kettleman wasn't wanted around here," Long continued. "The law wasn't after him."

"That's because they didn't know what he was doing," Brick said. "I done the community a favor if they just knew it."

"Mebbe," Long's voice was dubious. "It'll be murder, just the same."

"I ain't goin' to stay to find out what they call it!" Brick laughed. "We need some grub, Branch. We need a little outfit, an' my pardner needs a slicker. An' he needs another horse. That one he's got was stole."

Long said nothing.

"Well?" Brick snarled.

"Oh sure, Brick," Long agreed. "Sure. I'll fix you up."

"An' we'll watch you while you do it," Brick announced. "Branch, I don't trust you as far as I can spit. I've paid you plenty. I was told that you were all right. I stopped with you once before an' I had to leave in a hurry. I know what you'll do, Branch. The only thing I got to say is, don't be in a hurry to do it!"

"You know I wouldn't split off on you, Brick." Long appeared to be injured. "You know how I stand with you fellows."

"I know that Kettleman was holdin' down your place an' you didn't tell me," Brick announced. "Let's get that grub an' the horses, an' start. I'm right with you, Branch."

Long did not speak again. He moved around the cabin, collecting those things Brick had demanded. Salt pork, some flour, baking powder, coffee, salt—these went into a gunnysack. The smoky skillet, a pot and a smoke-blackened, five-pound lard bucket, together with two tin cups, went into another gunnysack. From several slickers that hung behind the door, Long selected one and tossed it to Thad who caught it.

"That all you want?" he asked.

"Two blankets," Brick said.

Long got two blankets from the bunk. "What else?" he demanded.

"Horses," said Brick. "Come on, kid."

Thad helped Brick put on his slicker. The injured arm in its sling hampered Brick. It was evident that the arm pained him. Thad put on the slicker that Long had given him and the three men went out of the cabin. It seemed impossible to Thad that they could be so calloused, and yet, save for that first brief inspection that Long had made, neither man paid any attention to the body in the room. Thad looked back as he came to the door. Kettleman lay, still on his face, sprawled on the floor.

There were horses in the corral. From these Brick selected two, asking Long whether or not they had been ridden, and examining the mounts carefully. Thad saddled both animals. All the while the rain dripped down from the lead-colored sky. When the horses were saddled, rolls were made of the blankets and the provisions and cooking utensils, and tied behind the cantles.

"How much do I owe you, Branch?" Brick asked.

"Five hundred dollars," Long answered steadily.

Brick Mahoney laughed. "You'd ruther have me owe it to you than beat you out of it, wouldn't you?" he asked. "Git on yore pony, kid. Show Branch how they fork a horse in Wyoming. An' after you've got on, *watch him!*"

Thad had been astounded at the sum Long named. He was more surprised at Brick's words. Long said: "I'll remember this, Brick. Don't think I won't."

"When yo're rememberin', don't forget to think about Kettleman," Brick answered, his voice as deliberately warning as Long's had been. "You set, kid?" Brick was at his horse's head. "Don't forget to watch him."

Thad looked at Long. Long stood still there in the corral, the rain dripping from the brim of his hat and running down the skirts of his slicker.

"If he moves his hands you know what to do, kid," Brick said. "Whoa! you damned jughead. Whoa!"

Thad continued to watch Branch Long. Long continued to stand, motionless.

"All right, kid," Brick announced. "Start out. *I'm* watchin' you now, Branch. I owe you five hundred dollars. I'll pay you . . . some day."

They were outside the corral now. Brick had opened the gate before he mounted. The horses in the pen followed the two mounted men out. Long moved to intercept the horses and Brick called, 'Let 'em go, Branch!" Long stopped. Thad's horse splashed across a puddle, heading down the canyon; Thad knew that Brick was behind him for he could hear his companion's horse splashing. When they were two hundred yards from the corral, Thad looked back. Branch Long was running back and forth, trying to pen a horse that did not want to go into the corral. Long's slicker flapped and hampered him and, as Thad looked, the man stopped and jerked off the slicker.

"We stopped him awhile," Brick said with unction. "He's got to catch a horse before he can ride."

"What will he do?" Thad asked.

Brick's horse moved, coming abreast of Thad. "He'll catch a horse," Brick answered, "an' then he'll ride like hell an' get some of Kettleman's friends an' they'll hold a pow-wow. Then they'll get word to Charlie Farrel and he'll come out an' they'll talk some more; then they'll give us a chase."

"Do you think that . . ." Thad began.

"Kettleman!" Brick interrupted. "I knew I'd have to settle with Kettleman some day. Him an' me been at outs ever since I was a kid. He thought he had it on me, damn him!"

"What was he doing?" Thad asked curiously.

"Stealing horses. Mebbe rustlin' some cattle," Brick answered. "He was the he-coon in this neck of the woods, or thought he was. He had a reputation as a gunman. He was supposed to be bad. I guess I softened him up some! Mebbe when they get to talkin' about gunhands they'll mention Brick Mahoney now. You're damned right they will!"

Looking with disbelief at Brick, Thad could see his companion's excitement. The exhilaration, the drunkenness still clung to Brick. His eyes sparkled and his cheeks were flushed. Thad felt sick, sick at what he had seen and sick that Brick Mahoney could boast so.

"And what about us, Brick?" Thad asked. "What will we do?"

"Make a lot of tracks," Brick answered. "It ain't just Charlie

Farrel an' the law followin' us now, Kid. Kettleman's boys are goin' to be pretty sore too. Likely they'll look for us awhile."

"We could have got out," Thad said. "I wasn't sick. I could have traveled."

"An' let Kettleman say that he'd run me off?" Brick demanded. "Not by a damned sight! We'll work south, kid. I got friends around Franklin. We'll get down into that country. An' then by hell, we'll show 'em all!"

They rode on steadily, working out of the hills. Brick stayed with the canyon and Thad stayed with Brick. The canyon widened as they rode, the pines on its slopes giving way to cedar, and presently they were out of the cedar and on the plains. The rain rung like a gray curtain and the wind flicked and whipped the rain. At the mouth of the canyon Thad drew rein. Brick's horse went on a few steps and then stopped, and Brick looked back.

"What's the matter, kid?" he asked. "See somethin'?"

"No," Thad answered and then, deliberately, "I'm not going with you, Brick."

Brick brought his horse back. "You ain't goin' with me?" he asked, spacing the words.

"No." Thad shook his head. "I'm not, Brick."

"Why not?" Brick's voice was sharp.

Thad jerked his head toward the canyon. "I can't," he said. "I . . ."

"You're goin' to split with me, huh?" Brick's eyes were narrow and his lips were thin. "You think you'll just run out on me?"

"That isn't it," Thad answered hastily. "I know what you've done for me, Brick. I know that you got me out of jail and I know that you stuck with me last night. I know that you'd be with Silk and Curly now if it wasn't for me. But I can't go on, Brick. I . . ."

"Yellow!" Brick snapped. "You lost your guts because a skunk that needed it got killed. Yellow! That's what you are!"

"I'm not," Thad refuted hotly. "I'm not a killer either. I'm just not going with you."

"You'll go back to Las Flores an' give yourself up an' tell Charlie Farrel all about me an' where to find me, huh?" Brick snapped. "That's yore program, is it?"

"You know I won't do that," Thad said steadily. "You know . . ."

"I know yo're yellow as a sunflower," Brick interrupted scornfully. "Why you little . . ." His voice rose angrily. Minutely, with a depth and breadth of profanity that Thad had never suspected existed, Brick cursed the boy, detailing his ancestry, himself, and his lack of courage. Under the lash of that flailing tongue Thad flushed and then, slowly but steadily, the anger arose in him until he rasped out one word.

"Stop!"

Brick, eyes still bleak, glazed with anger, checked his tongue. "That's enough!" Thad grated. "You can't talk to me like that!"

"You little yellow-bellied pup," Brick snapped. "I can't talk to you, huh? Why you . . ."

Brick's slicker, because of his injured arm, was open. Thad tore at the snaps of his own oilskin, pulling them open. "Go ahead!" Thad yelled, everything forgotten in his anger. "Get yore gun out. Get it, damn you!"

His slicker was open now. Hampered by it he reached for the Bisley Colt. Brick, eyes slitted, had already thrust his hand under his own slicker. Thad's horse was fighting its head, shifting, slipping in the mud. Thad's hand touched the Bisley. Brick's weapon was already clear of its holster, in his hand, free. And then Brick stopped. "Quit it!" he snarled, and then, more slowly, "By God, it would be murder. I can't do it!"

Sudden as his anger, sanity returned to Thad. There sat Brick Mahoney on a motionless horse, a gun in his hand, his eyes wide with comprehension. On Brick's face was an odd play of emotion. Anger struggled with something else, and then the red face smoothed out and the wide eyes were normally round again.

Thad brought his own hand out from under his slicker, empty.
Very slowly Brick put away his gun.

"All right, kid," Brick said. "You ain't yellow. I take it all
back. I apologize. Is that enough, kid?"

"It's enough," Thad said hoarsely.

"Then go on." Brick's voice was flat and lifeless. "I was
crazy, I guess. Yo're right. You ought to split off. You ought to
leave me. Go on, kid."

He said no more, but reining his horse around rode toward
the south. Thad followed the man with his eyes, quieting his
own nervous horse, tempted to follow Brick, tempted to ride
after him.

Brick must have sensed that temptation. He looked back at
Thad and through the rain Thad could see that Brick was smiling. "So long, kid," Brick called, and suddenly his horse began
to lope.

The curtain of the rain hanging between them made vision
poor. Thad watched that loping horse and rider recede and
grow dim in the rain; and then suddenly he kicked his own
horse with spurless heels and bent forward in the saddle as the
startled beast began to run, for Brick Mahoney's horse was down
and Brick lay, a limp yellow bundle in his slicker, on the sodden
ground. The horse scrambled up and ran a little distance and
faced about to stand, reins hanging. But Brick Mahoney did not
move.

When Thad reached Brick and flung himself down he saw
that Brick's face was a mask of agony. He reached out his hands
to pull the man up, and then stopped. "It's my damned arm,
kid," Brick gasped. "I've broke it this time."

Thad, holding one rein of his bridle, kneeling beside Brick,
got his hands under the man and lifted him. "I'll get you in,
Brick," Thad promised. "I'll stick with you."

"Yo're a good kid," Brick Mahoney mumbled.

Thad raised Brick, supporting him until he managed to sit
alone. He caught Brick's horse and brought the animal back.

He helped Brick mount, first adjusting the sling until Brick, through clenched teeth, said that his arm was fine and that he could ride. Then Thad mounted his own horse and fell in beside Brick, eyes alert and watchful, ready instantly to help his companion. Together they rode toward the south, bordering along the foothills, neither knowing where they were going, both knowing that they must keep on. The rain clung to the earth and the clouds were low and time went by endlessly until dusk began to fall. Far ahead, through that falling dusk, Thad Breathea saw a pinpoint of light and headed toward it.

Brick was reeling in the saddle when they reached the light. Thad was leading Brick's horse. Brick could not talk. When Thad asked him how he was, he answered, "All right," the words so distorted that Thad could hardly understand them. The light came from a little rock house set against the flank of a hill, and as they reached the house Thad's horse tossed up his head and neighed a greeting. Thad dismounted stiffly. Here was shelter. Here was light. Here was a place where he could take Brick, where he could make Brick comfortable and warm. Even as Brick Mahoney had done for him, so now Thad did for Brick. What reception he would meet he did not know, but he was grimly certain that Brick should have the things he needed. He opened his mouth to call to the house and the words checked upon his lips. It was unnecessary; the door of the house opened and a man called: *"Quien es?"*

"I need help," Thad called. "Come out here."

"Quien es?" came the call again, and a squat-bodied man appeared in the doorway, silhouetted by the light.

"Come out and help me!" Thad commanded. "I need help."

The man came from the door into the rain. Cautiously he approached Thad and Brick and the horses. A woman stood in the light of the door now, and Thad could see a child's head peering from behind the woman. The squat man was at the horses, looking at Brick, staring at Thad.

"Que quiere?" he demanded. *"Quien es?"*

"You've got to help me get him down," Thad said desperately. "I've got to have help."

The squat man turned to the house and called, *"Tercita! Ven acá!"* and the child that had hidden behind the woman, a thin girl of perhaps twelve, came running out into the rain. The squat man spoke rapidly in Spanish and the child looked up at Thad.

"My father esays w'at do you want?" she asked slowly.

"I've got a hurt man here," Thad answered. "I've got to get him to shelter."

The girl interpreted the words and the swarthy face of the squat man lighted and he smiled. *"Seguro,"* he said. *"Seguro,* señor."

"Help me get him down," Thad commanded, and reached up for Brick. The squat man moved to Thad's side. It was he who detached Brick's clenched hand from the saddle horn and, with Thad helping, eased Brick to the ground. Brick could not stand and Thad, just as Brick had done, put his arm under Brick's shoulder and half carried him toward the house, the swarthy man aiding and the girl pattering along beside them.

They took Brick into the little room and Thad lowered him to a bed while the owner of the house stood by and while a fat woman, dressed in calico and with her braids flapping, scurried back and forth.

Thad straightened from placing Brick on the bed, and looked from the woman to the man and then to the little girl. The man was speaking to the child, his Spanish swift and sibilant. The girl nodded, turned and faced Thad, her hands clasped behind her, her eyes shy and yet looking squarely into Thad's own.

"My father . . ." the girl said, "ees esay you are welcome, señor. You an' your fran."

CHAPTER SEVEN

We Like Cigars

THERE were vines on the porch of the Lazy 5 headquarters and in the summer it was a cool place, if any spot below the Rim could be called cool. The country below the Rim, being a thousand feet lower than the mesa whereon Las Flores was built, was always hotter than the upper country and in July the lower country might well have served as a prelude to Hell. Dale Krespin sat with his feet cocked on the rail of his vine-covered porch and beside him Ben Prince, thin cigarette between his brown fingers, stared moodily out across the yard and let smoke trickle through his nostrils. Krespin's mouth was drawn down at the corners, and deep-creased wrinkles about his eyes and indenting his forehead bespoke the older man's anxiety.

"I'll have to pay him," Krespin said, his voice nearly a groan. "There's no way out of it."

Ben Prince had a pleasant voice. It had been melodious even in the chapel choir at Stillwater when Ben occupied a cell in that distinguished penitentiary. It was still melodious as he commented to his employer, but the words did not make music. "You tried to save two hundred dollars on the Breathea kid," Prince stated flatly. "Now Croates is bracin' you for a thousand, an' that's just the beginnin'. You'll pay him and pay him, an' then Breathea will turn up and make good his claim on the estate. You're a damned fool, Dale, and you're too chinchy to live!"

Krespin did not answer his foreman's statement, and Prince amplified further. "You played it smart with old Jake. I'll give you that. You worked on him till he tore up his old will where he split his estate. You whined around and tried to get him to make a new will leaving it all to you. Before he could do that he died. You done all right then too; you got yourself appointed administrator an' you were gettin' things nicely into your hands until this kid turned up; then you lost what sense you had.

"You tried to kill the kid by givin' him that Diamond Bar bay. The horse reared an' threw himself back all right, but the kid got free, so you killed the horse." Prince flicked ashes from his cigarette and drew upon it again. "Then," he continued, "you took the kid to town. All you had to do was give him two hundred dollars. He'd of signed a release that would have cleared any claim he had on the estate. But you couldn't do that. The kid got into a jackpot and you seen a chance to get by without payin' the two hundred. You thought you'd saved a dime. Now the kid's out of jail an' what have you got? A headache, if you ask me."

"How was I to know?" Krespin snapped. "He was arrested for helpin' Mahoney an' his boys."

"You ought," Prince interrupted, "to of got him out an' paid him the two hundred an' got that release signed. Then you'd of been clear. In place of that you said you'd never seen him before. Oh, but you're a ripe damned fool, Dale!"

Krespin stared moodily out across the yard. Prince took a last drag on his cigarette and threw it away.

"And old Jake left all this," Prince said, "an' no will. An' the kid stands a chance to get it all. He's blood kin an' you're not, Dale."

"He won't get it," Krespin snarled. "I spent my life buildin' up this place. It belongs to me. Breathea won't get it!"

Prince grinned in sardonic amusement. "You ain't forgettin' that I'm your pardner, are you, Dale?" he asked.

"I don't forget nothin'," Krespin answered with asperity. "But this Breathea boy . . ."

"Now," Prince interrupted again, his fingers busy as he rolled another cigarette, "young Breathea is on the run. The law's after him an' after him hard. He's with Brick Mahoney and Brick is a slippery fellow to catch. An' Brick's smart. But there's ways of getting to Brick that the law don't know about. And the only way that you an' me can be sure of Thad Breathea is to have him out of the way."

Krespin darted a quick glance at his foreman. "How do you mean?" he demanded.

"You ain't never been on the dodge, have you, Dale?" Prince said slowly. "I know you ain't. You been busy doing what old Jake told you, all your life. It's different with me. I never was a home guard. I've been around. I know some boys that know Brick Mahoney, an' they'd know where he'll go. I'll get to 'em and they'll rub out Brick, and Thad Breathea along with him. It'll cost us, but it won't cost us as much as havin' Breathea come back here an' claim his granddaddy's estate. You'll have to put up some money, Dale, but it'll be worth it."

Krespin's eyes studied Prince's face. Slowly he nodded. "All right," he said grudgingly, "all right, Ben. But I don't want to know nothin' about it."

Prince smiled sardonically. "Squeamish, huh?" he asked. "All right. You won't know nothin' about it. Now about that letter: Ten High Croates wrote you that he had some documents of value to you and that they'd cost you a thousand dollars. He isn't goin' to hand them over for any thousand. He wants a cut. Well, he'll get it."

"You mean I've got to divide with him?" he demanded. "Do you mean I've got to hand over more money to him?"

"Every dollar you spend makes fifty cents less for me," Prince drawled. "I don't like to lose money any more than you do. The way to pay Ten High Croates is to get him out of the way!"

"You . . ." Krespin began.

"Me!" Prince snapped. "I won't leave the job to any bungler. I'll do it myself."

"But . . ." Krespin expostulated.

"There ain't any 'but's' about it," Prince said smoothly. "I'll do it and you can bet on it that nobody'll know. You an' me will be in the clear. Now here's what we'll do. There's a dance every Saturday night at Tony Lazolli's place in Las Flores. On Saturday you'll go into town an' you'll see Ten High, but you won't have the money. You'll tell him that you won't give him the money until that night an' that you'll meet him at Tony's dance an' hand it over an' take the documents. It'll be that letter that Thad Breathea lost. I don't know how Ten High got it, but he's got it. You won't go to Lazolli's. You'll hunt up somebody an' stay with 'em. You'll have an alibi. Ten High will go to Tony's an' when the dance breaks up he'll be dead."

"You . . ." Krespin began again.

"I'll stake out a horse every few miles between here an' Las Flores," Prince said. "I can make the thirty miles in just about an hour an' a half. I'll be with the boys at the branding camp. I'll tell them that I've got to come to the ranch. I'll ride out from camp an' I'll be gone long enough to go to the house an' back to camp, and in that time I'll go to Las Flores an' see Mr. Croates an' be back again. That's what I'll do. And if anybody asks any questions the boys at the camp will know where I was all the time."

Once more Prince threw away a burned cigarette. He looked at Krespin. "And if you try to go back on me, Dale," he said softly, "I'll slip a knife into yore belly an' let yore guts drag down around yore knees. You sabe?"

Dale Krespin shivered.

Prince got up. "Today's Monday," he said. "I'll ride up on top this afternoon. I want to make some connections. You get yourself ready to part with about a thousand dollars, Dale. It'll cost you that to get Brick Mahoney an' Thad Breathea killed. I'm goin' up an' locate a few boys I know. I'll be back day after tomorrow, I reckon, and the brandin' crew will just have to do without me. So long, Dale."

Ben Prince got up and left the porch. Dale Krespin watched his foreman's slim figure as Prince walked across the yard and turned the corner of the house to go to the corral. He was still looking at the corner when Prince reappeared astride his horse. Prince lifted a hand and rode on toward the north, and once more Dale Krespin shivered. As Prince was lost to view, the ranchman got up and went into the house.

For a long time he sat at Jake Breathea's old battered desk. Then the little ranchman grunted and half turned in the chair. "Do the dirty work," he growled, facing in the direction that Prince had taken. "Go ahead an' do it. But if you think I'm goin' to give you half of this . . ." Krespin stopped. An expression utterly evil, utterly malevolent, crossed his face. "You ain't the only one that can kill a man, Prince," he completed. "You ain't the only one!"

Ben Prince, leaving the Lazy 5, rode north until he reached the road that climbed the Rim. He followed that road leisurely but when the road turned south toward Las Flores, Prince went on toward the west. He crossed the Flores river at a little-used ford and, pursuing his way, came by dusk to the edge of the hills. There at a sheep camp he stopped and partook of boiled mutton and chili and then, because the day was long and darkness had not yet fully come, he rode on into the hills. He stopped that night beneath a pine tree, his saddle blanket for a mattress and his coat for a blanket, and he slept peacefully the while his hobbled horse grazed close by. In the morning Prince's breakfast was a cigarette and the morning breeze, and having so sustained himself, he caught his horse and saddled and rode on. By ten o'clock he was in the little rincon where Silk Gerald and Curly Winters had parted from Thad and Brick Mahoney. Skirting the rincon, Ben Prince rode out toward the west and continued on into the hills. Seemingly he knew the path.

At noon he stopped his horse above a valley in the mountains and then rode on down toward the smoke that arose in a lazy spiral from a house set close to the edge of the timber that bordered the valley. Reaching the house Prince dismounted and, letting his horse stand, walked as one sure of his welcome, toward the cabin door. He had almost reached the door when a man, bearded and unkempt, appeared and stood in the opening, surveying him hostilely.

Ben Prince stopped. "Hello, Arch," he greeted.

The unkempt man, so addressed, grunted surlily, and Prince resumed his walk. "Are Silk and Curly around?" he asked.

"Who are they?" Arch demanded. "I don't know nobody by that name, Prince."

Ben Prince laughed. "Arch," he commented, "if I told what I know about you, they'd hang you. Have you seen Silk or Curly?"

Arch did not answer. Silk Gerald came around the corner of the cabin, his hands hanging loose at his sides. He stopped, looked at the visitor and then spoke a greeting. "Hello, Ben."

"Hello, Silk," Prince answered. "I see you got here all right."

"I got here," Silk agreed. "Did you want to see me, Ben?"

"You and Curly," Prince agreed.

"Curly's comin'," Silk said.

Curly Winters came strolling from the timber, a rifle over his arm. He nodded to Prince as he came up, and rested the butt of the Winchester on the ground.

"Hello, Curly," Prince greeted.

"Hello," Curly answered.

"You look better than you did the last time I saw you," Prince spoke critically. "Seems like this climate agrees with you better than the climate at Stillwater."

Curly grinned. "It's a lot healthier," he agreed.

"Is Brick around?" Prince asked.

Curly and Silk looked at each other. Curly began to frown.

"I see he isn't," Prince said smoothly. "You boys an' Brick split up?"

"The damned fool pulled out on us," Curly said brusquely. "Brick's losin' his grip. He went off with some ring-tailed kid that we taken out of the Las Flores jail. Silk an' me are through with Brick."

Deliberately Prince sat down, cross-legged, on the ground. "Now listen, boys," he said, "you know me an' you know I've been right with you. I want to put you in line to make some money."

Curly likewise sat down. Silk stood, with his legs wide spread. "We're listenin'," Silk announced.

"There's a thousand dollars in it for the men that kill Brick

Mahoney an' the kid that's with him," Ben Prince said deliberately. "A thousand dollars, cash on the barrel head."

"On account of that Kettleman thing?" Silk asked, his eyes narrow.

Ben Prince had not heard of Kettleman's death but he concealed his surprise and nodded. "On account of that," he agreed. "Now I can't say any more, but if somebody would come ridin' in to the old Breathea ranch an' found me sittin' on the porch an' was to say, 'Brick Mahoney's dead an' so is that kid that was with him,' an' then could prove what they'd said, I'd say, 'Walk right in the office boys an' help yourself to the cigars.' And when they opened the box they'd find money in place of cigars in it."

"Kettleman," Curly murmured, "was a pretty fair friend of mine. I rode with Kettleman once."

"I've got no friends," Silk Gerald announced. "I don't ride with nobody. Arch has about got dinner ready, Ben. You'll eat with us?"

"Thanks," said Ben Prince, getting up. "I'll do that. I'm pretty gaunt."

The surly Arch had set dinner on the table. Ben Prince sitting down with the three men, talked easily of Las Flores, of the country below, of what was going on at Gato, Trinity and Albuquerque. After the meal, while Arch washed the dishes, Prince seated himself on a stool outside the cabin and smoked a cigarette. To him there came Curly and Silk.

"You ridin' back this evenin', Ben?" Curly questioned.

"Right away," Ben Prince answered.

"Me an' Silk like cigars," Curly announced. "Likely we'll drop in before long an' cadge a smoke off you."

"You do that," Ben Prince said serenely. "You're always welcome, Curly. I guess I'll pull along now. I've got a ways to go."

He walked out to his horse and, mounting, looked back toward the cabin. Silk and Curly stood beside the door and Arch was looking through it.

"So long, boys," Ben Prince called. "I'll see you."

"So long," came the answering chorus.

Ben Prince rode off toward the east.

When Prince had disappeared, Curly rolled a cigarette. "So we're goin' to snuff out Brick an' the kid an' collect some money," he drawled. "Wonder why Ben wants 'em killed. He never was a friend to Kettleman."

Silk continued to stare moodily at the spot where Prince had dropped from sight. "It ain't Brick he wants," Silk said. "He kept draggin' in the kid. It's the kid he's really after."

"An' we're goin' to do it?" Curly insisted.

"We said we would, didn't we?"

"A thousand dollars," Curly mused. "I could use a thousand dollars, but where would Ben Prince get that much?"

"He's workin' for a man that's got it," Silk suggested. "You know, Curly . . ."

"Yeah?"

"There might be more than a thousand in it. Ben wanted that kid out of the way mighty bad."

"So . . . ?" Curly took a long drag on his cigarette.

"So," Silk said, "we'll scout around a little before we do much. Brick will head back to Franklin anyhow, an' hole up there. It will take him a while to do that, an' we'll have to go to Franklin to find him. We might spend a little time findin' out a few things before we move."

Curly laughed. "You want to see Pearl anyhow," he accused. "Yo're stuck on her."

"What if I am?" Silk snapped. "Sure I want to see Pearl. An' I'll get her to pry around a little for us too. She's stayin' at Lulu Black's an' Lulu is a wise old bird."

Saturday was a gala day in Las Flores. On Saturday the ranchmen and sheepmen, the small farmers, came to town and tied their horses around the plaza and did their shopping. On Saturday they met acquaintances and the plaza of Las Flores was filled with rapid Spanish and the slower drawl of English. On Saturday afternoon Ten High Croates, pushing through Lulu's door, interrupted her slumber.

"He's bit!" Ten High announced jubilantly. "I seen him. He's bit!"

Lulu, sitting up and rubbing the sleep from her eyes, scowled at the dapper little man and then, as the import of his words came home to her, the scowl was erased.

"You got the money?" she demanded.

Ten High shook his head. "Not yet. I get it tonight," he answered. "He's goin' to meet me tonight in Lazolli's place, at the dance. He'll give me the money an' I give him them letters an' . . ."

"Don't be a damned fool," Lulu scoffed. "He'll give you the money an' you'll give him *one* of the letters. He'll have to give us more than any thousand dollars before he gets both of 'em. You give me them letters, Ten High. I'll keep 'em. I know how to get the money out of this."

Ten High, surveying Lulu's firm jaw, nodded his head slowly. "All right," he agreed. "Which letter will we give him, Lulu?"

"The one that Carl Breathea wrote to him," Lulu chuckled. "It's his, ain't it?"

Ten High's little eyes surveyed Lulu thoughtfully. "You know," Ten High said, "there ain't any need to give him either letter. We'll keep them both, Lulu. An' he can pay us for keepin' our mouths shut. That's what he can do!"

Propped up on one elbow on the bed, Lulu scowled. "You get the money an' don't forget my cut," she ordered. "Don't you forget that."

"Sure," Ten High agreed, and jauntily departed.

Two doors down the hall from Lulu's room he stopped, looked back to see that he was not observed and then tapped softly with his finger tips and opened the door. A henna-haired girl, make-up heightening the color of her face, turned in a chair and half arose as Ten High entered.

"What did you come in for?" she demanded, her voice a sharp whisper. "If Lulu saw you come in here . . ."

"She didn't see me, Pearl," Ten High interrupted, his voice

also lowered to a whisper. "Anyhow, after tonight we won't care a damn about Lulu. He's goin' to come across, Pearl."

"You mean that Krespin . . . ?"

"Yeah, I mean that Krespin's goin' to pay me for keepin' still about what I know." Ten High chuckled. "He don't want old Jake's grandson showin' up an' spoilin' his game. You get packed, Pearl. I'll get the money from Krespin tonight an' then we'll pull out for the south. How about it, honey? You an' me ought to do right well together down around El Paso or Silver City."

Pearl moved toward the man, her body sinuous. Placing her hands on Ten High's shoulders, the girl reached up and kissed him. "Won't Lulu froth at the mouth!" she giggled. "She'll be crazy mad."

Ten High thrust out his puny chest. "To hell with Lulu," he whispered. "You get packed. I'll meet you an' we'll pull out."

"You'd better go now," Pearl whispered, "Lulu might come in. Wait till I look out an' see if the hall's empty." She moved to the door and, opening it, peered out.

"All clear," Pearl whispered. With a grin, Ten High slipped through the doorway.

At ten o'clock Saturday night, Charlie Farrel sat in the sheriff's office in the Las Flores courthouse and sucked upon a long dead pipe as he considered the toes of his boot which were propped up on the sheriff's desk. Las Flores on a Saturday night was full of life and energy, and while Lon Popples, the town marshal, and his deputies as a rule handled whatever matters arose within the town, still Farrel stayed awake on Saturday nights. It might just be that Popples would need some help or—and this had happened before—things occurred that were within the jurisdiction of the sheriff's office.

Steps sounded in the courthouse corridor and Farrel removed his feet from the desk top. The door of the sheriff's office was open and through it a man walked into the light. "Hello, Charlie," the newcomer greeted.

"Why, hello, Mr. Krespin," Farrel answered. "Come in and sit down."

Dale Krespin advanced further into the office, chose a chair and seated himself. He brought two cigars from his pocket, passed one to Farrel and bit off the end of the other. Farrel struck a match and when the cigars were lighted, reseated himself. His eyes were narrow as he looked at Krespin.

"Anything on your mind, Mr. Krespin?" he asked.

Krespin puffed smoke, and nodded. "We're brandin'," he said. "Our calves ain't tallyin' out. I'm wonderin' about it."

Farrel puffed out a gout of smoke. "I thought," he murmured, "that when Kettleman was killed this calf stealin' would stop. I thought Mahoney did us a favor when he downed Kettleman, an' him an' that kid got away. We couldn't pin it on Kettleman but we had our ideas of who was stealin' cattle."

"You ain't found out a thing about Mahoney an' that kid?" Krespin asked.

"We're still lookin'," Farrel answered. "We got a tip today that we're goin' to look into tomorrow mornin'. We . . ."

He broke off. Again there were footfalls in the corridor. A man was runing through the courthouse, coming to the sheriff's office. Both Krespin and Farrel got to their feet.

The running man arrived at the door, clutched the door jamb and panted out his message. "Popples wants you right away, Charlie. There was a killin' down at Tony Lazolli's place. Ten High Croates got shot."

"I'll be right down!" Charlie Farrel announced briskly. "You'll have to excuse me, Mr. Krespin. I'll talk to you later on. I've got business now."

CHAPTER EIGHT

Flight

THAT night Breathea and Brick Mahoney occupied a cave. They had been in the cave for a week and were accustomed to the dim light and the rock walls and the sturdy smell of goat that pervaded the place. Occasionally a bearded billy or a nanny with yellow, black-slotted eyes appeared in the opening of the cave and stared curiously at the interlopers. By looking out the doorway of the cavern, Thad could generally see a kid perched, all four feet bunched together, on a sharp pointed rock, playing King of the Castle with others of its kind. When evening came Alfredo Vara or Rufina Vara or little Tercita came to pen the goats, driving them down the hill. Then, after the goats were penned, there was a long twilight and presently footsteps rattled on the loose rock and Alfredo or Rufina came trudging up the slope, always with Tercita accompanying them, and there was hot goat stew seasoned with chili, or frijoles seasoned with chili, or tortillas, hot with chili, for the occupants of the cave to eat. There was water in the cave, and two blankets, and the two saddles lay on their sides against the wall. It was pleasant enough, except for the goats, and even the goats afforded some measure of amusement. And too it was dangerous and there was a constant tension.

Brick, his arm splinted and in a sling, fretted against the restraint. Thad worried, hiding his worry from Brick. Little Tercita enjoyed the strange visitors and exercised her English on Thad. Rufina, always with the fat baby, Tomaso, astride her hip, came occasionally to look to the well-being of her guests, and Alfredo, squat and swarthy and friendly, spent long minutes squatted against the wall, conversing in Spanish with Brick Mahoney. But always there was a restraint, a bridled fear hovering over the cave in the hillside above Alfredo Vara's rock-walled house.

For the first few days Brick, his arm set and splinted, had been feverish and had required constant attention. Then, although the fever lingered, he was much better. Now the fever was gone and, in place of anxiety over Brick, another anxiety held Thad's mind. At first he had carried water for Brick to drink and to bathe Brick's face. He had learned to roll cigarettes for Brick, and he had performed a hundred small tasks for the red-haired man.

With money that Brick furnished, Alfredo had gone to town and there made sundry purchases: shirts, underwear, socks and Levi Strauss overalls, and tobacco. These had been brought to the cave. Rufina, giggling at some comment from Brick, had taken the soiled clothing and washed it and brought it back neatly ironed. Even Thad's suit trousers had been washed and ironed, but they were shrunk so pitifully that Thad could not wear them. Alfredo had provided a razor and Thad had shaved Brick and himself. All these things had helped to kill time, had helped to make life bearable in the cave, while Brick's arm set and while trains, visible from the mouth of the cave, puffed their way along the valley, and while wagons on the road that bordered the tracks, crawled beetle-like along. But for the most part Thad and Brick talked, long, drawling conversations that helped to while away the time and that gave the two something of a perspective of each other.

From the drawling talk Thad Breathea had painted a mental picture of Brick Mahoney, outlaw. It was not a bad picture, albeit it conformed to no pattern of lawfulness. Brick had stolen, he had raided, he had taken what he wished, and he recounted those adventures lustfully. But, interspersed with the adventures, with the highlights and the minor boasting, Thad had seen another picture grow. The picture of a youngster that hadn't much, of a lonely half-starved kid in an arid wasteland where he struggled for an existence and watched others, more fortunate, gain the things that were denied him. Thad saw that boy growing up, learning that the strong took what they wanted and that the weak did not survive, learning that the law was on the side of strength, rebelling against that knowledge and finally stepping across the thin line that marks the lawless from the lawful.

And so the days had passed with Brick's arm knitting and the wound apparently healing clean. And now the day was Sunday and once again Brick and Thad sat close by the entrance to the cave and Brick was talking.

"I was about sixteen," Brick drawled. "I worked for old man Cotton. Cotton didn't have the money an' when the Cross V pushed him he couldn't hire the men he needed. An' so we got licked. A few of us stuck with him when the showdown come an' we done what we could, but we got beat. So we run. The law was after us because the Cross V had hired 'em. Well . . . That's the way it goes. I made a livin' stealing Cross V cattle then, an' after that I kind of branched out. I'd do it again, too. Roll me another pill, kid, will you?"

Thad rolled the cigarette, put it in Brick's mouth and lighted it, and Brick puffed contentedly. "An' if Cotton had won," Brick said suddenly, "I'd of stayed with him. I'd of had my own place by now an' Kettleman an' them would of been the ones to run."

Brick looked narrowly at Thad when he said that name and Thad turned his head away. Kettleman! Thad could still see Kettleman sprawling on the floor, his hand reaching out for the gun at the tips of his fingers.

"It could easy of been me, kid," Brick Mahoney said.

"You think we're all right here?" Thad asked abruptly, changing the subject.

"For now," Brick answered. "Alfredo will look after us. You don't need to worry about Alfredo, kid." Brick grinned. "You don't sabe a Mexican. There ain't no better people when they like you. Alfredo figures that we're his company an' there ain't nothin' he won't do for company. An' I've give Alfredo some money too. Alfredo's all right."

"We can't stay here forever," Thad said.

"No," Brick agreed. "My arm's goin' to be all right. We'll travel pretty soon."

"Where will we go?"

"I belong around Franklin," Brick answered. "I got some friends there an' that's where we'll head. I ain't been in this country long. Just long enough to look it over an' scout out that bank job. Silk's the one that knows this country. Him an' Curly. He took us around an' showed us a few things. Silk knew about Branch Long's place an' he knew about another hideout over the hill. I guess that's where him an' Curly went when they left us. Silk didn't say that Kettleman was at Long's, an' Branch didn't say nothin' about it either, when you an' me got there. I wouldn't have gone to Long's if I'd known Kettleman was holdin' it down."

Brick's voice trailed away. Thad moved to the door of the cavern.

"You know, kid," Brick said suddenly, "you was right about you an' me. We're goin' to have to split up. You go south with me an' after we're clear of here, you get you a ridin' job. You wasn't cut out for this business."

Thad made no answer. He squatted by the mouth of the cave, looking out at the goats.

"You can't stay here," Brick mused. "They've got you tabbed. You're with me an' that makes you an outlaw."

Thad spoke rebelliously. "Why? I didn't do anything but hold the horses and I didn't know what was happening then. If Krespin had told the truth they wouldn't even have put me in jail."

Brick shrugged. He knew Thad's story. Knew it all. Thad had told Brick the tale, beginning in Wyoming and ending at the hitchrail in the plaza of Las Flores. "It's not what might of happened, but what did happen," Brick said. "This fellow Krespin lied. I don't know why he done it, an' neither do you, but he did. Mebbe he wanted to stay out of trouble. Mebbe he wanted you out of the way; we don't know. But he said he'd never seen you. An' so they put you in jail because you held our horses. But it ain't just that any more, kid. You was with me at Long's. It'll be murder now. That's what they want us for."

"I could go in an' give myself up," Thad said stubbornly. "I could get Judge Althen to come down from Fort Blocker. He'd tell them who I was. That would clear me."

Brick shook his head. "You went to jail in Las Flores once," he said. "Did they listen to you then? No they didn't. They slapped you around an' . . ."

"But Farrel didn't slap me around," Thad interrupted. "He treated me all right. He . . ."

"An' we come back an' took you away from Farrel," Brick snapped. "Who'd believe you now, kid? Nobody. Not a soul. It ain't that I want you to go bad, kid. You know I don't want that. But I know how this law business works. Yo're guilty until you prove yourself innocent an' you'd have a hell of a time doin' that. They want somebody to show for the bank robbery an' for that business up at Long's. If you went in an' gave yourself up they'd railroad you. That's what they'd do. Your chance is to stick with me an' get out of the country; then if you want to get yore Wyomin' lawyer an' come back here, you can do it. That's the way to work it."

Thad made no answer. His face was set in stubborn, obstinate lines. Brick, watching his companion, puffed on his cigarette.

"Just the same I'm goin' to give myself up," Thad said suddenly. "Alfredo's coming up the hill, headed here."

Alfredo arrived at the entrance of the cave, out of breath from the climb. He sat down in the shade, panting, grinned at Thad and, his breath recovered, spoke to Brick.

Thad could not understand a word that was said, but watching Brick's face he saw that Alfredo's words brought alarm to his companion. Brick said, *"Mil gracias,* Alfredo," and turned to look at Thad.

"Alfredo thinks we're located," he announced. "His cousin was here yesterday an' saw our horses. Alfredo says his cousin

can't be trusted an' he says that a deputy sheriff asked him a lot
of questions when he was in town gettin' that stuff for us. It
looks like we'd better leave, kid."

"I'm not going," Thad said stubbornly. "I'm going to give
myself up."

"I can't stop you," Brick snapped, "but you can take it from
me, it's a fool idea. I'm goin' to get out of here, kid, an' I'm goin'
right now. Alfredo . . ." He turned and spoke to Vara again.
Alfredo grunted, nodded, said: *"Si . . . si . . . yo se . . ."* and
getting up, went down the hill toward the house.

"Look, kid," Brick said. "You'd better come with me."

Thad shook his head.

Brick sighed. "Well then," he said, "if ever you want to get
hold of me, if this fool idea of yores don't work out an' you're
lucky enough to get away, you go south to Franklin. You get
hold of Arch Heibert at the Palace Saloon in Franklin an' you
tell him who you are. He'll know where I am an' he'll put you in
touch with me. I wish you'd go with me, kid."

"No," Thad said, but there was indecision in his voice. "I'll
saddle for you, Brick. Here . . ." He bent down and picked up
Brick's saddle, hesitated an instant and then lifted his own
saddle in his other hand.

Brick, carrying the bridles and blankets in his good hand had
stepped to the mouth of the cave. Thad, carrying the saddles,
also stepped out from their shelter. Brick was staring away
toward the south.

"There's men on the road," Brick said. "Headed this way."
He started down the hill. Alfredo was coming from the canyon,
leading the two horses. Down behind Alfredo Vara's little rock
house Thad saddled Brick's horse and then his own. Alfredo
talked to Brick and the redhead answered in monosyllables,
watching Thad narrowly. Alfredo went to the corner of the
house, looked out, and drawing back his head, made an announcement to Brick.

"It's the sheriff," Brick said. "Alfredo knows him."

Thad held out his hand. "So long, Brick," he said. "You'll have time enough. I'll ride out to them."

Brick seized Thad's hand. "Yo're a good kid," Brick said. "Mebbe it's the right thing to do, but I don't think so. Good luck, Thad, an' don't forget what I told you."

"I won't," Thad promised. He grinned at Alfredo, mounted, and rode out from behind the house, heading toward the south.

Brick waited an instant and then climbed awkwardly into his own saddle. Fumbling in his pocket he produced a bill and thrust it into Alfredo's hand.

"Mil gracias, amigo," Brick said. *"Yo creo . . ."* He stopped abruptly.

Thad's voice came floating up to the two men behind the house.

"I give myself up," Thad Breathea called. "I . . ."

A shot, flat and harsh, punctuated the words, breaking them. Brick Mahoney pulled his horse around and, without looking at Alfredo, rode out from the shelter of the house.

To the south, down on the flat, he could see Thad Breathea sitting his horse, his hand lifted in the old, old sign of the plainsman and the Indian: the peace sign. Beyond Thad the horsemen, five of them, had fanned out until they made a semi-circle and were coming on, coming fast. As Brick watched one of those advancing riders drew rein and lifted his arm until it was level. Again the report of a gun came across the flat and then Thad Breathea whirled his horse and, the animal running full out, came back toward Brick. With a curse Brick kicked with his heels and his horse leaped ahead. In a sweeping curve —for Thad had changed direction—Brick rode to meet his partner, and beyond them the possemen, hampered momentarily by a deep-sided arroyo, checked their horses and milled as they sought a crossing. Brick's horse, running at top speed, swept in beside Thad's mount and Brick's voice was shrill as he called.

"Come on, kid!"

Thad, bent low in his saddle, shouted back inarticulately,

the shout as shrill as Brick's own. Side by side they pounded toward the east and the posse, having found a crossing, followed, shooting as they rode.

Thad and Brick gained in that first wild dash. Their pursuers, delayed by the arroyo, their horses already a little tired because of the long trip from Las Flores, were no match for the fresh mounts of the men they followed. Brick, his jaws clamped because of the pain in his arm, looked back from time to time and presently pulled his horse into a slower gait. With wonder in his eyes Thad also pulled down his horse from mad run to slower lope. He too looked back. The posse was a mile behind them now, coming steadily, horses and men bobbing across the flat. Brick gasped words to his companion.

"Stay ahead of 'em. It'll be dark . . ."

Instantly the idea was plain to Thad. They could not run off and leave their pursuers. Horseflesh would not stand that, but they could at least stay ahead. Barring bad luck or an accident, they could maintain their lead. And after a while night would come and then they might shake off the posse. That was Brick's idea and it might work. It had to work. Thad rode close to Brick. He could see the agony that the pounding gait of the horses brought to the red-haired man. Brick's face was a twisted mask of pain but he held his saddle strongly and never for an instant did he slacken the pace he had set.

"Can you make it, Brick?" Thad demanded. "Can you?"

"What . . . happened?" Brick demanded, not answering Thad's question.

"I rode out to meet them," Thad answered. "I was going to give myself up. Before I got to them one of them shot at me. It was Krespin. I stopped and he shot again. Then I saw you come out and I circled back. Can you make it?"

"Hell . . ." Brick grunted, "I'm all right."

The two dropped into a fold of ground. Looking back, their pursuers were lost to sight. Brick turned north along the little ridge, crossed the depression and they topped out on the other side. Now once more they could see that dogged pursuit. Brick was holding his injured arm now, using his right hand to support it, his reins swinging free from the fingers of his injured hand. Apparently the support gave him some relief.

"I wish I knew the country better," he said. "There's a rimrock east of us. We went the wrong way. The hills would have been better."

"We can circle . . ." Thad began.

"An' be cut off," Brick stated. "We've got to go on."

Thad said no more. The country rolled away toward the east. Behind them the hills grew more and more distant but always, against those hills they could see the bobbing spots of black that were horsemen following them. Brick pulled down his horse once more and again Thad imitated his companion. The horses trotted, breathing hard, sweating. The bobbing dots of black came on.

"We're better mounted," Brick Mahoney said, "an' the horses are fresh an' it's two hours to sundown. We'll make it all right, kid. We'll get away."

"And to hell with them!" Thad said viciously. "I was goin' to give myself up. I was going to go back to Las Flores and send for Judge Althen and clear it all up. They wouldn't let me: they took a shot at me when I had my hands up. To hell with them! I'll go with you, Brick. I'll stick with you."

"We'd better shake it up a little," Brick Mahoney said. "They're gettin' closer."

CHAPTER NINE

Wanted!

BY dusk the two fugitives had shaken off the pursuit. The bobbing black dots were no longer visible behind them. Somewhere on that back trail, Thad Breathea and Brick Mahoney knew that the pursuit clung, following tracks, determined, relentless; but with the posse no longer visible the tension was eased. At dusk, too, they came to the rim, the broken country they rode through presaging the nearness of that great descent. Their horses were done, played out, weary with the race. Still the two kept their tired animals slogging ahead. They must go down below the rim; they must keep on. Only distance and time could help them and, in that country of mounted men, a man on foot was helpless and they must have fresh mounts. Neither man spoke of those things; they knew them and speech was unnecessary.

The rim broke off before them, a great lava caprock, crevassed by a hundred thousand winters, cracked and broken by a hundred thousand summers. Cedars grew in the lava where scanty earth had formed. Great chunks of lava had broken off and added to the entangling maze of rock. Go down they must, and so they sought for a pathway for descent and with but scant time to find it.

"We can make it here," Brick announced. "We'll have to lead our horses."

There was a possible path below them, a path that would tantalize a burro and be a highway for a mountain goat. Thad, dismounting, surveyed that path. "Think you can, Brick?" he asked, looking at his companion's injured arm.

"Hell," said Brick Mahoney, and laughing recklessly, "I got to!"

Thad went down first. Leading his horse, sliding and slipping over rocks, turning to coax the weary beast over some sheer drop where a boulder blocked the way. On a little bench he paused and by the sounds that came from above, estimated the progress of his companion. Brick too reached the bench and stopped, and in the waning light Thad could see the utter weariness and pain written on the man's face.

"Go on, kid," Brick directed.

Thad went on.

Here were no gentle slopes, no sweetly rolling hills; here was fierce nature and a drop that led to oblivion. "You coming, Brick?"

"Go on, kid."

Now the bench they followed dwarfed away. Now came a hillside, sheer and precipitous and covered with stones that slid beneath their feet. The horses hung back, drooping their heads, searching for footing before they stepped from one uncertainty on to the next. Above Thad the rocks rattled and Brick Mahoney's voice was sharp with pain. Thad stopped. Again the rocks rolled and as they checked, Brick spoke again.

"Go on, kid."

The rock slope conquered, there came the second rim, not so sheer as the first, but affording problems of its own, problems that must be answered and none too easily in the dying light. Below that second rim, Thad stopped. Here was a wide bench, dotted by cedars, and here, underfoot was a trail, a winding pathway made by moving cattle.

"Almost down," Thad Breathea announced.

Brick Mahoney made no answer.

They could ride now. It was better to ride than to walk. Even a weary horse may be surefooted and a man on a horse is not apt to have his mount slide down and step on him. Wordlessly Thad helped Brick to mount and then climbed into his own saddle. Mounted, he could see above the cedars and looking toward the north he saw a light blink and then grow steady on the plain beneath. There was a house below and where there was a house there would be people. People must be avoided but horses were a necessity and there might be horses at the house.

They rode on, following the winding cowtrack. It bent and twisted and passed closely beneath trees where a horseman could not ride because of the branches; but it went down and where a cow could go, a horse could follow, and cattle went to water. The wide bench narrowed and stopped and the cowpath zigzagged down a canyon side and leveled again. And now the horses, despite their weariness, cocked their ears and moved more rapidly. Overhead a star winked, clear and pale in the lighted sky, and all about was darkness for they were below the rim.

The horses stopped and then moved ahead once more, half

sliding down a steep embrasure in a bank. There were no rocks here but only earth. Then water gurgled about the horses' feet and the animals lowered their heads and sucked thirstily, and Brick Mahoney's voice was small and hoarse.

"I guess I stay here, kid. I guess I'm done."

"I saw a light," Thad said.

"I seen it too."

"Mebbe . . ."

"I've hurt my arm again. Seems like that bandage slipped when I fell back on the hill. Kid . . ."

"Yes, Brick?"

"You go on."

Thad's horse raised its head. Thad moved the animal until he was beside his companion.

"You an' me'll go on," Thad Breathea said. "There's sand on the other side. We'll rest awhile."

The horses splashed across the stream and stopped. Dismounting, Thad helped his companion to alight. He tied his own horse to Brick's saddle horn, Brick's horse to the horn of his own saddle. He stretched Brick Mahoney on the sand and then went to the creek and dipped water in his hat and brought it back. Brick drank thirstily and when he had finished, his voice was stronger.

"That's right. You an' me'll go on. We got to have fresh horses, kid."

"We'll get 'em," assured Thad Breathea.

Leaving Brick he went to the horses and replaced his temporary tie with hobbles, twisting loops of soft rope around fore pasterns, pulling off the saddles and blankets, removing the bridles. He lugged the gear back to Brick, dumped it down and standing over his companion asked a question.

"How's the arm?"

"It hurts like hell," Brick said matter-of-factly. "The bandage slipped an' the splint slipped out."

"Do you want me . . ." Thad began.

"There's nothin' we can do about it tonight," Brick interrupted hastily. Thad sensed that Brick wanted the arm left alone, that Brick was about at the end of his rope and that anything that Thad might do would be in the nature of injury rather than help.

"We shook 'em anyhow," Thad said.

Brick grunted. "They didn't reach the top before we were down," he said, speaking of the pursuing possemen. "They'd have taken a shot at us if they had. Come mornin' they'll find out where we went off the rim."

"And follow us?" Thad suggested.

Brick laughed grimly. "Not them. They got a respect for their necks. They'll find a trail an' then come down."

"So we've got a start," Thad said.

"A start, anyhow," Brick agreed.

"Then," Thad sat down beside his companion, "give me your makings and I'll roll you a smoke and we'll lie down in the sand an' get some sleep."

Again Brick's chuckle came, not grim now. "I'll go you one," he said. "You know, kid, you learn awful fast. A week ago you'd have sat up all night worryin'."

"I'll let the other fellow worry from now on," Thad said, and there was a new timbre, a new hardness in his voice. "Here you are, Brick. Wet the flap and I'll stick it down for you. I kind of wish I smoked. It's somethin' to do when you've got nothin' else."

A match flamed, briefly illuminating Brick's face. The smell of burning tobacco was pleasant, almost peaceful. "You said it was Krespin shot at you?" Brick asked suddenly.

"It was, damn him!" Thad's young voice was savage.

"It looks like," Brick drawled, "that Krespin kind of wanted you out of the way, kid."

Thad was silent for a long minute. "I was going to give myself up," he repeated once more. "I called to 'em. They shot at me. A man can't do the right thing, Brick. They won't let him."

Brick maintained his silence and Thad, his voice hard and more bitter than Brick Mahoney had ever heard it, spoke again.

"I'll go south with you," he announced. "I'll stick along. But I'm not going to split off and get a ridin' job. They've made me an outlaw! All right, I'll be one. I've got the name; I might as well have what goes with it!"

"Kid," Brick's voice was sharp, "you don't want to . . ."

"To hell with the law," Thad snarled. "The law's crooked. From now on I'm on my own. You told me what would happen, Brick, an' by God you were right!"

Morning came, cold, gray, cloudless. With the first faint streaks of dawn Thad was up, out of the shelter of the stream bed, wrangling the hobbled horses. The animals were fresher after the night's rest, but they were far from what Thad wanted in the line of horseflesh. Still they must do until others could be acquired, and Thad put on his own and Brick's saddles. Brick lay by silently while Thad saddled. His face was lined and Thad knew that the arm was paining. When they inspected the injury Thad drew a quick breath. The arm was swollen out of all proportion and was red and inflamed. It was easy to see that the bullet wound was infected, but Thad, replacing the bandage, could not tell whether or not the arm was broken again.

"Got to do something about that," Thad announced when he had finished. "That's got to have a doctor, Brick."

"No," Brick shook his head. His eyes were bright with the mounting fever in his body. "No doctor. Think I want to run my head in a loop?"

"We've got to outfit anyhow," Thad said sturdily. "Where's a town, Brick?"

"Concha," Brick answered slowly, "is just against the Texas line. Mebbe . . ."

"We'll go there," Thad decided.

Brick looked at the boy and was about to expostulate, but closed his lips on the words. There was a new look about Thad, a new competency in his very posture. It was as though Thad Breathea had suddenly graduated from a youth into a man.

"An' here's where we get some horses," Thad announced. "There's a bunch workin' in to water."

He helped Brick mount and, leaving the red-haired man under the creek bank, rode out on the flat. There was a horse band coming toward the creek and Thad, circling them, drove them in toward the water. He was pleased to note that the horses bore saddle marks, showing that they were broken. In his present condition Brick could not ride a bronc.

The horses went into the creek bed and Thad drove them downstream. Brick fell in with the horses, turning them, and they went into an angle of the cut bank, some hundred feet of sand and gravel separating them from the water. Thad and Brick dismounted and Thad took Brick's rope from the saddle and got his own rope.

"They're gentle," he said, and walked toward the horses.

Brick stood by while Thad, looking over the animals, made his selections. For Brick he roped out a bay with black stockings, and led him out, tying him to a clump of brush. For his own horse he selected another bay, almost a twin to the one he had roped for Brick. Brick let the rest go and they trotted off as Thad began to change saddles. When he had effected the change, shifting Brick's saddle as well as his own, he mounted Brick's horse and rode him back and forth through the sand. Brick watched, and despite the pain in his arm could not repress a grin. Thad Breathea was uncorking his companion's horse and doing a business-like job. Thad, seemingly, had undertaken to look after Brick Mahoney.

Satisfied that Brick's horse would not buck, Thad mounted his own animal. This horse too, full of vigor as he was, did not offer to pitch, and Brick, climbing unsteadily on his horse while Thad held the animal's head, grinned again.

"And now what?" Brick asked.

"Now," Thad replied, "we'll haze these horses we rode along and drop 'em where they won't be too easy picked up. We're pretty close to a house, the way I figure, and there's no use of leavin' sign."

"You learn fast," Brick praised, and fell in behind the two riderless horses.

The two men rode on east, driving the free horses until, in a clump of pinon trees on a little point, Brick moved to drop them. They had come a full ten miles from the creek and there was not much chance that the horses would be picked up soon. Leaving the animals the two companions struck on through the pinons and out onto the plain again, still working east. They were hungry and tired, stiff from their riding and from their almost sleepless night. Neither mentioned the fact. Thad watched Brick with anxious, covert glances. Brick clung grimly to the business of getting along. Black smoke against the sky attracted the attention of both, and Brick said: "That's the E.P. & S.W. We're gettin' close to it."

"Where's Concha?" Thad asked.

"East, along the tracks," Brick answered vaguely.

At noon, with the sun high overhead, a wagon road curving up from the south came to march beside the tracks. Thad and Brick followed the road. They came presently to a cross road, a grade crossing traversing the tracks and joining the road they followed. There was a telegraph pole beside the crossing and a white painted sign, its cross-bars bearing the black lettering: "Railroad crossing. Look out . . . the cars." On the telegraph pole there was a white cardboard square and Thad, riding close, looked at the sign and then pulled it from its tacks and rode back to Brick.

"Look," he directed.

In heavy black letters across the white of the cardboard was the word, "WANTED," and below that, in smaller print, "For Bank Robbery and Murder: Thomas Mahoney, alias Brick Mahoney, alias Red, alias Colorado Mahoney; and Thaddeus Breathea, alias Thad Breathea, alias Wyoming Kid." A description followed and then: "A reward of two hundred dollars each will be paid by the sheriff of Dos Piedras county for information leading to the apprehension and arrest of the above."

"They didn't get my name right," Thad said carefully. "It ain't Thaddeus; it's Theodore. I'd better tell 'em about that."

"You can thank Branch Long for that 'Wyoming Kid' business," Brick commented. "He heard me say you were from Wyoming an' he heard me call you 'kid.' "

"The Wyoming Kid," Thad murmured the words. He tossed the poster aside and looked at Brick through narrowed, glinting eyes. "Let's go on," he said tersely, and the words were an order. Brick made no answer other than to start his horse again.

By mid-afternoon, still following the railroad, they saw against the hazy eastern sky the black bulk of a water tower perched on stilts above the railroad grade. That water tower was Concha, Brick said, and continued with the statement that they had better not ride in in the daylight but wait for night.

"The stores will be open," Brick continued. "It's a little town an' they won't close up. You'd better buy what we're goin' to need, Thad. My red head kind of marks me."

Thad nodded his agreement and Brick, holding his reins in his injured hand, drew money from his pocket and handed it to his companion. Thad took the proffered bills and put them away, and they rode on, looking now for a place to hole up until darkness came.

They found what they wanted in a stone-lined culvert that crossed under the tracks. The stone arch was set at an angle, bending sharply just beyond the tracks and a trickle of water running through the culvert showed why the railroad builders had placed it there. Beyond the angle of the culvert the two stopped and dismounted. The horses drank and then stood patiently waiting while their riders also quenched their thirst. Then, with their backs against the stone of the culvert, Thad and Brick sat down. Brick smoked a cigarette that Thad rolled for him, and they spoke of their future plans.

"We'd better," Brick said, "turn these horses loose an' get the train out of here. This is the E.P. & S.W. an' it runs right into Franklin. We can hit a train an' go south. I'm goin' to have to lay up awhile till this arm gets well."

"You mean buy a ticket?" Thad demanded. "They'd . . ."

"I mean hop a freight," Brick interrupted, and grinned. "We'll ride a box car south."

"Oh," Thad said.

"But first," Brick announced, "we've got to eat. I'm about half starved."

Thad too was feeling the pinch of hunger. He nodded. "Will we turn the horses loose out here?" he asked. "An' what about the saddles, Brick? They . . ."

"Yo're ridin' a stolen saddle an' I expect that mine belonged to somebody else one time," Brick said. "Don't worry about the saddles. But I don't think we'd better walk in. We'll take the horses an' just leave 'em in town. Somebody will want 'em an' anyhow we'd better have 'em handy in case we need to leave before a train pulls out. I wish this arm didn't hurt so damned bad."

"Let's put some cold water on it," Thad said. "Maybe that would ease it some."

Brick bared his arm, tenderly lifting it from the sling, and Thad, using a handkerchief, bathed the inflamed surface with water from the little stream. Brick said that the water felt good.

When sundown came they mounted once more and leaving the friendly haven of the culvert, they rode on east. The water tank came closer and Brick, pulling his gun from its holster, pushed the weapon down inside his waistband under his shirt. "You'd better hide your gun, kid," he advised. "They don't like for you to carry one in town an' we'd better not have the law lookin' at us."

Following Brick's example Thad slipped shells from his belt, placing them in a trousers pocket. They hung the gun belts on their saddles.

"We'll eat," Brick anounced. "An' I want a drink. I can use a drink of whisky, kid."

Thad nodded. He had taken but one drink of liquor in his life, a drink that his father had given him when he had come from a long ride, cold and wet through.

"An' a big steak," Brick continued. "We'll buy a little canned stuff, too, so we can have somethin' to eat in our box car."

It was dusk when they reached the outskirts of the town.

Brick turned his horse toward the railroad and nodded his satisfaction. A switch engine was chuffing busily back and forth in the railroad yard and there was a locomotive on the track from the round-house, its nose pointed toward the east.

"Looks like we're in luck," Brick commented.

"Why?" Thad demanded.

"They're makin' up a train. That engine's headed the way we want to go."

Thad grunted. This was all new to him. He watched the puffing switch engine, filing away for future reference the information Brick had given him.

"An empty box car is goin' to look mighty good to me," Brick said. "This is all right, kid. We'll tie the horses to that hitchrack an' go get our drink an' our meal. Come on."

They were in the middle of the town now, the street they traversed flanking the tracks of the railroad. Further along they could see the bulk of the depot and its lights. Opposite them was a hitchrail already holding three horses, and behind the rail a store. A little further down the street was a saloon, and between the saloon and the depot a restaurant. Dismounting, Thad watched Brick get down, and then fastened both horses to the hitchrail.

"Don't tie a tight knot," Brick admonished. "We might want 'em."

They went around the rail and, boots thumping on the board sidewalk, Brick's spurs jingling, went on to the saloon. Pushing open the door they went in, and a heavy man, hair plastered against his head and neatly parted in the middle, put down the towel and glass he held and advanced along the bar toward them. Brick tipped back his hat, grinned at the barman and said: "Whisky."

The bartender's round, inquiring eyes sought Thad's and Thad nodded. The bartender set out a bottle and two small glasses.

Thad watched Brick. When Brick poured his drink, Thad did likewise, and when Brick said: "First today!" and shot the whisky down his throat, Thad also picked up his glass, made the same small gesture Brick had made and tossed the whisky into his mouth. It gagged and burned him and he swallowed convulsively.

Brick said, "That was good. We'll take another."

Once again the drinks were poured and taken and Brick placed money on the bar.

The bartender, taking the bill, turned and made change from the till. He put the silver on the bar top and spoke to Brick. "Been travelin'?"

"Some," Brick agreed. "We come in from Texas. Is there anythin' goin' on around Concha? Anybody hirin' hands?"

"They're workin' cattle," the bartender announced. "You might catch on with a wagon. Looks like you'd got hurt."

"Horse fell with me," Brick said casually. "It ain't bad."

Thad could feel the whisky warming him, the warmth suffusing from his belly up through his body. His tongue felt thick and furry where, for the time, the alcohol anæsthetized it. Brick, too, was feeling the two quick drinks on his empty stomach.

"Have another little shot?" the bartender asked, moving the bottle suggestively.

"Sure," Brick agreed, taking the bottle.

"I've had enough," Thad said. "I'm hungry, Brick."

Brick's eyes shot a warning and Thad realized what he had done. Brick put down the bottle.

"I guess I won't," he said elaborately. "I'm hungry too. Come on, Bud."

They went out of the saloon. On the sidewalk Thad said: "I'm a damn fool. I didn't think what I was doin'. Silk or Curly wouldn't of done that, Brick."

"Silk an' Curly ain't here," Brick said shortly. "I don't think he noticed. Let's eat."

They went on to the restaurant. While they waited for their steaks Brick read a paper that was on the table. It was an old paper, its edges frayed and the corners curled. Brick read slowly and then pushed the paper across to Thad. "I'm glad that fellow Curly downed in the bank didn't die," Brick said, low-voiced.

Thad read the headlines and the story. There was a detailed account of the bank robbery in Las Flores.

"We didn't get what they said we did," Brick murmured. "We didn't get but about a thousand dollars. We had to run before we got to the vault." Thad made no answer for the waiter was coming, bearing the steaks.

The whisky, coupled with their long fast, had given Thad and Brick the appetites of wolves. They ate rapidly, hardly able to restrain themselves and chew the meat that they cut and put into their mouths. The steaks seemed to melt away. Brick wiped his mouth with the back of his hand, drank the last of his coffee and glanced at Thad. Thad was already finished. At the counter, as he paid the proprietor, Brick jerked his head toward the railroad yard across the street.

"They haulin' much freight?" he asked.

"Pretty good," the restaurant man answered. "That's a west-bound drag they're makin' up over there. They . . ." He stopped. Two railroaders had come through the door, an engineer and a fireman evidently, their clothing bespeaking their trades.

"Put me up a lunch, Tom," one overalled man directed. "Make it snappy, will you? You want a cup of coffee, Jack?"

The other nodded and the two went to the counter and sat down. Thad and Brick exchanged glances. Brick in the lead, they went on out to the sidewalk.

"You go up to the store, kid," Brick instructed. "Get some canned stuff. Get some canned tomatoes so we'll have somethin' to drink. I'll wait for you."

Thad nodded and turning, walked toward the store in front of which their horses were tied. Brick leaned back against the wall. Down the street a short distance a street lamp burned, yellow in its glass box. The box leaked air for the yellow kerosene flame flickered.

There was a customer in the store, a woman who seemingly required an endless amount of attention. She debated with the proprietor while Thad fidgeted. When, finally, she was satisfied and went out, Thad had already made his selections and gave his order tersely to the merchant. Canned tomatoes, canned beans, sardines, a box of crackers—these in turn were placed upon the counter and, at Thad's behest, taken from the counter and shoved into a sugar sack that the storekeeper produced. Thad paid for the goods, picked up the sack and went to the door. As he stepped out on the sidewalk he heard the crash of box car couplings coming together. He glanced to the right to locate Brick, and at his elbow a man spoke.

"These your horses, bud?"

Instantly Thad sensed danger. He turned, saw that the speaker was a tall thin man with a dark mustache, and that there was a star on his coat, and behind the officer Thad saw another man.

"What horses?" Thad asked, and shifted the sack.

"Right there," the officer said. "I think you rode in to town on 'em. The barkeeper down at the Blue Ribbon heard you call a man 'Brick.' Yo're under . . ."

On the tracks a whistle sounded two short blasts. Thad saw Brick push himself away from the wall of a building and step out into the light. Again couplings clashed and wheels groaned as they began to move.

"Run!" Thad yelled, and swung the sack. The canned goods crashed against the thin man's face, driving him back into his companion. Thad dropped the sack and sprinted across the street. Glancing back he could see Brick coming, running after him. He slowed for Brick to catch up and heard Brick's panting call.

"Go on, kid!"

In front of Thad cars were sliding past. The black open door of a box car was immediately in front of him, moving sedately. Thad flung himself at that black opening. He heard shots crashing into the darkness, felt the edge of the car floor against his belly, and with a heave and a squirming, sprawled into the car. Scrambling up, he looked out of the door. Brick was nowhere in sight. He must have reached the train. Behind Thad, in the street, he could see men running across the light of the street lamp. He cowered back from the door. Under him the wheels were clicking as the train picked up speed. Up ahead the whistle sounded again, and risking another glance, Thad saw a light waving in little concentric circles far down the train. He drew back and squatted beside the door, making himself small. The car was rolling steadily, bouncing roughly, gaining momentum. Thad Breathea drew a deep breath and let it go.

CHAPTER TEN

Chief Deputy

ON Sunday morning Charlie Farrel was busy. A lean, tireless man with a smooth melancholy face, he went from place to place, summoning those men he wanted for a coroner's jury. Later, while the coroner and the county prosecutor questioned witnesses and while the jurymen viewed the mortal remains of Ten High Croates, Farrel held his place, motionless, against the wall of the room and listened to the testimony, his eyes bright and alert and watchful as the witnesses appeared. The jury, after a brief intermission, gave their verdict. Ten High Croates had come to his death by gunshot wounds inflicted by a person unknown to the jury. Gus Hoffman, always politic, stepped out with the jurymen and Charlie Farrel went into the sheriff's office. He was there, sitting at the desk, his head tipped back and his pipe between his teeth, when Hoffman joined him.

Gus Hoffman was fat, and in the heat of the day his skin was oily. He was sheriff because of his politics and because he had married Maria Villareal and the whole clan of the Villareals voted him into office. Sometimes Gus took his sheriff-ship seriously, but more often he was inclined to let Farrel run the office. Farrel could see that this was one of the times when Gus wanted to be sheriff, so he sucked on his unlighted pipe and prepared to be patient.

"We're goin' to have to do somethin' about this killin',
Charlie," Gus said importantly. "We're goin' to have to do
somethin' right way. This murder right on the heels of the
bank robbery an' that jail break don't look good. In fact, the
whole thing's bad. Mahoney tyin' you up an' takin' that kid out
of jail, and Kettleman gettin' killed an' . . ."

Farrel straightened in his chair and looked at his superior
officer. "I'm an officer, Gus," he interrupted, "but I'm not a
damned fool. Mahoney wanted that kid and he had a gun on
me. I was mistaken about the kid and I'll admit it, but I'm not
goin' to be a damned fool when a man's got the drop."

Hoffman waved that aside. "Anyhow we're goin' to have to
do somethin'," he said again.

"And what had we better do, Gus?" Farrel questioned gently.
"You heard the testimony at the inquest."

Hoffman sat down. He took a cigar from his pocket, bit off
the end and lighted the cigar. He did not offer one to his sub-
ordinate. "Somethin'," he said around the brown cylinder.
"Now I think that Croates was killed by somebody that had a
grudge against him. He had trouble with Joe Pierce an' Walt
Davis on the train the day he got here. Now I think . . ." Hoffman's voice droned on. Charlie Farrel had already telegraphed
Albuquerque and received reports on the activities of Mr. Davis
and Mr. Pierce. Pierce was in jail for disturbing the peace and
Mr. Davis was no longer in residence at Albuquerque, having
been invited to go further south by the alert officials of that thriv-
ing city. Charlie Farrel had received this information about four
o'clock in the morning. Hoffman was an annoyance as he always
was when there happened to be work to do, and Charlie Farrel
wanted to think. He swiveled the chair around.

"Why don't you take a posse and look into that tip we got
from Andreas Montoya?" he asked suddenly. "Andreas said
that there were some strange horses out at Alfredo Vara's goat
ranch and that Alfredo was feedin' somebody. Remember?
Maybe Mahoney and the kid are holed up at Vara's."

Gus Hoffman seized the idea, as Farrel had know he would.

Hoffman liked to appear important, he liked to lead a posse, and he liked, when things tightened up, to pass the buck to Farrel's broad shoulders.

Hoffman came up from where he sat, and slapped his leg. "That's right!" he exclaimed.

"I was goin' to ride out to Vara's place today," Farrel said. "Mebbe it would be better if you went. I'll stay here and work on this Croates business."

Gus Hoffman was like a pup offered the end of a sack. He seized the idea that Farrel had extended, and worried it. "Mahoney!" he said. "If he's out there I'll get him. That would be somethin'. After all, Croates was just a tinhorn gambler. Now Mahoney . . ."

Farrel lost the rest of the sentence. He was tipped back in his chair again, thinking. Gus Hoffman bustled about the office and presently went out. After a time Farrel heard a disturbance outside the courthouse and, going to the window, saw Hoffman riding away. There were four men with Hoffman, Dale Krespin among them.

"He's got some good company," Charlie Farrel said comfortably, and went back to his chair.

For a long time he sat there, eyes closed, meditating. He was a good officer and he kept his county as clean as he could with the help that he had. That was a task. The county was a hundred miles broad by a hundred and twenty long, and the help inadequate. Hoffman was a nonentity save only in politics, and the deputies that Hoffman appointed were picked for the votes they would draw and not for their ability in law enforcement. Charlie Farrel checked things over in his mind.

He knew, as he should have known, that there were black spots in the county. He knew that Branch Long would harbor an outlaw, indeed had criminal connections. Knowing and proving were different things and Charlie Farrel grudgingly admired Brick Mahoney for having settled with Kettleman. That did not keep him from wanting Brick Mahoney behind bars. Farrel knew, too, that there were officers in other adjacent counties that were less scrupulous than he, and less efficient even than Hoffman. Hoffman was a politician but he was fairly honest. Some of those others were not. For example, Farrel had heard rumors of Arch Ratcliff's cabin across the county line. It was out of Farrel's jurisdiction. What could he do about it?

Like all good peace officers, Charlie Farrel had his connections, some of them shady, some not. Police work depends upon painstaking effort and stool pigeons, and of those last Farrel had a well-trained loft. But there was something amiss, something awry with all this business. The bank robbery had been unforeseen insofar as the sheriff's office was concerned, and still rumor had filtered through to Farrel that Lon Popples and his deputy town marshal had been expecting just such an occurrence and had been more or less prepared for it. Farrel expected and got no co-operation from the town marshal. Popples was on the other side of the political fence from Gus Hoffman.

And then there was the killing of Kettleman. Dolf McBride was the deputy sheriff in that district and Farrel had long suspected that McBride was seeing some Kettleman money. He couldn't prove it but he suspected it. Gus Hoffman would listen to no word against McBride who was foreman for the J Cross T and controlled a lot of votes.

Now had come this murder in Las Flores itself. Someone had thrust a gun through the window of Tony Lazolli's dance hall and pulled the trigger three times. Ten High Croates was very, very dead and there was no reason for his being killed, as far as Charlie Farrel could see. The gray-haired deputy shook his head. There was no connection between the happenings, between the bank robbery and the deaths of Kettleman and Croates. No connection at all. It was just one of those things that happen to bedevil honest and hard-working officers. Farrel got up from his chair, picked up his hat and pulling it down over his eyes, walked out of the sheriff's office. He was going out to ask a few questions.

Leaving the courthouse Farrel took his way along the plaza

and turned at the east corner. Following down that street he came presently to Lulu Black's establishment. Las Flores had a Sunday closing law but Farrel, walking around to the back of the building, pushed open the door and entered. Reaching the barroom he found Buster presiding behind the bar. Two customers drinking beer at the bar recognized the newcomer and departed hastily.

"Where's Lulu, Buster?" Farrel asked.

"Out back," Buster answered surlily. "Look, Charlie, everybody opens up on Sunday. You ain't goin' to . . ."

"I want to talk to Lulu," Farrel interrupted. "Go get her."

Buster went out a rear door of the long room, and finding a chair beside a table, Farrel seated himself and waited.

Lulu was not long in answering the summons. Buster was not with her. Seeing Farrel she smiled placatingly and came toward him.

"Hello, sheriff," Lulu greeted affably.

Farrel nodded. "How are you, Lulu?" he answered. "I saw you at the inquest this mornin'. I thought I'd come around and talk to you a little."

Lulu's blue eyes were hard and wary. "I told all I knew about Ten High at the inquest," she announced. "He was stayin' here an' last night he went out an' said that he was goin' to Tony's. The next thing I knew Lon Popples was here tellin' me that Ten High had been killed and that I had to come to the inquest. That's all I know, sheriff."

"Let's visit awhile," Charlie Farrel suggested. "I haven't seen you for a long time, Lulu. You've stayed out of trouble pretty good."

Lulu assumed a virtuous air. "I won't stand for drunks in my place," she said. "I run a nice respectable beer parlor an' . . ."

Farrel waved a hand. "I know what you run," he said grimly. "There's nothin' a man can't buy in your place, from cards and bad whisky to marijuana. Did you ever hear of Leavenworth, Lulu?"

Lulu's eyes grew wide. "Leavenworth?" she demanded. "Are

you tryin' to scare me, Charlie? Leavenworth? Why, that's a Federal penitentiary. That's where the Government sends people."

Farrel nodded. "Let's sit down an' talk about Leavenworth a little," he said.

Lulu flopped into a chair. "Leavenworth!" she said again.

Farrel took off his hat, put it on the table. "Yeah," he drawled. "Leavenworth. I haven't cracked down on you, Lulu. Popples runs the town and I know that you pay Popples for protection. That's his business. Oh, maybe I can't prove it." He spoke hastily, forestalling the words that were on Lulu's lips. "I'm not out to reform the world, Lulu. I'm not a parson. The business between you and Popples is between you and Popples; but this other is murder and I'm interested. Now what do you know about it?"

Lulu's lips set in a stubborn, obstinate line. "I told what I knew at the inquest," she answered again.

"All right." Farrel reached for his hat. "There'll be a U. S. deputy marshal callin' in on you pretty soon now. Of course, he's goin' to be interested in the fact that Benny Tafoya and Salomon Garcia an' that bunch got their marijuana here. He . . ."

"But I never sold it to 'em," Lulu shrilled. "You know I never. It was . . ."

"They got it in your place," Farrel interrupted. "The deputy marshal ain't goin' to go further than that. Particularly when I tell him . . ."

"Now look," Lulu leaned forward across the table, the edge creasing her ample bosom. "Now look, Charlie. You know that I shipped Juan Salas out of here as soon as I found out what was goin' on. You know . . ."

Mentally Farrel filed the name Juan Salas for future reference. He had not known about Salas. Farrel's voice was dry as he said: "Tell it to the deputy," and put on his hat preparatory to leaving.

"Wait, Charlie!" Lulu's voice rose high. "I don't want a U. S.

marshal around here. I never done nothin'. I don't know who killed Ten High."

Farrel settled back and took off his hat again. "What was Ten High into, Lulu?" he asked conversationally. "He talked to you, didn't he?"

"He had some trouble with Joe Pierce an' Walt Davis on the train when he came here this last time," Lulu said.

"And one of them is in jail and one is in El Paso," Farrel said. "It wasn't them, Lulu. Ten High talked to some of his friends about how much money he was goin' to get. Where was the money comin' from?"

"I don't know," Lulu answered. "I'll tell you what, Charlie. I'll take you down to Ten High's room. You search it. Maybe you'd find somethin'!" There was a cunning gleam in Lulu's China-blue eyes.

Farrel's lips twitched sardonically. Lulu was going to make sure that he found something. He followed the ample woman out of the room.

Lulu padded down the hall. Wanting to give Lulu time to make her plant in Ten High's room, Charlie Farrel stopped to speak to Buster who was returning to the barroom. Lulu knew a great deal that she wasn't going to tell in words; of that Farrel was certain. And he was lucky to get any information at all. The talk about marijuana had been a bluff and Farrel was surprised that it had gone over so well. He left Buster and went on. Lulu was inside the room at the end of the hall. She gestured as Farrel entered.

"His grip is under the bed," she said. "All his other stuff is in the closet. You look around, Charlie."

"I'll do that," Farrel agreed. As he came down the hall he had heard a ringing sound as of something striking against the brass bedstead.

Lulu stood by while Farrel casually looked around the room; while he went into the curtained corner that served for a closet, and glanced about. Farrel came out from behind the curtain, approached the bed and bending down pulled out Ten High's grip. The room had been searched before, he knew, he himself having dispatched a deputy to make a search. But now he expected to find something. When he opened the grip his expectations were realized. There, on top of the tangle of soiled clothing, was an envelope. Farrel picked it up, noted that the return address on the envelope was that of some lawyer in Wyoming, and pulling out the papers the envelope contained, opened them and read them through.

Lulu watched the officer narrowly but Farrel's face was inscrutable. "Did you find anything, Charlie?" she asked.

"Not much," Farrel answered, returning the letters to the envelope and placing it in his coat pocket. "Not much, Lulu. I guess it was just one of those things. I'll go on back to the office."

"About that United States marshal . . ." Lulu began.

"I don't expect one in for quite a while," Farrel said. "Don't put too much confidence in Lon Popples, Lulu. He doesn't always do what he says he will."

"Popples!" Lulu spat the word. "I wouldn't trust that man as far as I could throw a bull by the tail. Why, you know what he done . . ."

"You take it up with Popples," Charlie Farrel said. "So long, Lulu. Stay out of jail."

He walked out of the room and going down the hall let himself out of the building into the sunlight.

Back at the courthouse again he sat in the sheriff's office and once more read the letters through. When he had finished he tapped thoughtfully on the desk with the folded papers and considered facts.

Charlie Farrel knew that Jake Breathea had died intestate. He knew that Dale Krespin claimed the estate and that Krespin was almost sure to get it. Farrel had first been an officer under old Jake and while Breathea had been a hard taskmaster, Charlie Farrel bore a lasting affection for the old man. Too, he had known Carl Breathea. Carl Breathea had surrendered himself to Charlie Farrel after killing Tom Parkes.

Charlie Farrel had told Carl Breathea good-by when Breathea left the country for an unannounced destination. The kid who had held the horses for Brick Mahoney and those other bandits had said his name was Thad Breathea and had called on Dale Krespin to identify him. Charlie Farrel had been interested in that, and in Krespin's declaration that he had never seen the boy before. Given a little time and Farrel would have probed that angle, but he had not had the time. Mahoney and those others had come back, had held him at the point of a gun, tied him up and made a jail delivery. That had firmly fixed the conviction in Farrel's mind that the youngster was connected with Brick and that he had lied. But now, here in his hand, was proof that it was no lie, that the youngster was actually old Jake's grandson and had spoken the truth.

"Well," Charlie Farrel said musingly, "it was worth killin' a man over. Old Jake had three thousand head of cattle and the Lord knows how much land." Again he tapped with the letters on the desk top. Krespin! that was the man. Dale Krespin! He stood to lose a fortune and Ten High Croates had these letters and was using them.

"But hell!" Charlie Farrel said aloud, sitting bolt upright in his chair. "Dale Krespin was in here when Ten High was killed. Right in this office."

He slumped down again and thought further. Lulu was not telling all she knew. He had to get a little more from Lulu. He had to find out . . .

Charlie Farrel got up and reached for his hat. Once more he left the office. This time he went around the plaza and down another street into a respectable section of the sprawling little town. Along the street he went until he reached a dwelling house and there he paused. Grinning faintly, he went up the walk and knocked at the front door. A man in shirt sleeves came to the door and Farrel jerked his head toward the porch. The man came on out, a portly, gray-haired citizen.

"What's on your mind, Charlie?" he asked.

"I'm after a little information, Colonel," Farrel answered.

"Anything I can do . . ." the man said.

Farrel nodded. "Lulu Black," he said, and noted that the portly man's ruddy face paled, "is holdin' out a little information we need. I'd sure like it if she came in and talked to me."

"I'm sure I don't . . ." the portly man said.

"You've got a lot of influence, Colonel," Farrel said significantly. "I hope you'll use it."

The Colonel was suddenly affable. "Won't you come in, Charlie?" he asked. "It's hot and my daughter's made a pitcher of lemonade. Come in."

"No, thanks, Colonel," Farrel refused. "I'll go along. Stop in at the courthouse and see me when you're down that way." He nodded then, and leaving the Colonel on the porch, went down the steps and back toward the plaza. It was not pleasant, being an officer. A man learned a lot of things that weren't particularly agreeable. Sometimes he had to use his information. The Colonel was a respected citizen, a widower, and he had a couple of fine kids. If the Colonel only knew it, he was as safe as he would be in a church; but the Colonel didn't know it.

Back in the sheriff's office Farrel produced the envelope once more and studied its surface. Presently he grunted and opening a drawer brought out paper, a bottle of ink and a pen. The ink was dried in the bottle, thick and heavy, and the pen scratched. Charlie Farrel, squirming occasionally because this was hard work, wrote a letter, addressed it, referring to the envelope that he had found in Ten High's grip, sealed his own envelope and stamped it. He had just finished that task when he had visitors.

Tony Lazolli was a fat man and excitable. The man with Tony was disheveled and dirty. Farrel knew the disheveled man. He was Roy Morrison and Las Flores' official drunkard. Mothers, wishing to frighten their children into paths of rectitude, said: "Do you want to be like Roy Morrison?"

"Come in, boys," Charlie Farrel greeted. "What's on your mind, Tony?"

"Tell him!" Tony exclaimed, shoving Morrison forward. "Tell him w'at you told me!"

Morrison, battered hat in his hands, stared at the floor. "Well," he said hesitantly, "I was drunk last night, Charlie. I'd got some money for haulin' a load of wood to old man Apple's an' I went to Tony's an' . . ."

"Never you mind that!" Tony shrilled. "You tell him!"

"I am tellin' him, ain't I?" Morrison demanded. "Just as fast as I can. I . . ."

"Get along with it, Roy," Farrel commanded, forestalling another outburst from Lazolli.

"Well," Morrison continued, "anyhow I was drunk. But I wasn't clear passed out. Tony put me out when the dance started. He said he didn't want me around. So I went outside an' I was layin' down by the buildin'. I thought I'd go back. It ain't fair to sell a man whisky to get drunk on an' then throw him out when he gets drunk. I was goin' back in but that barkeeper that works for Tony is a tough customer an' . . . well, I lay down an' I guess I went to sleep."

"Tell him," Tony shrilled. "You go all around an' you don' tell nothin'. You . . ."

"Go on, Roy," Farrel interrupted quietly.

"Well," Morrison said, "there was some shots woke me up an' I looked around an' I seen a man runnin' away. I got up an' started to foller him but I tripped over some wire an' fell down. Tony don't clean up around his place. It's a wonder I didn't break my neck. Anyhow this man run . . ."

"Did you see him?" Farrel asked quietly.

"Kind of," Morrison admitted.

"Who was it?"

"It looked like Ben Prince," Morrison said. "I know Ben an' . . . well, it kind of looked like him."

"I told him he's crazy!" Lazolli shrilled. "I told him that he's drunk an' he's crazy. You tell him, Charlie. He's drunk, huh?"

"You must have been drunk, Roy," Charlie Farrel said. "I wouldn't go around spillin' talk like this to anybody if I was you. Nobody'd believe you an' you might get into trouble."

"I guess I was drunk," Morrison said contritely. "It was dark anyhow. Yeah. I guess I was drunk all right. It couldn't of been Ben Prince."

"He's spoiling my business," Lazolli shrilled. "Prince an' all them Lazy Fife cowboys come to my place. They . . ."

"All right, Tony," Farrel broke in. "Roy said that he was drunk. He's not goin' to say anything more about this, are you, Roy?"

"I guess I was drunk," Morrison said again. "I was mistaken all right. I'll keep my mouth shut."

"That's right, Roy," Farrel said. "And now, Tony, I'll tell you something: Roy's right. You got no business sellin' a man liquor to get drunk on an' then throwin' him out. The sheriff's office don't have much to say about how things go in Las Flores, but if I was you and wanted to keep my place open, I'd stop that. I sure would."

All the wind went out of Tony Lazolli. He glared malevolently at Roy Morrison, seemed about to say something, and then, turning, stamped out of the office. Roy Morrison twisted his hat. "Did you want me for anythin', Charlie?" he asked.

"Not a thing, Roy," Farrel said gently. "Just don't talk too much and if I was you I wouldn't take a drink at Lazolli's place. I wouldn't go around there."

"I ain't goin' to," Roy Morrison declared. "The damned cheat!" Turning, he shambled out of the office.

Charlie Farrel put his feet on the desk after Morrison was gone and thoughtfully surveyed his boot toes. "An' Ben will have an alibi a mile long," he surmised. "Well, there's no use in gettin' Roy killed. I guess I done the right thing." He scowled at the boot toes. "I'll ride down and check on Ben a little anyhow," he said. "Just as soon as Gus gets back."

Patience and perseverance, those two things make up the majority of police work. Charlie Farrel knew that; still it is hard to be patient: to wait for a letter to be answered; to wait for influences, hidden and tortuous, to work; to wait until waiting seems no longer possible.

Gus Hoffman did not get back until noon, Monday. He came into his office walking with feet wide spread, sore from his ride. He carried information and excitement with him. They had, he told his chief deputy, jumped Brick Mahoney and the youngster with him, at Alfredo Vara's goat ranch.

"The kid rode right down to see who we was," Hoffman said. "Boldest thing I ever saw. He rode right out toward us."

"An' then?" Farrel prompted.

"There was an arroyo between us," Hoffman continued, looking around at his companions for corroboration. "Krespin took a shot at the kid. He just sat there. Krespin took another shot an' the kid turned his horse an' run. Mahoney come out from behind the house and hooked up with him. They went east. We followed them but their horses were fresh an' we lost sight of 'em."

"They got away then?" Farrel said.

"Yeah. They hit the rim an' went down a place where a goat couldn't travel. We saw it this mornin' when we were cold-trailing 'em. We stopped at the Y B last night an' got fresh horses there this mornin'. They got across into Bernal county all right. Likely they're in Texas by this time. When I get rested up I'm goin' to get hold of Vara. He . . ."

"Come here a minute, Gus," Farrel nodded his head toward a corner. The sheriff, answering the nod, moved across the office and Farrel, lowering his voice, spoke into his superior's ear.

"About Vara," Farrel said. "I wouldn't be too hard on him, Gus. You know all them Varas live together up above Pacheco, an' well, likely Mahoney an' that kid held a gun on him an' scared him to death an' made him hide 'em. I wouldn't be too hard on Alfredo, Gus."

Fat Gus Hoffman grunted, but Farrel knew that the words had gone home. There were a lot of Varas and they had a lot of votes.

"Anyhow," Hoffman said, "I'm goin' to talk to Alfredo."

"Sure," Farrel agreed. "What became of Krespin, Gus?"

"He went home," Hoffman answered. "There wasn't any need of him comin' to town so he went home."

"I see," said Charlie Farrel. "Yeah, I see. He went home."

CHAPTER ELEVEN

Hanging!

GRADUALLY Thad's eyes became accustomed to the darkness of the box car. He remained beside the door, staring out into the night. The last lights of Concha had flickered away and now the dark expanse of country stretched out beside the train. Somewhere back of him, in another rolling car, Brick Mahoney was hidden. Thad was sure of it. The feeling strengthened him. Despite his recent experiences, despite the hardness that had grown up in him, Thad Breathea was still a kid, borrowing from Mahoney's matureness for strength and for assistance. The car rocked and jolted and Thad spread his legs out and leaned against the door. From the far end of the car a jocular voice came from the darkness.

"We got company, Chink. Come on back an' be sociable, sonny."

Instantly Thad was alert. The jocularity in the voice alarmed him more than harshness would have done. "Who's there?" he demanded.

"Now is that nice?" the voice asked. "We didn't go askin' you who you were when you piled into our carriage. Come on back, sonny. We ain't goin' to hurt you."

Thad remained beside the door, staring toward the source of the voice, trying to pierce the blackness. There was a rasping sound as though someone scraped a foot in moving, and Thad's hand went to his waistline, reaching in under his shirt and clutching the butt of the Bisley Colt.

"Aw what's the use of foolin' with him, Red?" another voice rasped. "Let's look him over."

"Now Chinky," the jocular voice said, "you wouldn't go an' be rough, would you? He's a nice little boy an' he's got money in his pockets an' tobacco for us to smoke, an' he's goin' to give it to us. Ain't you, sonny?"

Still Thad said nothing. The rasping sound came again. The car lurched and a man grunted. "Damn hoghead's tryin' to shake the liver out of us," Chink exploded, and cursed the engineer's ancestry.

"Well, kid," all the jocularity was gone from the first voice now, "are you goin' to pony up? Me an' Chink seen you an' yore friend eatin' in the restaurant. Yore friend didn't make the train. They was shootin' at you, wasn't they? Me an' Chink won't shoot. We'll . . ."

Thad had pulled his feet under him. The door opposite the one beside him was closed and there was a wedge of lighter darkness stretching across the car. Thad with a single motion pushed himself up and leaped, striking against the further door.

"What good is that, sonny? Red scoffed. "Do you think you can dodge me an' Chink in here? Why sonny . . ."

The Bisley was in Thad's hand. A switch stand flashing past threw a red glare into the car for an instant and then came darkness again. The red light winked from the dull blue of the gun, and Thad, finding his voice commanded:

"Stay where you are."

"Hell!" Red cursed. "He's got a gun, Chink!"

"Stay back," Thad warned.

The train was round a curve, gradually picking up speed as the engine struck a down grade. Thad braced his shoulders against the car door. At the end of the car there was an indistinct murmur. "Listen, kid," Red said, his voice whining, "we was just foolin' with you. We're just a couple of harmless bums."

"You stay where you are." Thad gained assurance from the wheedling voice. "I've got a gun."

"We know you got a gun. We ain't goin' to do nothin' to you. We was just . . . Take him, Chink!"

The whine of the flanges against the rail, the rock and rattle of the train had made hearing difficult. Thad caught a glimpse of a black bulk lunging toward him. Instinctively he ducked, dodging aside, and in his hand the Bisley crashed. A man squealed, high and frightened but with no hurt in the yell, and then Thad was caught by an arm that swept across his chest. He swung the Colt, the gun in his hand thumping down against bone, swung another blow and felt the encompassing arm drop away from him. Wheeling, then, Thad lifted the gun, the hammer pulled back, his finger tense on the trigger.

"You killed him!" Red's voice was shrill. "You killed Chink!"

Shoulders against the car door, Thad slid along toward the rear of the car, feet braced, eyes searching. He could see in the partial light that came through the open door, a bulky bundle stretched on the car floor. Out of the dimness now and in complete dark, Thad stopped. On the floor the man who had attacked him stirred but uttered no sound.

"Come up to your pardner!" Thad ordered. "Come up to him or I'll cut loose at you!"

"Now kid . . ." Red whined, "we wasn't goin' to hurt you."

"Come up!" Thad's voice was inexorable.

There was movement other than that of the car and a second figure appeared beside the man on the floor. "See if he's hurt," Thad commanded, keeping the gun trained steadily. "Look at him."

The man who had come from the rear of the car bent down. Presently he straightened, pulling up the body of the other. "He ain't dead," Red announced surlily.

As though to corroborate that statement the man who had been prone groaned, shifted in Red's grip, and braced himself with his hands.

"What hit me?" he demanded. "What . . . ?"

"I hit you!" There was a ring and a snap to Thad's voice. "I've got a gun on you now."

"Lissen," Red was pleading, "we didn't mean nothin'. We
. . ."

"Pull him up," Thad ordered. "Get him to his feet."

Red hauled at Chink's shoulders. Chink came up, took a lurching step and seized the edge of the open door for support. "Now get off!" Thad snapped. "Jump!"

Red's voice was a wail. "We're goin' too fast. You'll kill us."

Indeed the train was speeding now, the car rocking and lurching as the engineer made time down the slope of a sag. Thad could see the blackness of the landscape flashing past, and relented a trifle.

"Jump when he slows down," he ordered. "I don't trust you."

The speed of the train lessened as they passed the bottom of the sag and began the ascent of the other side. The tattoo of the wheels diminished. Up ahead the engine labored.

"Now!" Thad commanded. "Jump!"

"Lissen, mister," Red whined. "We got our turkeys at the end of the car. We didn't mean nothin', honest. We was just havin' a little fun . . ."

"Jump!" Thad ordered.

"We'll be killed," Red wailed.

Thad moved swiftly out of the darkness into the gloom of the door. The Bisley was shoved forward, pointed at the two. It was not hardness but rather fear that drove Thad, that made his voice savage.

"Jump or I'll . . ."

Chink, at the car door, let go of the edge and leaped. For an instant he was a flying blur against the dark sky and then he was gone. The train was barely moving now, panting up the grade.

"Jump!" Thad ordered again.

"Damn you!" Red snarled. "I'll get even with you. I'll . . ." He, too, took a step and jumped into the night. Thad, listening, could hear nothing but the beat of the engine's exhaust and the rattle of the car. He sat down, his back against the door. Had he killed them, he wondered. The train was moving slowly but . . . The Bisley Colt lowered, rested against his leg. Thad sat trembling.

They passed the top of the climb and rocking and swaying

hurried down the other side. Occasionally the engine wailed: *Whooooo . . . Whooooo! Whoo . . . Whooo!"* Thad held the gun in his lax hand and stared at the square of dimness that was the open door. How long he sat there he did not know. There was no way of measuring time. Then the speed slackened and there was a grinding sound beneath the car. Again the speed was checked, the jerk throwing Thad back, and then with a great clanking the train stopped. Thad sat still. A jerk almost threw him to the floor as slack went out of the couplings. The car moved ahead, stopped and from the engine came the muffled thudding of the air pump. Thad, gathering himself, got up, went to the car door and peered out. Away down the track he could see a lantern bobbing, and the lights of a switch stand. He sat down on the door edge and lowered himself to the cinders.

Moving back along the train, feet crunching in the ballast, Thad called cautiously: "Brick . . . Brick . . ." Beside each car he called and stopped to listen. No answer came. If Brick was on the train he must be behind the car Thad had taken. Thad knew that. He went on back toward the lighted caboose, still cautiously calling, still stopping to listen. Somewhere to the south a whistle wailed, faint and far away. At the car in front of the caboose Thad paused.

"Brick . . . Brick . . ." No answer.

Turning, he went back forward again. There was a rumbling roar coming now, growing stronger. Again the whistle, shrill and clear. Thad hurried. There was a lantern coming toward him down the train. He reached the open door of his box car, hoisted himself up and sought the security of darkness. Sound and vibration beat against the sides of the car, the roar grew, swelled to deafening pulsation, and then died away. At the car door the lantern winked.

"Come out of there, you bum!" a voice rasped. Thad, the Bisley hidden, moved forward.

"Think you can ride without payin' for it, do yuh?" rasped the man on the ground. Thad peered out. A brakeman stood in front of the car door, lantern lifted, brake club gripped threateningly.

"Come awn now!" the brakeman ordered. "If you want to ride you got to pay or else you get off."

"How much?" Thad asked.

"How much you got?" the brakeman snapped.

Thad felt in his pocket. "I've got half a dollar," he said.

The brakeman lowered the brake club. "Hand it over," he ordered. "I'll let you ride but if the brains or the hind shack comes along they'll throw you off. Come on. Gimme."

Thad dropped the half dollar in the brakeman's open palm.

"You'd better get up in the end of the car," the railroader announced. "Stay there where it's dark."

His feet crunched against the ballast again and the light was gone from the door. Thad retreated to the end of the car. His boot struck something soft and bending down he felt a blanket wrapped bundle. Was this what they called a turkey? Thad sat down on the bundle.

His back was braced against the end wall when the engineer put slack into the train. The jerk when the slack went out almost knocked Thad unconscious. He did not know what was coming and his head snapped back against the wall. The freight pulled out of the siding, stopped while the switch was closed, started again and once more the rattle of the car and the clicking of the wheels encompassed Thad. He sat on the bundle, the jolts lessened a little by its bulk. Gradually his head drooped. Where was Brick, he wondered. Where was Brick and where were Silk and Curly? Would he ever see Brick again? Would he ever see Curly and Silk? His chin touched his chest and he jerked his head up. Droop forward . . . jerk . . . droop . . . jerk . . .

"Come outa there, you bum! Come out now!"

Thad opened his eyes. He was sprawled against the end of the car. There was a blanket bundle under his head, torn and filthy. He sat up stiffly. Daylight was flooding into the car and, thrust through the open door, barely clearing the car floor, was a broad red face that held a pair of snapping black eyes.

"Come outa there!" the face ordered. "This ain't no passenger train!" Stiffly Thad got up.

The black eyes widened. "Hell," the face said. "You ain't nothin' but a kid. It's a good thing I found you, kid!"

Thad walked to the car door.

The man on the ground was as broad as his face. Broad shoulders, thick neck, short thick arms. He stared at Thad and Thad stared back and suddenly the black eyes twinkled. "Where'd you get on?" the trainman asked.

"Back there," Thad said.

"Well here's where you get off," the brakeman announced.

"I gave a man fifty cents," Thad informed. "He said I could ride . . ."

"That damn Ryan," the brakeman growled. "Knockin' down on bums again. Was that all you had, kid?"

Thad made no answer. The trainman gestured with one broad flat hand. "You get off," he ordered. "We're outside the yard limit an' it's lucky for you. They got the toughest railroad bull in Alta there is this side of Franklin. Git off, kid, an' take to your feet; an' don't let Sloan Whitless get hold of you."

Thad slid down to the car floor and dropped to the cinders. "Thanks," he said. "I . . ."

Again the broad hand waved. "Beat it, kid," the trainman ordered. "Here." Something flashed through the morning light. A quarter tinkled on the cinders at Thad's feet. "Cake money," said the brakeman. "Now, g'wan an' beat it!"

Thad stooped to pick up the quarter then walked on along the train.

"Get off the right-of-way," the trainman yelled after him. With an answering wave of his hand Thad turned to the left and dropping down over the little embankment, left the tracks.

On down the tracks, a wagon load paralleling them, there was a town. Thad debated about going into the town. It was early morning and the sun was half hidden in a cloud bank. Around the clouds the sky was clear and a deep blue. Hunger overcoming caution, Thad trudged down the road. As he walked, the train jerked into motion and rolled smoothly past him. On the steps of the caboose the broad-shouldered man lifted a hand in a parting gesture. Thad returned the wave.

He found a restaurant close to the edge of town and went in. The counterman eyed him curiously but went back to get the coffee, bacon and eggs that Thad ordered. Thad looked at himself in the mirror that was behind the counter. He was dirty, disheveled, his eyes red-rimmed. The counterman brought the order and Thad ate ravenously and paid for his meal.

"You don't want to stick around town, kid," the counterman advised. "The town marshal is hell on hobos."

Thad nodded his thanks and left the restaurant. He went on down the street and finding a store open, went in and bought a clean shirt. He had to give the merchant a twenty-dollar bill and the man eyed the bill then glanced sharply at Thad before he made change. Carrying the shirt Thad went on his way. The town was awakening and he believed that he had better not stay. He wished devoutly that Brick were with him. He needed Brick. Brick would know what to do. But Brick was not there.

On the further edge of town where the houses gave way to prairie, there was a clump of trees. Walking past the stockyards, Thad made his way to the little grove. There he found water and peeling off his soiled shirt Thad washed, rubbing his fingers over the stubble of beard on his chin. When the pool cleared following his splashing, he used it for a mirror and combed his hair with his fingers. His hair was long, grown unkempt since his last haircut. When had he last had a haircut? Thad remembered. It had been in Fort Blocker, just before he took the train south. He leaned back against a tree and moodily stared at the unpainted boards of the stockyards and at the rolling green country that was all about. Thoughts raced through his mind as he sat there. Uppermost among those thoughts was Brick Mahoney. Thad did not realize, had not known, how much Brick meant to him. Now Brick was gone. Thad was on his own. He wondered if word of the bank robbery and the killing close by Las Flores had come so far. This town was Alta and probably the law in Alta was as anxious to see him as the law in Las Flores or in Concha.

Wagons going by, headed toward town, attracted Thad. There were three of them, men sitting beside their wives on the spring seats, youngsters crowded into the wagon boxes. Thad stared after the wagons. There was only one thing for him to do: go on to Franklin and find the Palace Saloon and Arch Heibert, and ask for Brick. And Brick would not be there; Thad was sure of it. But what else could he do?

A little party of men rode by, going to Alta. There were lots of people on the road, and all going in the direction of Alta. Thad wondered what the attraction might be in town.

The sun climbed on up and the shade around the water lessened. Three milk cows, evidently belonging to people in town, came down and stood some distance away, afraid to come into the water because Thad was there. A train, going south, paused at the Alta yards, chuffed and puffed a good deal and then pulled slowly past Thad. He looked with longing at the red box cars. He wished that he were on that train but he was afraid, afraid to run out and climb on. Anyhow it was going too fast. More people passed along the road going to town. The sun was full above and it was noon. Thad stood up. Certainly with so many people in town one more would not be noticed. He was hungry and it was noon and he would go in and eat a meal. He had missed a great many meals recently.

The outskirts of Alta were deserted. Thad went on toward the center of town. A two-storied, red brick building was at the town's center and as Thad neared it he encountered the crowd. There were no women in the crowd, but only men, and they blocked the sidewalks about the red building, filled the streets. Thad hovered on the outskirts, staying back. Men came up behind him, blocking him off. He heard voices, words that were meaningless, and then he was standing beside a smooth-faced young fellow of about his own age.

"What's going on?" Thad asked.

"They're hangin' Rusty Dunneman," the smooth-faced boy

answered, and pushed forward. There was an eddy in the crowd that moved Thad. He came to the edge of the sidewalk and stopped. The two-storied brick building was a courthouse and there on the grass beside the courthouse, the raw yellow wood of a scaffold stood out like an open, running sore.

"What they hanging him for?" Thad asked.

The smooth-faced youth looked at him curiously. "Rusty held up an S. P. train," the boy answered. "Him an' his gang. The conductor and the express messenger was killed. You just come to town?"

Thad nodded. The youth, pleased with a fresh audience, retailed information. "Rusty got caught," he said. "One of his gang told the officers where he was. They had a big fight an' Rusty was brought in an' tried. He appealed the case but they finally turned him down. He's goin' to be hung at one o'clock. They . . . Here they come!"

There was a stir in the little clump of men beside the courthouse door. Through that group came another compact body of men closely surrounding a tall, hatless fellow that held his head defiantly. At the steps of the scaffold the group broke and the hatless man and three others began to climb the steps. The men behind intrigued Thad. There was one man, short, heavy-set carrying a sawed-off shotgun. Another was clothed in ministerial black and a third, long and lank and with a bony, prominent-nosed face, wore a derby and was smoking a cigar with quick nervous puffs.

"That fellow with the derby is Sloan Whitless," Thad's acquaintance murmured. "Railroad officer. He's the one that caught Rusty."

On the platform of the scaffold the three men were busy about the fourth. Quickly the rope loop that dangled from the heavy crossbeam was placed about the hatless man's head. The black-hatted man stooped and buckled a belt about Rusty Dunneman's knees; then, straightening from the task, the black-hatted man turned Dunneman until he faced the crowd.

The preacher was talking, low-voiced, and Dunneman shook

his head. The black-hatted man stepped forward, held up his hand for silence, and drawing a paper from his pocket, read the sentence to the tense crowd, his voice rolling flatly.

"First hangin' that Kleg Peter's ever had," Thad's companion murmured.

As the reading finished there was a stir and mutter from the crowd. Thad felt men behind him pushing forward and braced his shoulders against the movement. In front of the crowd men turned, spreading out their arms, holding back the surge of humanity. These were special deputies. Thad could see the bright star on the vest of the man who was in front of his particular section.

"Lots of folks liked Rusty," Thad's companion murmured. "If they'd . . ."

The stirring in the crowd ceased. Peter, the sheriff, had held up his hand once more. He was half turned, looking at the man on the trap. "Have you got anything to say, Dunneman?" he asked.

There was utter silence in the crowd.

On the scaffold Dunneman touched his lips with the tip of his tongue. His eyes looked to right and left. Thad had seen that same hunted, frightened look in the eyes of a trapped coyote. Dunneman's voice was curiously light and clear as he spoke.

"Yo're hangin' me," Dunneman said. "All right. Yo're hangin' me. An' I'll see you all in hell. I'll be at the door waitin'. Turn loose yore wolf, sheriff."

He stopped then, his lips closing firmly, only the jerking of a muscle in his cheek showing his strain. The sheriff, fumbling in his pocket, produced a black bag which he placed over Dunneman's head, and then stepped back. For a moment there was ab-absolute quiet and then, sudden as the fall of a plummet, Dunneman's black-clad body shot down and was lost to sight beneath the scaffold. From the crowd a concerted high-pitched sound arose as men who had held their breaths expelled them. Again silence reigned. For perhaps four minutes the silence remained unbroken save for the stamp of some horse as he struck at a fly, or the movement of booted feet on the board sidewalk. Then a sharp voice exclaimed: "I pronounce this man dead!"

Instantly bedlam broke loose. Behind Thad a man was sick, his retching, as he vomited, a gulping nauseating sound. Thad found that he was holding his throat with his hand and that he was sick, terribly, strainingly sick. He fought down the sensation and rising on his boot toes, saw a pudgy red-faced man standing in front of the dangling body beneath the scaffold. From the crossbeam the rope hung tight, vibrating a little still.

"Who's that?" Thad demanded, and found that his whilom acquaintance had been pushed away by the movement of the crowd. Someone else, close beside him said, "Doc Flarity's pronounced him dead."

Gradually the crowd thinned. Men, sick with what they had seen, excited, eyes wide and their faces white, passed by Thad, stumbled against him, pushed him as they moved. Saloon doors flapped and banged. One man, already drunk, was crying and his companions surrounding him drew him away. Still Thad waited. He saw a knife flash against the rope and heard the thump of Dunneman's body as inept hands dropped it.

Thad shoved himself back until his shoulders touched boards. He leaned against the building, bracing himself. The crowd thinned further and then there was a stir and a disturbance. Thad could see men carrying a body, limp, hanging from their hands like a meal sack. He turned until he faced the building, braced an arm against it and leaning his head on the arm fought down the sickness that was in him. Behind him feet tramped on the boards of the sidewalk and voices babbled. Thad did not look. He knew what was being carried past.

CHAPTER TWELVE

A Hand from Texas

AFTER a time Thad straightened from the wall. The gnawing hunger that had brought him into town was gone, but he could not go back to the trees beyond the stockyards. He could not leave the company of people. People, the duly accredited representatives of the people, had done the thing that Thad had just witnessed, had afforded the grisly spectacle that he had seen. Paradoxically he must stay with people, securing from other shocked individuals about him a measure of comfort. Thad walked down the street, not looking back at the courthouse and the empty scaffold, from the crossbeam of which a limp rope now dangled, but keeping his eyes firmly ahead.

When he came to the corner he hesitated. Dregs of the crowd that had witnessed the hanging still eddied along the street. Men came out of stores or saloons and talked to other men and re-entered doors. Now an occasional woman or child showed among the crowd and Thad heard the shrill voice of one small boy persistently plaguing his father for details of the tragedy. As he stood, undecided as to what to do, a tall man, black-mustached, the hair at his temples touched with gray, came from the store behind Thad and crossed the sidewalk to a buckboard. The man helped his companion, a girl of perhaps sixteen, into the buckboard and standing beside the wheel spoke to her.

"I'll be back in a minute, Childress," he said. "I've got to get a man to go out with us." He stepped up on the sidewalk again and the girl said: "All right, Dad."

The tall man moved toward an adjacent saloon and two men, coming from the saloon stopped and spoke to him. "How are you, Mr. Vermillion?" one asked, and the other, apparently an acquaintance, said: "Are you goin' right out, Morgan?"

"As soon as I get a man," Vermillion said. "We're haying."
He stood exchanging pleasantries with the two and Thad listened with half his attention. He was looking at the girl. She
was young and sweet. Her dress, of some flowered stuff, was
crisp and becoming, and her small cameo-like face was tilted up
toward the sky like the face of a flower. Nothing touched the
girl; Thad could see that. All the turmoil, all the soiled things
that walked or ran or crawled or wound torturously through
people's minds, would never touch her. She was so clean and so
sweet, and Thad's eyes lingered on her reverently. With a start
his attention was drawn from the girl back to reality. A heavy-
paunched man wearing a black hat, and another leaner edition
of the same man, were hustling two disheveled specimens along
the walk. Thad stepped back to be out of the way. One of the
men being pushed along was slight and red-haired. The other
was larger, black bearded. Both were dirty, their clothes and
skin grimy. Both were expostulating and there was no mistaking
the whining voice of the red-haired man. He was Red, the man
of the box car, the man whom Thad had forced to jump. Perforce the other must be Chink.

"We ain't done nothin'," Red whined. "We're tryin' to get
to California. We're just a couple of 'bos."

The fat man, pushing Red along, growled deep in his fat
throat. "Concha wired us to be on the lookout for you. Yo're
Brick Mahoney, that's who you are. Don't try to lie!"

"I ain't!" Red shrilled. "I ain't . . ."

He was past Thad now but he turned to look at his captor
and catching sight of Thad, struggled to free himself. "There
he is!" Red shrilled. "That's the one!" The fat officer jerked
him around and pushed him along, but sudden terror struck
Thad. Red had recognized him. He took a swift step back,
reached the side of the saloon and was seized by an idea. Morgan Vermillion was still in front of the saloon, he and his two
acquaintances watching the progress of Red and Chink along
the street. Thad spoke to Vermillion.

"I heard you say you needed a hand," he managed, his throat dry and his voice a little edged with his tension. "I'm a good hand in hay."

Vermillion's eyes were very black and very sharp. They searched Thad's face, passed from that on to his broad shoulders and on down along narrow hips and long legs to booted feet. A glint came into the black eyes. "What's your name?" Vermillion drawled.

Thad thought rapidly. "Ted . . . Smith," he answered. "I've made hay. I can drive a mower or a rake or stack. I . . ."

Vermillion's lips curved a trifle and the amusement was plain in his black eyes. "You want a job pretty bad," he said. "You've done a little ridin' too?"

"Yes, sir."

"Where are you from?"

Again Thad thought rapidly. "Texas," he answered.

Vermillion laughed and the two men with him grinned. "And you're pretty hungry and you want to eat," Vermillion said. "I never saw a cowboy that was worth a damn at anything but ridin', but I'll give you a job. Got a bed?"

"No, sir," Thad said.

"I can fix you up, I guess," Vermillion announced. "You go crawl into the back of that buckboard over there. Tell Childress you're going to work at the ranch. I'll be along in a minute." He chuckled at some deep mysterious joke, his companions laughing with him, and then pushed on the half-shutter doors of the saloon and went in. Thad walked across to the buckboard.

"I'm the man that's going to work at the ranch," he told the waiting girl, and stepping from the walk, went around and climbed into the bed of the vehicle.

Vermillion came out of the saloon wiping his lips with a handkerchief. He nodded to one or two men, untied his team, and climbing to the seat of the buckboard, backed the conveyance from the hitchrail, cramped the wheels to turn, and then straightening out the team drove along down the street toward the south. At the edge of town Vermillion followed a road that angled off toward the east, crossed the railroad tracks and let the horses trot along. Turning his head so that he looked over his shoulder he grinned at Thad.

"Texas, huh?" he said, and chuckled.

"Yes, sir," Thad answered.

"You never saw Texas," Vermillion grinned. "You don't have the kind of talk that comes from Texas. You come from the north—Colorado, likely."

Thad maintained a wise silence.

"And your last name is no more Smith than mine is," Vermillion gibed. "Don't pick Smith the next time, Ted. Better use Jones or Brown."

"Yes, sir," Thad said.

"Why'd you leave Colorado? Get into trouble?"

Thad saw the amusement in the black eyes. He grinned. "I robbed a bank," he said gravely. Vermillion burst into laughter.

"You don't need any more lessons," he said. "I don't guess your trouble was very serious. Probably you had a fight with your dad and decided to pull out on your own. Well, I'll make a hay hand out of you."

"Yes, sir," Thad said once more.

The buckboard rattled on southeast. From time to time Morgan Vermillion spoke to Thad, from time to time he had a word for his daughter. The girl answered, her laugh rilling like the trill of a meadowlark. There were long companionable silences too, when the rattle of the harness and the whir of the wheels and the steady plop of the trotting horses seemed to make the quiet a friendly pleasant thing.

With the sun low behind them they reached a stream and followed down it. The stream became a series of holes in wide grasslands and Vermillion looked back to Thad and said, "Is that hay enough to do you?"

Thad agreed that there was enough hay to keep him busy awhile and had hardly spoken the words before they swung across a vaga, the wheels silent on the soft earth and, rounding a low point, came upon a house and barn set about by hay stacks and corrals.

"Unhitch, Ted," Vermillion directed. "Turn the horses into the big pen and put the harness in the barn, and then come on up to the house."

He climbed down, grinned at Thad, helped his daughter alight and then, man and girl burdened by packages, walked toward the house. The door opened and a gray-haired motherly woman came out on the porch and kissed both Vermillion and the girl. Thad took the lines, drove the buckboard under the shed, backing it in expertly, and then alighting, unhooked the tugs and drove the horses to the barn.

He had unharnessed the team and was hanging up the harness when a man, gray-haired, elderly, appeared at the door and said casually, "I'll turn the horses out, kid," and possessing himself of the bridles led the bay team away.

Thad finished with the harness and came out of the barn to see the gray-haired man turning the horses through a wire gate. Over by the bunkhouse four or five men loafed, leaning against the wall, the small drawl of their voices drifting across to Thad, and from the cook shack beside the bunkhouse an aroma of cooked food and hot coffee came to crinkle Thad's nose and bring the saliva flowing in his mouth. He was ravenously hungry. He started toward the house and the gray-haired man, coming from the wire gate, intercepted.

"Ted Smith, ain't you?" the man asked, a little humor in his voice. "I'm Carl Logan. Vermillion said that you could come up after you'd ate supper. It's about ready."

Substantiating that statement the cook stuck his head from the door of the cook shack and drawled: "Come on an' eat, you fellers." Thad followed Logan to the cook shack.

At the table, where Logan occupied the end, there were casual introductions. Thad met Shorty Coventry, Ben Nichols, Murray Blane, Ken Moore, Walt James. They ate and ate, Nichols and Blane on either side of Logan. Logan evidently was the foreman, Blane and Nichols the riders. The talk was small, dwarfed by weariness and appetites. The cook, Patsy, hovered over the table, pouring coffee, bringing in more bread. Finished, the men stacked their dishes, carried them to the kitchen, dumped plates and cups in one pan; knives, forks and spoons in another.

"Now we'll go to the house," Logan said, and fell in step beside Thad.

Vermillion, the motherly woman, and the girl Childress were on the porch, Vermillion smoking a cigar comfortably. He nodded to Thad, said: "This is Ted Smith, mother," and turned to Logan. Mrs. Vermillion looked at Thad, smiled and said: "I've got some blankets for you, Ted. You need to borrow a razor."

"Yes, ma'am," Thad agreed.

Vermillion said: "You get a dollar a day and your board, Ted. Give him a rake to drive tomorrow, Carl."

Thad felt that he was dismissed. He gathered up the clean blankets from the porch steps, said, "Good night," awkwardly, and walked back to the bunkhouse. At the cook shack door he paused. "Have you got enough hot water for me to take a bath, Patsy?" he asked the cook.

Patsy grunted but Thad could see that the cook was pleased. "Haul in that tub outside," Patsy directed. "I'll have plenty of hot water. An' if you want to wash yore clothes I'll loan you a pair of overalls."

Thad said, "Thanks," and carried his blankets into the bunkhouse.

Later, in the kitchen, he scrubbed his clothes, his nakedness covered by a pair of cook's voluminous overalls. Then, filling the tub he dragged in from outside, he tempered the cold water with hot from the cistern on the stove and reveled in soap and the silken flow of water against his skin. Up on the porch Carl Logan, reporting to Vermillion, drawled:: "He asked Patsy for hot water an' soap. He washed his clothes an' he's washin' himself now."

In the shadows Vermillion's wife said: "I knew he was a good boy." And Morgan Vermillion chuckled.

"You have to see them, don't you, mother?" he gibed. "Likely he's an outlaw on the dodge."

"He's a good boy, just the same," Mrs. Vermillion said placidly. "Go to bed now, Childress."

Thad went to bed in the bunkhouse. There was a brand carved in the wall above his bed, the same brand that he had seen on the team coming out: a Flying V Bar. He went to sleep looking up at the place where the brand was carved and with the gentle snores of his companions about him. For the first time since his father's death, Thad felt a tranquillity, an ease all about him.

In the morning the feeling persisted. Morning came mighty early at the Flying V Bar; four o'clock heard the cook's call of, "Roll out," but even with the sleepiness and stiffness that that early hour brought, Thad felt at peace. Four o'clock wasn't very early. It was just a good getting-up time. He went with the others to do the chores, watched Murray Blane ride out on a wrangling horse to bring in the remuda, saw the horses come in and watched when Logan, the foreman, pointed out his team. Back at the bunkhouse he took his turn at the washbench, ate breakfast and then went with the others to the pens once more. He harnessed his team and with satisfaction walked behind the chunky horses down to the shed and hooked them to the buckrake that Logan said he was to handle.

From the headquarters the hay crew proceeded to the nearest vega. There, while two mowers began the round, Thad helped set the stacker. Vermillion had come down with the others and only Blane was riding. Everybody worked on the Flying V Bar and when they were haying everybody worked in the hay.

There was hay on the ground, cut the day before. The rake men waited for this to be freed of the night's moisture by the ascending sun and when it was dry enough, Coventry bunched it with a dump rake. Nichols and Logan were driving mowers. Vermillion himself had the stacker team and Walt James was on the stack. That left Thad and Ken Moore to buck the hay into

the stacker. Thad swung his team out, dropped his rake and began to pick up hay. When he had the rake loaded he drove in,
swung his team expertly to land his towering load on the teeth
of the overshot stacker and, backing them off, started out again.
He noticed that Vermillion watched him closely with the first
few loads that he brought in and after that paid no more attention to Thad than he did to the other hands. The hay was odor-
ous with the smell of freshly cut grass. Thad's team, working at
either end of the buckrake, were old enough to know how to
handle their job and young enough to have plenty of life. Thad
could drive a team, had handled teams and horses all his life
and when he came in with his sixth load he was whistling and
Vermillion grinned at him. The overshot stacker banged away,
throwing hay up on the stack, Vermillion drove the stacker team
and cleaned up around the stack with a fork, and James, on top,
handled the hay and stacked it, keeping the middle packed and
the edges even. It was mighty good to be in the hay field, mighty,
mighty good.

About ten o'clock Childress came down from the house,
mounted on an upstanding, spotted horse. She had a whole sack
of doughnuts and everybody knocked off for perhaps ten minutes to eat doughnuts and drink cool water from the burlap-
wrapped jugs, and relax a little. Then the girl was gone and the
work was taken up once more. At noon teams were unhooked
and taken to the barnyard where they were grained, gunny sack
morrales hung over their heads and their wise eyes peering over
the sacking for all the world like kids peeping over a lowered
blindfold. Dinner was hot and plentiful and there was time to
stretch and light pipes and cigarettes before returning to the
field.

Back in the field again the stacker was moved and staked
down and the endless round of haymaking went on. About four
o'clock Childress came down again, this time with lemonade,
cool from the spring house, and at six o'clock when work ceased,
Thad unhooked Buck and Bess from their singletrees, climbed
up on Buck's broad back and, with his hand on the hames, rode

back to headquarters, at peace with the world and with himself, and for the moment his cares forgotten in sheer physical weariness and the sense of a day's work well accomplished.

One day marched into the next without pause, without intermission, without friction. Gradually the tension in Thad's mind eased, gradually he relaxed. No one asked him any questions, no one pried, he was accepted as a workman, a man who had a job and who could do it, a peer among his fellows. At the end of the week they had finished the first big vega and were ready to go to the next, and at the end of the second week Morgan Vermillion paid his hands in good hard money and green bills. Carl Logan was going to town and by Logan Thad sent in for shirts and socks and another pair of overalls and a neckerchief.

On Sunday the Flying V Bar rested. Only Thad and Shorty Coventry were left at the place, the others having departed on various missions. Walt James had gone to see a girl at Alta; Logan was in town. Blane and Nichols departed upon an unstated mission, Ken Moore went home to visit his folks, some fifteen miles away. Even fat Patsy, the cook, had an errand in town and went to do it. On Sunday Thad and Coventry ate dinner at the big house with motherly Mrs. Vermillion presiding at the table and Morgan carving the roast and watching Thad with twinkling black eyes. After dinner there was a long quiet afternoon before it was time for the others to come back and the chores to be done, and Thad and Coventry loafed in the bunkhouse. Coventry wanted to talk and Thad let him, and presently the talk shifted to Vermillion and the Flying V Bar.

"He's been here a long time?" Thad asked. "He isn't very old, is he?"

"Fifty, mebbe," Coventry answered. "He's older than he looks. He's only been here since Childress was born. He settled down when she come."

Thad glanced at the other man. Coventry was perhaps fifty years old himself and looked his age, whereas Vermillion appeared to be about forty.

"Morgan," Coventry said, "bought this place then. He's

added to it right along an' he's got a real outfit, but before that he was an officer."

"An officer?" Thad lifted his eyebrows.

"An' a good one," Coventry said. "Morgan Vermillion done it all. He was a U. S. marshal over in the Indian Territory; he was a peace officer up in Kansas right at the end of the trail drivin'. He was just about everything."

The older man stopped and filled a pipe, lighted it and then drawled on. "Morgan," he said, "arrested me for stealin' cattle an' got me sent up for four years. When I came out he was waitin' for me an' he brought me out here an' give me a job. I've been workin' for him ever since." He puffed away at the pipe, eyeing Thad.

"But . . . weren't you sore at him?" Thad demanded. "Didn't you . . . ?"

"Hell," Coventry waved an arm, "it was Morgan's business to catch me. He was sheriff in Alta then. He's been a damned good friend to me, Morgan has."

Thad sat still, digesting that. Outside the bunkhouse a horse went past, the steps uneven. Thad, getting up, went to the door. Childress was riding her bay paint pony toward the barn, and Comanche, the paint, was limping. Thad stepped out and walked toward the barn.

When he reached the building Childress had dismounted and was looking at Comanche. Comanche was a gentle enough horse, cowpuncher-gentle anyhow, even though he would not have been exactly safe in an Eastern park. "He's lame, Ted," the girl announced as Thad came up. "I went for a ride down the creek and he went lame, so I came back."

"Whereabouts?" Thad asked.

"His left front foot."

"Can you pick up his feet?" Thad asked practically.

"We had to throw him to shoe him," the girl answered. "I've never tried to pick up his feet."

Thad walked over to Comanche. The horse cocked his ears at the approach of a stranger and Thad's voice was very soothing as he spoke. "What's the matter, huh?" Thad drawled. "Got a rock, did you? Need a li'l help, huh? Now look: I didn't do that to you. That was a couple of other fellows. I wouldn't hurt you on a bet."

His voice droned on, comforting, soothing. His hand slipped from Comanche's bay neck, down over his white shoulder, across a bay forearm and on to white pastern and fetlock. Thad eased his shoulder in against the horse, talking all the time, pulled on the fetlock and up came Comanche's foot.

"Got a nail in it," Thad announced. "He picked one up in the barn probably. You get the shoein' outfit."

Childress hurried away into the barn and Thad continued to talk to Comanche and to hold up his foot. On the porch of the big house Morgan Vermillion watched the scene and smiled broadly. Comanche was letting Thad get away with something that he would have resented in anyone else. Comanche was plenty touchy around the feet.

"Look here, mother," Vermillion said, and his wife, getting up from her chair, came to the end of the porch.

Childress brought the shoeing box and put it down. Thad drawled words to Comanche and Comanche listened with cocked ears while Thad got the nippers out of the box and pulled the shingle nail out of the pinto's foot.

"There you are," Thad announced. "It was the nail, not me that hurt you." He put the foot down and, tentatively, Comanche tried his weight on it.

"Nothing very bad," Thad assured Comanche's owner. "It got into the quick a little, but it isn't bad."

Childress was beaming. "I'm glad of that," she said. "Can I ride him now?"

"I wouldn't till you see if it's going to make trouble," Thad advised, speaking of the nail. "I'll unsaddle for you an' turn him out."

The girl nodded her thanks, and Thad led Comanche away and stopping beside the saddle room, pulled off the saddle and blanket.

When he came back after turning the horse into the horse pasture Childress was still waiting at the barn. "Thanks," she said, smiling frankly at Thad. "You come on up to the house. I baked a cake yesterday and I'll give you a piece. It isn't very good."

"I'll bet it is," Thad answered, and walking beside the girl, made for the kitchen.

On the porch Morgan Vermillion spoke to his wife. "There's a pretty good boy, mother. And he's a hand with horses. I wouldn't be surprised if I didn't find something for him to do after we're through with the hay."

Grace Vermillion smiled placidly at her husband and continued to darn the sock in her hand. "I thought you would when you brought him out," she said. "I think he's a nice boy, Dad."

CHAPTER THIRTEEN

He Who Runs

SUNDAY evening saw the return of the wayfarers. Ken Moore came back first, shortly followed by Murray Blane, Ben Nichols, and James. Thad and Shorty Coventry did the chores, the milking and the feeding, and they had finished that when Carl Logan arrived in the ranch buckboard, accompanied by Patsy. Patsy had viewed the sights of Alta unwisely and too well. It required two of the boys to get the cook into his room and to bed, and in the excitement of Patsy's advent and trying to keep him quiet, all else was forgotten. It was not until late, after an impromptu supper cooked by Shorty, that Logan gave Thad the clothing he had purchased. Thad put the package under his bed without unwrapping it. He grinned ruefully to himself as he did so. It seemed to Thad that he was always buying clothes and going off and leaving them, running away, and he hoped that his most recent purchases would not suffer the same fate.

Logan, now that Patsy was attended to, was full of news.

There was a good deal going on in Alta and Logan retailed it. Uppermost in interest was the story he had concerning a joke on the Alta sheriff's office. According to Logan everybody was giving Kleg Peter and his deputies the horse laugh.

"They arrested a couple of fellows the day that Dunneman was hung," Logan said. "Kleg had a telegram from Concha to look out for Brick Mahoney and his pardner the Wyoming Kid. They was supposed to have jumped a train an' come south. One of the fellows that was arrested was red-haired and the other was young and kind of big and Kleg thought he had Brick an' his pardner. He throwed 'em in jail an' called the officers at Las Flores to come over. Charlie Farrel got to Alta this mornin' an' said that Kleg was all wet. He had a couple of bums. The worst part of it for Kleg was that the redheaded hobo had tried to tell him that the Wyoming Kid was in town an' standin' right on the sidewalk when the deputies taken these bums in. Now Kleg don't know what to do. The redhead seen this Wyoming Kid and Brick eatin' supper in a restaurant in Concha an' he seen 'em get on the train. An' a brakeman said that he seen a young fellow that answered the Kid's description get off a train ouside the Alta yards an' go in to town. It'll just about ruin Kleg when election time comes around."

"What's Kleg goin' to do about it?" Coventry asked.

Logan shrugged his shoulders. "What can he do?" he answered. "He's let 'em both slip through his fingers an' arrested a couple of hobos that he had to let go. Kleg's pretty sick about it."

The talk went on, full of surmise and conjecture as to the probable actions of Brick Mahoney and the Wyoming Kid. The bank robbery at Las Flores was recounted and embellished and the killing of Kettleman was commented upon.

"They're salty, both of 'em," Murray Blane stated. "I wouldn't like to bump up against Mahoney or the other one either. They'd think no more of killin' a man than they would a gopher."

"I don't think . . ." Thad began, and stopped short. All eyes were turned toward him.

"What don't you think, Ted?" Walt James asked.

"Oh nothin'," Thad answered lamely. "I was just going to say I don't think they'll catch those two."

James grunted, and Shorty Coventry made comment. "If the boss started after them you bet he'd catch 'em."

"Yeah, he would," Logan agreed.

The talk went on until Logan, announcing that he was going to bed, walked out of the big room to go to his own smaller one that, as foreman, he occupied. After Logan's departure the others quieted and, undressing, went to bed. Thad lay awake a long time after Coventry was snoring, looking up at the blackness overhead and pondering over what he had heard. He could run, he knew. He could make a break and get away, but if he did it would cause a lot of talk and undoubtedly put Kleg Peter on his trail. The sheriff would want to know why a hay hand working for Morgan Vermillion pulled up stakes and disappeared just as soon as he heard that the sheriff's office was looking for Brick Mahoney and the Wyoming Kid. It was better to stay and not run until he had to.

In the morning the hay crew moved to the upper vega. Because of the distance from the house they took along a wagon and a lunch and did not come in at noon. There was a water keg, and feed in the wagon for the horses, and when noon came the men loafed in the wagon's shade. Again there was talk concerning the mistake made by the sheriff's office in Alta. In this talk Vermillion took some part, asking a few brief questions but not commenting on what he heard in reply.

That night when the crew was finished with the day's work, Vermillion drove the wagon in. He called to Thad as he climbed to the wagon seat and directing the youngster to tie the team to the wagon's endgate, gestured to the seat beside him. "Come on and ride with me, Ted," he ordered.

Thad, after fastening the team, climbed up to the wagon seat and they started for the ranch. The wagon was the end of the procession and Thad watched the others riding ahead. James was mounted on one of Coventry's horses, Coventry on the other. Beyond those two the other teams were strung out, each teamster riding one of his horses.

"You know, Ted," Vermillion said suddenly, "I think maybe I can use you after we're through with the hay. Did you ever break any horses?"

Thad nodded. "I've broke horses," he said.

"Both my riders are getting kind of old to saddle a bronc," Vermillion commented. "Murray is a good hand with a horse and so is Ben. They can teach a horse something but I'd like to have somebody younger to kind of take the edge off. Want to try your hand at it?"

"Yes, sir!" Thad agreed eagerly. He had been worried as to what he would do when the hay was finished. This brief interlude, this breathing spell in his flight had seemed a paradise to him. He had, for a little time, lost the wild fear of the hunted man and had felt a certain security but he knew that the safety was temporary. Once away from this haven and he must run again. And here was Vermillion holding out a hand and showing him a vista of future peace.

"I saw you with Childress' pony last night," Vermillion said. "Comanche is gentle enough an' safe or I wouldn't let the girl have him, but he's a fool about his feet. I'll let you have a try at snappin' broncs. I've put off startin' 'em till right now hopin' I could find a good bronc rider."

"I'll try my best," Thad promised.

The wagon rolled along. "You weren't in very bad trouble, were you, Ted?" Vermillion asked suddenly, and then, without waiting for Thad to answer, "A kid like you is mighty apt to think a thing's bad when it ain't." He looked at Thad narrowly as he spoke and Thad turned away and watched the prairie country slide past.

"You know," Vermillion said conversationally, "a man that's goin' to amount to anythin' usually gets into a jackpot or two.

Generally there's a time when he can step one way or the other. He's got to make up his own mind. Sometimes he kind of gets on the wrong side of the fence an' has to go back an' start over. That's all right if he does it."

"Suppose he don't do it?" Thad ventured.

Vermillion's face was stern. "Then he goes clear bad and in the end it gets him," the ranchman said. "Look at Rusty Dunneman. He wound up by gettin' hung. Take Brick Mahoney and this Wyoming Kid; take the fellows that were with 'em, Silk Gerald and Curly Winters. They started out likely, just like a lot of young fellows start, not doing anything that was very bad but just bein' ornery. Then they got in deeper and deeper and now they've robbed a bank and killed a man. They can't go back an' start over. They're in too deep."

"What'll happen to them?" Thad asked, managing somehow to keep his voice level.

"They'll get caught," Vermillion prophesied. "Sometime they'll slip up and the law will get them. Then they'll get what Dunneman got. Every man that believes in the law will be against them. They can't buck the world. They might get by for a while but sooner or later they'll slip. A man like that is generally a wolf." Vermillion's lips were a grim straight line and his eyes were bleak. After an instant he spoke again. "A young fellow can generally go back and clean up whatever little mistake he's made," he said, and the grim lips curved. "You think it over, Ted. You've got some friends, you know. Mother likes you and you've made a good hand for me in the hay."

"Yes, sir," Thad answered automatically.

When they reached the ranch Thad unharnessed both teams and attended to them. When he finished that he washed up and went to supper. The first edge off the crew's appetites, talk sprang up around the table, reverting, naturally, to the recent excitement in Alta. Opinions were expressed freely and Thad, finishing his meal, stepped back over the bench, carried his plate out to the kitchen and then went on outside. He sat down against the wall and the talk floated out to him.

"There's a reward out on Mahoney and the Kid," Carl Logan announced. "Five hundred dollars for their apprehension an' arrest. Maybe that's why Kleg is so sore."

A laugh went up at that and after the merriment had subsided Walt James asked a question. "You sure about the reward, Carl?"

"I've got a hand bill if you want to see it," Logan answered.

Silence followed the announcement. Evidently the reward notice was being passed around. Coventry said: "This description of the Wyoming Kid would fit a lot of people. It would pretty near fit you, Ken, an' it's a dead ringer for Ted."

Again there was laughter. Ken Moore announced: "Well I was over to my folks' place the day the bank in Las Flores was held up. I guess that lets me out."

And Murray Blane with the sharp humor of the rider, answered Moore: "Yore folks might have to testify, Ken. Mebbe Kleg will want that dinero so bad he'll pick you up."

A general scraping of the benches and the rattle of dishes in the wreck pan announced the end of the meal and the men came trooping out of the cook shack. It was not quite dark and Coventry walked over beside Thad and stuffing his pipe; lighted it and sat companionably smoking.

"What you got lined up when we're through hayin'?" he asked.

"Mr. Vermillion said that he'd put me to starting broncs," Thad answered.

Coventry nodded. "An' he'll have somethin' else for you to do after that," he prophesied. "Morgan likes you an' when he likes a man he'll stick with him."

Thad made no answer and Coventry said: "There's a ring around the moon. It's changin' too. We'll have a rain tomorrow." Knocking the dottle from his pipe, he got up and went into the bunkhouse.

Coventry's prophecy came true. In the morning there was a gentle drizzle that, before noon, grew to a storm in volume. No man makes hay in the rain and the Flying V Bar hay crew stayed in out of the wet. When after dinner the storm broke and the clouds cleared away it was too wet to go in the field, and Logan put his men to work about the place doing various odd jobs that a ranch always has available.

Thad's chore was to grease the wagon. He got the vehicle up on blocks under the shed, took a wrench and removed a wheel and was liberally daubing on the axle grease when Childress came down from the house and stood watching him. Childress, wearing a clean gingham dress, looked like a home-made angel fresh out of the kitchen. Thad stopped work and smiled at the girl.

"You've got grease on your cheek," Childress announced.

Thad reached up a hand and touched his cheek, thereby adding more grease. Both of them laughed.

"Dad says that he's going to put you to riding broncs," Childress made announcement, "as soon as the haying's done."

"That's right," Thad agreed.

"Did you ever ride broncs?"

Thad had put back the first wheel and was busy with the second. The nut was stuck and he labored with the wrench, so intent on what he was doing that he paid no thought to his reply. "Sure," he said. "I rode broncs in Wyoming. Before I came down here I always had a bunch of green horses."

Childress sat down companionably on a box. "I wonder what it's like in Wyoming," she said. "Is it like down here?"

The nut turned and Thad banged his knuckles against the hub and put them to his lips for he had skinned them. "About the same,". he agreed absently. "Different kind of grass an' there's mountains."

"I'd like to go there," Childress mused. "I'd like to travel on a train. Dad said that he'll take me back to Kentucky when I'm older. Tell me about Wyoming, Ted."

Sharp anxiety shot through Thad. No longer abstracted by the wheel he knew that he had said the wrong thing. "I wasn't up there long," he said awkwardly. "I come from Texas you know."

"Then tell me about Texas," Childress commanded.

"Well . . ." Thad had never been in Texas and was caught again, ". . . it's a pretty kind of country. You know Texas is awful big an' it's hard to tell about it."

"But just where you came from," Childress insisted.

There was no backing out. Thad had to talk. He hated to lie to this eager girl sitting there so prettily but he had to say something. In desperation he invented a Texas that never was and will never be. "There's lots of mountains," Thad said. "Big high ones with snow on 'em. They go away up. There's . . ." Walt James came around the corner of the shed. He looked at Thad through narrow eyes for a long minute and then passed on without a word, going toward the house. Thad wondered if James had been behind the shed all the time.

"Go on," Childress commanded.

"Oh, there isn't much to tell," Thad said. "It's just a place."

"Some day," Childress said, "I'll go there."

She stayed on the box while Thad finished the greasing. He was replacing the last wheel when the girl got up. "I wonder where Walt is going," she said, stepping out from the shed.

Thad came from the wagon and joined the girl, wiping his sleeve across his forehead, for the afternoon was hot and the shed even hotter. Walt James was riding off across the vega, heading northwest.

"Maybe Dad sent him to town for something," Childress said.

"Maybe," Thad answered and went back into the shed.

He finished with the wagon and helped Coventry set two posts in the corral. By that time the sun was low and Logan said that they would knock off. The men cleaned up. Thad, changing to his newly purchased clothing, loafed until supper was ready and after the meal they went out to do the chores.

Thad finished with his team and was going back to the barn with the empty morrales when Childress came down from the house again. She followed him straight to the barn and stood in the door while he hung up the feed bags. The other men had finished, all save Coventry who was milking, and Thad and the girl were alone in the barn.

"You aren't an outlaw, are you, Ted?" Childress blurted. "Dad said at supper that . . ."

Grace Vermillion's voice came from the house: "Childress! . . . Childress . . . !"

"Mother wants me," Childress said. "You aren't, are you?"

Thad turned slowly. "I . . ." he said.

"Childress!" the call came again.

"I've got to go," Childress said. Turning she ran toward the call. Thad stayed in the barn. He watched the door and no one appeared. Carefully, always watching the door, he went to the ladder and climbed into the loft. In a corner of the loft under a pile of old hay, he delved with his hands and brought out a cloth-wrapped bundle. He had hidden the Bisley Colt and his spare shells in that bundle the day he came to the Flying V Bar. Now he slipped the gun into his waistband, hiding it under his shirt as Brick had taught him, and put the spare shells in his pocket. Descending the ladder he saw that there was still no one in the barn. He knew now why Walt James had gone to town. He knew why Morgan Vermillion had sent James in.

There was bitterness in Thad, a kind of hatred. All he had asked was to be let alone. He had made a hand, a good one. He had done nothing to Vermillion or to James or to any one of these men. But James had heard him mention Wyoming and had heard his fabrications concerning Texas, and James had gone to Vermillion who had sent James to town. Thad remembered the hardness in the ranchman's face when Vermillion said: "A man like that is generally a wolf."

The Bisley Colt nestled against Thad's belly. "Every man that believes in the law will be against them," Vermillion had said, and too: "A young fellow can go back and clean up his mistakes," and, "You've got some friends, you know." Morgan Vermillion! The first inkling, the first suspicion he had that Ted Smith was Thad Breathea, alias the Wyoming Kid, Vermillion had sent a man to town for the sheriff. If Childress had only . . . No, Thad couldn't be angry with Childress. Childress hadn't known. Childress hadn't believed. She had come to him demanding the truth. Childress . . . sweet and clean and loyal to her friends . . .

Thad Breathea stepped out the back door of the barn and slid it shut after. He walked deliberately to the stack yard and through the stacks. On the far side he climbed the wire fence and in the dusk that now had fallen, he dropped off the level land into the bottom of the creek that ran through the horse pasture. The moon was up and shed a faint light. Back in the Flying V Bar headquarters men sat in the bunkhouse and probably there was a pitch game in progress with Coventry and Logan and Nichols playing. Up at the big house Mrs. Vermillion would be at work on her knitting or darning and Morgan would be sitting on the front porch and Childress washing dishes. Thad followed the creek toward the west. There was a long walk and many a climb ahead of him but not as long a walk or as steep a climb as those short thirteen steps he had seen Rusty Dunneman take. Over west there was a railroad and trains that ran toward the south and Franklin and Brick Mahoney— always supposing that Brick had gotten clear. Brick was the only friend he had; Brick was the only one who had stayed with him.

Thad grunted as he stumbled over stones, steadied himself and tramped on. For a while he had thought . . . Well, what was the use of thinking? The little time of peace was past and he must run again. Run like any other hunted thing, until, trapped at last, he would turn and face his hunters and pit his puny strength against them.

CHAPTER FOURTEEN

Thirty Days

CHARLIE FARREL sat on the front porch of the Flying V Bar ranch house and puffed slowly on his cigar. Vermillion occupied a rawhide-bottomed chair beside him and Grace Vermillion's rocker made a pleasant creaking sound. Childress was on the top step, hands locked together, thin girlish arms extended, back bent so that her chin rested on her arms, occupying a position that only the very young and very supple could achieve.

"I wish you'd come out yesterday," Vermillion said.

Farrel puffed on his cigar and nodded. "So do I," he agreed. "But it rained yesterday mornin' an' the road was bad an' Kleg wanted me to stay in town."

"He was here yesterday," Vermillion said, and paused.

"Yeah," Farrel drawled. He was quiet a moment after that and then spoke again. "I've been tryin' to find him. I've worked pretty hard at it. Funny how a break will come. If Kleg hadn't arrested those two bums an' if I hadn't come over to identify 'em an' then come out to visit you I'd never have hit his trail. Funny how things work out. I'm just a day late."

Vermillion tossed the stub of his cigar away and looked at Farrel. "Walt James heard the kid talkin' to Childress yesterday," he commented. "The boy's tongue slipped and he said that he was from Wyoming. Then he back-tracked and said it was Texas and told Childress all about the high mountains with snow on 'em." He laughed, a short, harsh bark. "James came leggin' it up here to say that the boy working for me was the Wyoming Kid. I told James he was crazy."

"He's a good boy," Grace Vermillion announced from her rocker. "I said so when I first saw him."

"Sure he's a good boy," Charlie Farrel agreed. "When he was

picked up he claimed that somebody gave him those horses to hold. Then Krespin said that he'd never seen the kid, and when Mahoney and them came back and tied me up and took the kid out of jail I felt sure that the boy was with 'em. You'd have thought so yourself, Morgan."

Vermillion nodded.

"Now," Farrel took his cigar from his mouth and eyed it contemplatively, "I know that the kid was tellin' the truth. There was a Mexican in the plaza that saw the kid take the horses an' heard what was said. An' there's been some things come up . . . Krespin is tryin' to cheat the kid out of what he's got comin'. I've got a letter from a lawyer up in Wyoming. He's comin' down. I'm goin' to have a poor time with him. I'm goin' to have a poor time all around. You see it's murder that I'm workin' on."

"Yeah," Vermillion drawled, "you told us."

Farrel paid no attention to the comment. "I sweated Branch Long a little," he recounted. "I wanted the truth about that Kettleman thing. Branch said Mahoney killed Kettleman. He said the kid got up an' dressed, that he was in bed when the trouble started. I don't see how the kid could have had much to do with that. A naked man generally ain't in on the shootin'."

"You told us that too," Vermillion reminded.

"And so," Farrel said, ignoring Vermillion's statement, "I come over here an' get a rig from the livery and ride out to see you an' stumble onto the kid's tracks. Funny, if I hadn't been a friend of yours I'd never of come out an' I'd never known how close I missed him."

"If Walt James had kept his mouth shut and hadn't gone leggin' it off to town the boy would still be here," Vermillion said darkly. "Walt is too good a hand at puttin' his nose in other people's business. That's why I sent him back to town with Kleg Peters this mornin'. I haven't got a place for a man like James, even if it does leave me short-handed with the hay crew."

"Ummm," Farrel said, around his cigar.

"And when you do find the boy, *if* you find him, I want to

know about it," Vermillion stated. "I liked the kid and I'll back him up."

"He's a good boy," Grace Vermillion said again with conviction.

Childress' voice came from the step, light and clear and sweet. "I wonder where Ted is now," she said.

"That's what we'd all like to know," her father answered.

And where was Thad Breathea? He was sitting on the sand, a mesquite bush, long and black-ridged, behind him and a fire blazing in front. There were three others besides Thad about the fire, battered, unkempt men, dirty faces covered with beard stubble, almost like animals as they sniffed the stew that was cooking in a bucket on the blaze.

"Mulligan's good," one grunted, and the cook, squat, long-armed as an ape and with the simian face of an ape, stirred the stew and made answer.

"You put everythin' into a mulligan except the bread an' the coffee. How's the coffee comin', Frisco?"

The first speaker was Chicago Dave, lanky and a little contemptuous of the others for he was the oldest on the road. The Rambler was cooking and Frisco Shorty now got up from where he sat and peered into the lard bucket that held the coffee.

"Pretty near ready," he said.

"The mulligan's *all* ready," Rambler announced. "Let's eat." Selecting a coffee can from the pile beyond the fire he dipped it into the fragrant stew, carried it a short distance away and squatting down, produced a spoon from a pocket of his ragged coat. Frisco and Chicago Dave were also selecting cans and Thad, getting up, walked to the can pile, took a can and helped himself to the stew. Having no spoon he bent a can top and used that for a conveyer to shovel the stew into his mouth.

"How long you been on the pike, kid?" Rambler asked, looking at Thad.

"Not so long," Thad answered and reaching out a long arm lifted the coffee from the fire. "Coffee's boiled," he announced.

"Just a damned gaycat!" There was contempt in Chicago Dave's voice. "We oughtn't to let you eat with a real stiff."

Thad looked steadily at the speaker. He did not like Chicago Dave and made no effort to hide his dislike. "Try to stop me," he snapped, and ladled in another can top of stew.

"The pike's gone to hell," Dave deplored. "A kid like you talkin' like that! Why ten years ago . . ."

"You told us all about ten years ago," Thad interrupted.

"Don't be so ringy, kid," the Rambler counseled. "Dave's been up an' down the road plenty. Where you from?"

"Where I come from," Thad retorted.

Rambler, an advocate of peace, changed the subject. "I wish we was out of Franklin," he observed. "Franklin's a hard town on 'bos."

"These country cops don't want to get tough with me!" Frisco boasted. "I know how to take care of them." His hand went in under his shirt and came out holding an eight inch knife that glinted evilly in the firelight. "Just a little of this an' they get pretty soft," Frisco declared.

"For Pete's sake put that up!" Rambler urged. "You don't never want to let one of these Franklin laws ketch you with a knife or a gun on you. I seen Denver after he'd served some time in Franklin. Denver had a gun on him when they caught him an' they like to beat him to death. Put it up, Frisco, an' have some more stew."

Frisco grunted and put the knife out of sight with a flourish. "Just the same . . ." he began.

"They give a man thirty days an' put him to work," Rambler stated, and shuddered at the thought of work. "They're makin' a sewer system. Lord, but them shovels are heavy, an' it's hot as hell too."

A hard voice out in the dark said: "All right, you bums. Stand up an' put your hands up."

"The law!" Frisco snarled and leaping to his feet made for the shadows. A shot cracked sharply. Frisco stopped his swift

retreat, lifted his hands well above his head, and turned around
slowly.

"That's right," commended the hard voice. "The rest of you
act nice an' there'll be no trouble."

Thad was in the shadow. He was caught and fairly; there
was no chance of his getting away. The mesquite blocked him
to the rear and he had to cross the firelight to make his escape
in any other direction. Still the mesquite gave him a chance. Sur-
reptitiously drawing the Bisley Colt from under his shirt, Thad
dropped it in the sand under the mesquite just as another voice,
higher than the first but equally hard, demanded: "You there!
What're you doin'?"

Thad stood up and lifted his hands shoulder high. A man
came from the shadows into the firelight, a gun held low, not
pointing at anything in particular but very prominent in his
hand. "Line up!" he ordered. "I'll look 'em over, Lanky. Line
up, you!"

Thad joined Frisco, Chicago Dave and the Rambler, standing
in line. The man with the gun passed behind them, feeling of
their pockets, tapping them under the arms and around the waist.
From Frisco he took the knife that that traveling man had
flourished and tossing it away into the darkness, stepped back
a half pace.

"Carry a shive, do you?" he questioned and dispassionately
slapped Frisco with the barrel of his gun. A red welt leaped
out along the side of Frisco's face and he staggered. The officer
slapped again with the gun and this time Frisco went down.

Out in the dark Lanky commended his partner. "That ought
to learn him, Babe."

Babe went on, completing his search, paying no attention to
Frisco who got to his feet, holding the side of his face with
his hands. "All right," Babe barked, "now make for the track
an' go on to town. The Judge is goin' to be glad to see you tomorrow. We're still diggin' a sewer." He chuckled malevolently
and fell in behind his captives.

Before they reached the track Thad thought of escape. It was full dark now that they had left the fire and there might be a chance. As though sensing his thoughts the man behind him dug a gun into his ribs and spoke.

"I'm right behind you. Keep goin'."

Thad kept going.

The little procession passed the lighted depot where numerous bystanders all had comments to make on its progress; on up through town, presently to halt before the jail. There was no formality at the jail. Thad, Chicago Dave, Rambler and Frisco Shorty, blood running down his neck from the welts on his head, were shoved unceremoniously into the bull pen and the door clanged shut behind them.

There were about ten men in the bull pen, some of them sleeping on benches against the wall, others awake, some standing, some sitting. The arrival of Thad and his companions caused but little disturbance. The sleepers continued to sleep and those awake and sober enough to be interested asked a few desultory questions. A turnkey coming to the door, looked through the grille and said: "Shut up, you!" and the bull pen lapsed into quiet. Thad picked out a place on the floor, lay down and despite the hardness of his bed, was soon asleep.

In the morning the four were arraigned before a police judge. That swarthy official, his English a broken, crippled thing, was brief and to the point. Thirty dollars or thirty days was his judgment and, except for two drunken cow punchers whose foremen appeared and paid their fines, all the occupants of the bull pen were stuck. Thad kept still when he came before the judge. He was afraid to speak out, afraid to say anything. He gave the name of Ted Smith to go on the blotter and aside from that and to say that he did not have thirty dollars, he maintained a discreet silence. He had decided that he would much prefer to be Ted Smith, serving thirty days for vagrancy, than Thad Breathea, wanted in New Mexico for bank robbery and murder.

Following the arraignment and sentencing the men were

taken back to jail. There Chicago Dave was told off to clean up the bull pen, empty the slops and otherwise care for the primitive sanitary arrangements; and the others, under the care of four guards, were marched out and along the street. Thad was surprised at Franklin. He had never been in a town of any size save only Denver and his brief sojourn in the depot at Denver had hardly been instructive. Franklin sprawled among the hills. These were bleak, dotted with sparse desert growth, and to the southwest Mount Franklin scowled down forbiddingly upon the town. Northward the smoke of the smelter mushroomed up against the sky, copper-colored in the sun. There was smoke too above the railroad yards. The buildings were low, one- or two-storied with an occasional three-story sky-scraper bordering the sidewalks. There were hacks at the curbs and a yellow trolley car banged past, causing Thad to shy almost like a frightened horse. As they marched they caught glimpses of the brown and sluggish river and the talk that came to Thad's ears was drawling English or rapid sibilant Spanish.

"All right," the guard commanded, "you take shovels!" His finger singled out six of the prisoners. "You others get you a pick apiece. Come on!"

Thad, in possession of a shovel, climbed down into a trench under the guard's direction and laboriously began to throw dirt up on the ridge above the narrow cut. At either end of the trench a guard sat, one under a big striped umbrella, both with shotguns across their knees. The guns were Winchesters, Model 1897 pump and were sawed off until the barrel was no longer than the magazine. The other two guards patrolled the side of the trench, looking down at the men beneath them. They too carried sawed-off guns and occasionally their voices rose harshly as they cursed a malingerer.

Thad shoveled dirt that Frisco loosened with his pick. There were brief intermissions when he rested and Frisco swung the pick, longer intervals when he lifted the long handled shovel, loaded full, and tossed the dirt out of the pit. The sun beat down like a sledge hammer, pounding on the men in the trench until the blood in their heads throbbed in aching pulsations. Rivulets of sweat ran from wet foreheads to join larger streams on chests and backs. Thad could feel the blisters growing on his hands.

"Come on! Shovel it out!" the guard rasped.

At noon they were marched back to the jail. There were beans and bread and something that passed for coffee. For a short intermission they sprawled in the bull pen, the more fortunate who possessed tobacco smoking cigarettes, the others, utterly weary, stretched on the floor. The stifling jail felt cool after the beating sun. Then back to the trench and the waiting shovels they went, to resume their unending labor.

Evening was a relief. After a supper of beans, bread and coffee, they were herded into the bull pen and left to their own devices. And while the benches in the bull pen were hard and the floor even harder, still there were compensations. The jail was not verminous and there was water with which to wash and there was always the chance that the evening would bring diversion. The town was hard, booming, tough as only a border town can be tough, and the police net caught some queer specimens. Then too there was the kangaroo court presided over by the bully of the bull pen and attended by his sycophants. Thad fell prey to that rough court and perforce whipped the bully of the bull pen, beating him unmercifully. After that he was left alone and as long as he stayed, the kangaroo court lost some of its sinister aspects.

At first the labor in the hot sun was almost unbearable; then Thad hardened until his hands were like iron and his muscles were ribbons of steel that played under his sweaty, dirty skin. Some of the others were not so fortunate and some were more fortunate. Some of the prisoners fawned upon their guards and bought favors with that fawning. Some of them broke under the strain.

Frisco was one of these. Working in the trench under the hot sun, he lifted his pick high and, with it poised in the air, collapsed. A guard cursed him and then climbed down into the trench while the others stood by. The guard bent down over the prone Frisco, lifted the man's limp head, pushed back an eyelid with a calloused forefinger and then climbing out bade Thad and Rambler lift the man. Two other prisoners carried Frisco away and Thad never saw the man again. Whether Frisco lived or died he did not know.

There were thirty men in the bull pen at the time of Frisco's collapse. The trench was long and not too deep, perhaps six feet. They had progressed from their first site and were further toward the town, following the line of stakes that engineers had set in the alley. The morning of the day following Frisco's removal, Thad, marching with his fellows to work, glanced at the back of a two-story brick building. They had just entered the alley as he looked up and he saw in a window of the building a pale face topped by flaming hair. There was no mistaking it: Brick Mahoney was looking out of the window. Thad stared at Brick, almost stopping in mid-stride. Brick looked down and then ducked hastily back from sight. He had not recognized Thad under his growth of beard and in his dilapidated, dirty clothing.

"Go on, Smith!" a guard growled.

Thad climbed down into the trench.

It was about ten o'clock when the break came. Thad, swinging a pick, struck rough boards and he pried at them, working them loose with the pick. A board and tattered, moldy cloth fell into the bottom of the trench and Thad, striking again with the pick, pried off another piece of board. Now a skull, a bit of hair still clinging above the ear hole and several vertebrae together with the flat-ridged bone of a scapula, tumbled into the trench. Thad stepped back.

"Hey," he called to the guard above him, "we've hit a graveyard."

The guard came to investigate. Thad passed up the skull and the scapula, pried again with the pick and was rewarded with the small bones of a wrist and hand, and the radius of an arm. Something glinted and bending down he picked up a heavy gold ring that evidently had come from the fingers. The guards had assembled above him and one of them demanded: "What you got there?"

Thad climbed up out of the trench and handed over the ring. The guard that was holding the skull dropped it and it bounced back toward the high board fence that lined the alley. Thad went to retrieve the skull but the attention of the guards was centered on the gold ring. Thad stooped, picked up the skull and was about to step back when he saw that he was opposite a gate in the fence and, more to the point, directly behind the fence was the brick building in the window of which he had seen Mahoney's face. Thad pushed on the gate, it opened, and with a step he was through and the gate closed behind him. Dropping the skull he ran toward the back of the building.

The windows here were barred with long iron rods but there was a door and it was open. Thad went through that door and into a room that smelled of beer and stale liquor. There was a stairs to his left and he moved toward them only to be stopped by a harsh voice.

"What do you want?"

Thad turned. A man in a white apron, his face hard, was standing at the inner door.

"Brick's up stairs," Thad panted. "I've got to get to him; I've got away."

As though to vouch for that there was a shout in the alley, a clamoring of voices. The hardness left the face of the man in the white apron. "Brick?" he snapped.

"I'm his pardner," Thad panted. "I'm . . ."

"The Wyoming Kid," the man in the apron finished. "Here, kid, duck down here. They'll be lookin' for you." He pulled up a trap door as he spoke and Thad caught a glimpse of darkness and steps that led into it. Then he was on the stairs, going down and the door closed above his head. Thad reached the bottom step and crouched.

He heard feet tramp back and forth overhead. He heard voices but could not distinguish the words. A long time went by, hours it seemed to the waiting Thad; then the trap door lifted. "Come on out," directed the white-aproned man, looking down. Thad climbed up the steps.

The saloonkeeper caught him by the arm as he reached the top. The saloon man was fat and had a round, moonlike face and a pair of the smallest eyes Thad had ever seen. "They sure missed you, kid," he said, his face wreathed in a smile. "I met 'em at the back door an' told 'em you'd run west and went over the fence. They're still lookin' an' you'll have to be careful. Come on now an' I'll take you up to Brick."

With the fat man's hand guiding him, Thad found the stairs and began the steep ascent. At the top landing the saloon man knocked twice and then once. A key turned in the door they confronted and it opened slowly. Thad stepped into a room. Brick Mahoney, a gun in his hand, was just beyond the door, partially screened by it. Brick was in shirt and trousers and the shirt was tucked in little folds where the left arm should have been. For a long moment the two eyed each other and then Thad, taking a step forward said, "Brick!"

Brick Mahoney lowered the hammer of the gun. "Oh kid!" he said.

CHAPTER FIFTEEN

The Last Job

THEY shook hands briefly after that, Brick putting his gun into his waistband to free his hand. And then they walked together to the cot that was against the wall and sat down. The saloon man remained beside the door, his round face smiling. Brick looked from Thad to the saloonkeeper and grinned.

"It's the kid all right, Arch," he said. "Thad Breathea. Kid, that's my brother-in-law, Arch Heibert."

Thad got up and shook hands with Heibert and thanked him. The grin never left Heibert's face. "Brick was worried about half to death when he didn't hear from you," he said. "I'm glad you got here. What are you goin' to need, kid?"

"I'd like to clean up and shave and get some clothes," Thad said. "I've been in the jug and digging sewers. I need to clean up."

"I'll see about gettin' you some clothes," Heibert promised. "Brick's got a razor an' you can get a bath in a barber shop after you shave an' change clothes. I'll leave it to you two fellows. You'll want to talk." He went out the door and closed it after him. Brick crossed the room after him and locked the door, and then came back to the cot.

"What happened to you, kid?" he demanded.

"What happened to you first!" Thad said. "How'd you get here? You didn't get on that freight I caught."

Brick shook his head. "I knew what was happenin'," he announced. "I saw those fellows shootin' at you an' I yelled at you but you didn't hear me. I caught the end of a car and went right across the coupling an' hit the ground an' run for the coal chutes. I hid in the chutes an' then I caught the blinds on an eastbound passenger an' went over into Colorado. By the time I got there I was pretty sick. Then I worked west an' hit the Santa Fe an' bought a ticket an' come straight here. I came right through Las Flores."

"You did?" Thad's face expressed his incredulity.

"I was travelin' on a Pullman an' I laid in a berth," Brick grinned. "You see this arm I lost was really givin' me hell then. I could say I was sick an' not be lyin'."

Thad nodded understanding.

"When I got here Arch an' my sister met me an' we went across to Mexico. The arm was infected an' a doctor over there took it off. He said he had to or I'd check out. I'd just about as soon of died as lose it but they didn't give me much chance to say what I wanted to do." Brick's eyes were morose.

Thad put his hand on Brick's shoulder. "You'll never miss it," he promised. "Not while I'm with you."

Brick got up, went to the barred window and looked out

briefly. "Arch has been stakin' me," he said. "Arch wants me to go to South America. I can locate down there. Some of them big outfits need men that can handle cattle an' speak Spanish. I wouldn't go till I'd heard from you." He swung back from the window and looked at Thad. "A damned cripple," he grated.

"You ain't a cripple," Thad refuted hotly. "South America sounds all right to me."

"You'd go with me?"

"I'll go any place you go," Thad promised.

The old sunny grin broke across Brick's pallid face. "What happened to you, kid?" he demanded. "You took a hell of a time to get here."

"An' had a poor time doin' it," Thad said. "I'll tell you."

Briefly then he recounted his adventures, the ride on the train to Alta, the hanging of Rusty Dunneman, his job with Morgan Vermillion, his flight, his arrest in Franklin, and his work in the sewer trench. "I saw you this morning, looking out the window," Thad completed. "I knew then I was going to make a break. We dug into an old graveyard and I had a chance and took it. Now I'm here."

Brick's eyes were filled with curiosity as he looked at Thad. "Yo're hard, kid," he commented. "You were just a kid when we first hooked up. Now you're hard as I am, harder maybe."

"Who wouldn't be?" Thad shrugged. "One thing sure. Brick, they'll never take me; not now, not after what I've seen and what's happened to me. They pick up a man for being a bum and give him thirty days in hell. Then if they can get him again they stick him again. There's no square deal about any of it. Look at me: I never did a thing wrong, not a thing. What's happened to me was framed on me. Now, by Glory, I'll take care of myself."

"Yeah," Brick nodded slowly, "you will."

There was two taps on the door, a pause and then a third tap. Brick crossed to the door and turned the key. Thad saw that Brick pulled his gun immediately after unlocking the door. The door opened and a woman came into the room. She closed the door behind her, put her shoulders against it and reached out toward Brick. Brick bent and kissed her. The woman was young, red-haired and blue-eyed, the rich blood in her cheeks showing through her milky white skin.

"I thought that was you, Ellen," Brick said. "This is the kid. He got here finally. Thad, this is my sister."

Thad bowed awkwardly, conscious of his bearded face, his worn, dirty clothing, the dirt and stink upon his body. Somehow he could not quite make this true in his mind. He had always pictured Brick as alone. To find that Brick had a family was a shock.

"Arch said that you had come," Ellen Heibert's voice was low and musical. "I'm glad. Now Brick will get away and out of danger."

"I haven't been in danger," Brick spoke quickly. "Not with you an' Arch lookin' after me. Don't the kid look good, Ellen? Ain't he all right?"

Thad was favored with a slow scrutiny of the blue eyes. Ellen Heibert nodded. "He's your friend, Brick," she said gravely.

"We'll get him cleaned up an' he'll look swell," Brick promised. "What's been happenin', Ellen?"

The woman shook her red head. "Nothing," she answered. "I came to see you and to see your friend. When will you be ready to go, Brick? We'll have to make arrangements."

"Pretty soon," Brick answered. "The kid's goin' with me."

"I'm glad!" Ellen thrust out her hand toward Thad in an impulsive gesture. "You'll look after Brick, won't you?"

"I'll stay with him," Thad promised.

"Arch is coming up," the woman said. "He has some clothes. I'll have to go now."

Again there came the tapping on the door. Ellen stood back and opening it, admitted Heibert. Heibert had clothing laid across his arm. "I rustled some duds," he announced. "You better slip along now, Ellen."

The woman flung a flashing smile at Thad, kissed Brick, and

went out. Heibert tossed the clothing down on the bed. "Help yourself, kid," he invited.

When Heibert had gone Brick sat down on the cot, Thad, stripping off his dirty clothing, washed as best he could with water from a bucket, and then with the aid of a small mirror, a pair of scissors and Brick's razor, freed his face of its growth of beard. His skin was pale as he emerged from beneath the growth and Brick laughed and joked with him. "Yo're as pale as I am, kid," Brick said. "But you look a lot better than you did."

"I feel better too," Thad agreed, dressing in the clothing Heibert had brought. "But I'm not clean yet."

Brick's eyes narrowed. "There ain't any reason why you can't go out," he announced. "Nobody knows you here. Cleaned up an' dressed the way you are, they'd never recognize you."

Thad nodded and finished his dressing.

For the remainder of the afternoon he sat on the cot with Brick. They talked, recalling the things that they had done together, reliving old adventures, harking back to the cave behind Alfredo Vara's goat ranch and the wild ride across country to the rim. Gradually the light in the room diminished and presently Heibert came up with food for both of them. He looked with approval at Thad.

"You look a lot different," Heibert said. "If I hadn't brought you here I wouldn't know you."

"Think it will be safe for the kid to go out?" Brick asked.

Heibert studied over the question and finally nodded his head. "I think so," he said. "They've quit askin' about you, Brick. The marshal hasn't been around again. They probably think you've gone to Mexico. Nobody knows the kid here and I think he'll be safe."

"I want to get a haircut and a real bath," Thad announced.

Once more Heibert nodded. "I think it will be safe," he said again. Accordingly the saloonkeeper waited while his guests ate the meal he had brought and then carrying the tray and with

Thad following him, left the little room. They went downstairs together and Heibert placed the tray on a beer keg and
took Thad with him on into the saloon.

There were no patrons in the place and only a bartender on
duty. Heibert spoke briefly to the bartender and then drawing
Thad aside, asked him if he had any money. Thad replied that
he had none and Heibert supplied the lack from his pocket.
"You can pay me back whenever you get it," he said casually.
"If you never do it's all right."

"I'll pay you," Thad promised.

"There's a barber shop two doors up the street," Heibert
directed. "Have you got a gun, kid?"

Thad shook his head. Going behind the bar Heibert returned
and passed over a short-barreled, hammerless Smith & Wesson.
"It's a lemon squeezer," he said. "A .32. . . . I don't think you'll
need it but it's handy."

"Thanks," Thad said gratefully. "I'm making you a lot of
trouble."

"No," Heibert shook his head. "Brick set me up in business
in this place. Brick's sister is my wife. Yo're Brick's friend. Anything I do ain't any trouble. You go on and get yore bath an' a
haircut. When you come back I'll have a place fixed for you to
sleep upstairs."

Thad nodded and left the saloon.

When he came back he was really clean, his hair cut and himself feeling as though he were a different person. Only the hat
and boots remained of his original outfit and both of those
needed replacement; still he did not feel inclined to spend any
more of Arch Heibert's money on himself.

Heibert was behind the bar when Thad came in and there
were several patrons in the saloon. It was not until these had
left that Heibert had time to go upstairs with Thad. He accompanied Thad to Brick's room, Brick admitted them and Heibert
pointed out bedding and another cot that had been brought up
during Thad's absence.

For two days Thad stayed close in the room with Brick. They

were fed by Heibert and visited daily by Ellen. On the afternoon
of the third day the woman commented on Thad's boots and his
hat, saying, in her husband's presence, that this apparel should
be replaced. Heibert agreed and when Thad demurred, Brick
took a hand. Accordingly Thad reluctantly agreed that he would
buy new boots and a new hat, and Heibert said that he thought
it would be safe enough for Thad to go out and get them. Boots
and hats are articles that require fitting and they could not be
purchased and brought in.

Thad did not go out until late the following afternoon. He
and Brick spent the morning talking about South America, dis-
cussing what they would do and how they would get there. Brick
was filled with enthusiasm and Thad caught the contagion from
Brick. There was a change in Brick, Thad noted. Where before
Brick had been hard and not inclined to regard consequences,
now he seemed less calloused and more apt to weigh results.

About three o'clock Thad left Brick and went downstairs.
Heibert had supplied him with money and Thad went along the
street to a clothing store. There, in place of boots, he bought a
pair of riding shoes. They were less expensive and he could get
a fit in them. Thad found no difficulty in securing a hat. His
selection was a small beaver-belly Stetson, the sort of hat a
brush-popper from the pear country would buy, and paid for
both purchases. When he left the store he did not immediately
return to the Palace Saloon. Franklin interested him, intrigued
him, and the fact that he had passed a man who had served as a
guard to the sewer gang and received no more than a casual
glance, had made him bold. If the guard had not recognized him
no one else would. Thad stood on a corner under the shade of
a tin awning and watched Franklin pass by, the clanging trolley
cars, the hacks with their coatless drivers, the shuffling, som-
breroed Mexicans, the troopers from Fort Blossum, all the life
of the town moving sluggishly in the afternoon heat. He did not
see two men come from the saloon behind him, pause and survey him closely and then step back into the saloon. Had he seen
those two he might not have so boldly walked back to the

Palace when six o'clock came, for the two were Silk Gerald and
Curly Winters.

Silk and Curly stayed in the bar. They watched the tall youngster through the half shuttered doors and when Thad left the
corner Silk and Curly came from the saloon and, half a block
behind him, followed along the street until they saw him enter
the Palace.

They gave Thad a little time and then casually went into the
saloon. Heibert's bartender was behind the bar and there were
two men drinking beer and talking to him, but Thad Breathea
was not in sight. Curly and Silk each bought a glass of beer,
talked casually to the bartender and then left the place. Outside
the Palace they stopped.

"That was him, sure," Silk stated.

"It was," Curly agreed.

"An' that's Brick's brother-in-law's place," Silk amplified.
"One time Brick was talkin' an' he said his brother-in-law run
a place in Franklin an' that his name was Heibert. You heard
who the bartender said his boss was, didn't you?"

"Uhhuh," Curly grunted. "Heibert."

"The kid went upstairs," Silk announced. "That's the only
place he could of gone."

"Unless he went out the back," Curly offered an alternative.

Silk shook his head. "I don't think so," he disagreed. "I'll
watch the front for a while, Curly, an' you go around to the alley
an' watch the back. See who comes out."

Curly nodded his head and departed.

Half an hour later he came back and rejoined Silk. "A waiter
from the restaurant just went in the back with a tray," Curly
announced. "I watched him go in the back door."

Silk's eyebrows lifted. "Then one of them is there for sure,"
he stated.

"Both of 'em," Curly said positively. "There was too much
on that tray for any one man."

"So what do we do?" Silk asked.

Silence fell between them for a time and then Curly offered

a plan. "Let's go in an' ask about Brick," he suggested. "After all we was with him, wasn't we? We want to hook up with him again, don't we?"

"Try it anyhow," Silk said. "We'll wait awhile an' then go in."

Thad and Brick were in their room playing cribbage when the knock came. The time was tedious and they had resorted to cards to break the monotony. Brick was almost recovered from the amputation of his arm and was fretting at the restraint placed upon him, and Thad too was restive, beginning to hate the narrow confines of their hiding place. A few more days and they would leave. Arrangements were already made for them to cross the river and there pick up horses. They planned, once in Mexico, to work along toward the south and eventually reach Vera Cruz. There they could get a boat and go on to their ultimate destination: Argentina. Both were sanguine concerning the proposed venture. There was, of course, the possibility that they would stay in Mexico, providing opportunity offered. But they had become thoroughly imbued with the idea that Argentina was the place to go. The name intrigued their imaginations, and Arch Heibert had brought books and maps and the two had pored over them avidly. Thad had just counted a twelve hand when the knock came on the door, two taps, a pause, then the third tap. He got up from the table and, crossing to the door, unlocked it. Heibert stood at the threshold and behind Heibert, Silk Gerald and Curly Winters. Instantly Thad was alert.

"Hello, kid," Silk said, not giving Thad time to say a word. "We didn't know you were here. We came to see Brick." As he spoke he stepped past Heibert and entered the room. Curly too passed Heibert who stood just at the door. Thad looked at Heibert inquiringly.

"They're all right," Heibert said. "They were with Brick. I know that."

Brick's voice, greeting the two, forestalled anything Thad might have said. Brick was cordial. As Thad turned he could see Brick shaking hands with Curly, and grinning. Thad nodded curtly to Heibert and stepped back into the room. He did not like this; he did not like it at all.

"You remember Curly an' Silk, kid," Brick said jovially. "Remember when they took you out of jail?"

"Sure," Thad agreed. "I remember." He did not say that he also remembered that Silk and Curly had ridden off and left Brick and himself, but his eyes were dark with the recollection.

Silk came up and put out his hand. Perforce Thad took it. "We been tryin' to hook up with Brick ever since we split off," Silk said. "How did you make out, kid?"

"All right," Thad answered briefly.

"You had tough luck, Brick," Curly said. "Losin' that arm was a bad break."

Brick nodded soberly. "I'm about well of it now," he announced. "When did you boys get in?"

"Just now," Curly answered. "We had a hell of a time. We been on the dodge ever since we split up. We worked south an' when we got this far we looked for you. You remember one time you were talkin' about Franklin an' we kind of figured you'd be here. Silk remembered what you'd said about yore brother-in-law an' so we come."

"I'll leave you fellows," Heibert spoke from beside the door. "There's a pretty good crowd downstairs an' I'd better get back."

"Come up when you can, Arch," Brick called.

"Sure," Heibert answered, and went out closing the door behind him. Automatically Thad turned the key.

Silk sat down on a cot. Curly took one of the chairs beside the table and looked at the cribbage board. "Gets kind of tiresome hidin' out," he suggested. "Gettin' pretty tired of it, Brick?"

"Damned tired," Brick corroborated. "It won't be long now, though. Me an' the kid are leavin' poco pronto."

"So?" Silk said. "Where you goin'?"

"South America." There was pride in Brick's announcement.

Silk whistled softly. "That's a long ways off," he said.

Curly toyed with the cards on the table. "You got a stake that will get you there?" he asked.

"We can get one," Brick answered. "Arch figures that he'll stake us."

Thad had not seated himself. He stood beside the shaded window, leaning back against the wall, watching the two visitors. Somehow Thad could not feel that this was a friendly visit, that the intentions of these two were as above-board as they seemed. Now he interjected a word. "Brick staked Heibert," he said. "Arch told me all about it. Brick's got it comin'."

Curly disregarded Thad's comment. "Silk an' me been thinkin'," he drawled. "How'd you like to pull out of here with a stake of yore own? One that you didn't owe to nobody?"

"What have you got on yore mind?" Brick asked quietly.

"I'll tell you," Curly answered. "Me an' Silk got a job staked out. We need some help. We want a couple of boys that we know we can count on an' we thought of you an' the kid. How'd you like to make five thousand dollars, Brick?"

Brick's eyes brightened and then faded again. "I ain't any good," he said. "This arm . . ."

"We'd ruther have you without no arms at all than anybody else," Silk assured. "It's yore head that we want, Brick. We need some help plannin' this."

"What is it?" Brick asked.

"A payroll," Silk announced. "There's a bunch of mines up around Gato. The payroll goes out to 'em twice a month an' it's a sweet pot. We would kind of like to look at that payroll, Brick."

"Gato," Brick said musingly.

"Up above Las Flores," Curly amplified. "Silk an' me know that country like a book. They haul the payroll out on a train. What do you think about it, Brick?"

"Gato," Brick said again. "That's a bad country for me an' the kid to go into. You know that Kettleman business . . ."

"Nobody is crowdin' you about Kettleman," Curly interposed hastily. "They kind of figure up there that you done 'em a favor."

"It would be a nice little stake," Brick mused. "It wouldn't cramp Arch any."

Thad knew that Brick had been worrying about taking money from Arch Heibert. Heibert was willing to give it to Brick; in fact, insisted that he give Brick sufficient money for the proposed venture. But Brick did not like it that way.

"Now this is the way we kind of planned it," Silk said. "We can get horses an' a little outfit. We take our time gettin' up there. By the time we reach the north end of the country you'll be feelin' all right; then we'll look it over an' do the job, an' we'll all have money enough to do what we want. There's anyhow thirty thousand dollars in that payroll. We split it four ways."

"It sounds kind of good," Brick admitted.

"Then you'll go?" Silk's question was quick.

Brick looked at Silk and then at Curly, his eyes narrow. "Yeah," he said deliberately, "I'll go."

"Good!" Exultation was in Silk's voice. "How about you, kid?"

"I side Brick," Thad said quietly. "All the way."

"An' that's good too," Curly said heartily. "We'll have a drink on it."

"Go down stairs an' bring a bottle, kid, will you?" Brick asked.

Without a word Thad went out and down the stairs. When he returned Arch Heibert was with him. Heibert brought the bottle and the glasses and set them on the table. "Celebration?" he asked.

"Kind of," Brick admitted. "Did the kid tell you?"

"He said you wanted a drink," Heibert answered.

Brick took the opened bottle and poured drinks into the small glasses. "I won't be needing that money from you, Arch," he said. "I'll make my own stake."

A worried look came into Heibert's eyes. "You goin' to pull a job?" he asked bluntly.

"Silk an' Curly an' the kid an' me," Brick answered.

"You don't need to, you know," Heibert said. "You know how welcome you are, Brick. You know . . ."

Brick had taken his drink. He grinned at Heibert. "I know I ain't goin' to sponge on you no more, Arch," he announced.

Heibert seemed about ready to push his point, then thought better of it and, with a nod to the men about the table, went out.

"We'll plan a little now," Brick announced. "Have you boys got any money?"

"I've got enough for what we need," Silk said. "All right, let's plan it."

The talk went on, a discussion of horses, outfit, routes to follow, all the details of getting into the northern country. Thad took no part in the talk other than to listen. Brick gave information concerning the acquisition of horses, spoke concerning the men who could be trusted and those who could not, mentioned the things he believed essential. Silk and Curly added details. Thad said nothing but listened and as he listened he watched Silk and Curly with narrow, distrustful eyes.

"All right," Silk said finally. "Tomorrow night then. We'll have it all lined up. We'll be ready to go."

"An' so will we," Brick promised.

"Then we'll pull out an' start to work," Curly said. "The sooner the quicker. We'll have another drink and go." Once more the glasses were filled and once more the four men drank; then bidding Thad and Brick "so long," Curly and Silk made their departure.

"What do you think of it, kid?" Brick asked when the others were gone.

Thad's answer came slowly. "I don't trust those two as far as I can throw an anvil; I'm not strong for it, Brick. Why did they want us?"

"Because"—the drinks and some inner exultation had taken hold of Brick and made his eyes bright and his voice strong—"they know I've got the brains. They know they need me on a job like this. I thought I was done, kid. I thought I was finished when this arm went, but I guess I'm not. I guess there's some life in the old horse yet."

Thad was about to speak again and then checked himself. He could not cast doubts on Brick's enthusiasm. It would not do. Brick was more like his old self, more the happy-go-lucky, come-what-might, don't-give-a-damn Brick Mahoney than he had been since Thad rejoined him. Thad could not bear to tear down that feeling.

"Yeah, I guess that's it," he agreed.

It was later that night that Ellen came. Thad admitted her and she went straight to Brick and, throwing her arms about him, held him close. "Arch told me," she said. "Don't go, Brick. Don't do it. Don't go back into danger again. You can have everything Arch and I have. You know you can. You don't need . . ."

"Now honey!" Brick interrupted. "Now Ellen, this ain't goin' to be dangerous. This is just one last job to put the kid an' me in the clear an' take us out of the country."

"But it's stealing," Ellen said. "It's . . ."

"You don't even know what we're goin' to do," Brick said harshly. "Don't talk about stealin', girl. Arch owns this place an' you got a nice house, an' all because I gave you a little start. You know where that start came from."

Ellen drew back from her brother. "I know," she said, a choke in her voice. "I've hated it, Brick. Please don't go."

"Why," Brick said. "I've promised. I told 'em I'd go. You wouldn't have me go back on that, would you?"

There was a finality in his voice that forbade further argument. Ellen looked at her brother as though she were seeing him for the first time, as though he were a stranger. "Then you will do it?" she said dully.

"I said I'd go," Brick stated.

The woman made a little hopeless gesture and turned to Thad. "You . . ." she began.

"The kid had nothin' to do with it," Brick interposed swiftly. "He's goin' with me, that's all."

Ellen's blue eyes were wide as she looked at Thad. "You're going too?" she asked.

Thad nodded.

"And you'll stay with Brick?"

"I'll stay with him," Thad promised. "Yes, ma'am."

The red-haired woman walked over to Thad and placing her hand on his arm, spoke earnestly. "You'll look out for him?" she asked. "You will?"

"I'll be lookin' out for the kid, more likely," Brick scoffed.

Ellen paid no attention to her brother. She continued to look into Thad's eyes.

"I'll look out for him," Thad promised.

CHAPTER SIXTEEN

Stingy Gun

WHEN men are in camp there is little that they can keep hidden from one another. Thad Breathea, Brick Mahoney, Silk Gerald, and Curly Winters had been camping for two weeks. They were across the Pecos and in the rough country along the Canadian, and still Thad kept his secret. Why he had kept it to himself he did not know; why he should continue to keep it, was a question. But for two weeks Thad had secreted the little "stingy gun," the .32-caliber Smith & Wesson that Heibert had dubbed a lemon squeezer. During the day it rode in Thad's waistband under his shirt and at night it was close beside his hand when he turned in. His belt gun swung at his hip, plain for all to see, but the little Smith & Wesson stayed out of sight.

The two weeks had been easy. There were the four saddle horses and two bed horses and a horse that carried a pack; these were transportation. As for the rest, the beds were thin enough, but who cared? And the pack carried an ax and a skillet and a coffee pot and a Dutch oven and enough food to suffice.

The food supply had been replenished once. Before they crossed the Canadian, Brick and Silk Gerald—Brick because he had the best Spanish—rode into a little native placita, and from the storekeeper there bought tobacco and coffee, the two essentials that were getting low. When they returned Brick was chuckling. The storekeeper had a daughter and Brick had flirted outrageously with the girl.

The trip so far had been leisurely. There were days when they stretched out and hit the ball, forty or fifty miles lying behind them when night came. There were other days when they stayed in camp and let the horses rest, not moving save to cook or change to a more comfortable position. There were days when the sun shone bright and days when the rain fell, and always they were going north and always Brick was regaining his strength and growing red from the sun once more, and brighter eyed and more happy. Thad watched Brick and he watched the others. He rejoiced that Brick improved so, and gradually his ingrained suspicion of Curly and Silk was lulled. They were hearty and simple and, so Thad came to believe, real friends of Brick. But on the night they made camp north of the Red River, Thad was tense. That day, following the crossing of the river, Thad had seen a little bunch of cattle. Two of the cows were branded Lazy 5. The brand in itself was enough to put Thad on edge.

They made camp in a rincon among the rough breaks that led down to the river, hobbling the horses, spreading down the beds, cutting wood and building a little fire. Thad, his belt gun laid aside, took the axe and cut enough wood for the night and morning necessity, and brought it in. Returning with the wood, he placed no significance in the abrupt cessation of earnest, low-voiced conversation between Silk and Curly when they noticed his approach.

Brick, growing more handy daily with his single arm, fell to work cooking, and Curly and Silk looked after the horses. After the sun was gone they gathered about the fire and ate the salt pork, the biscuits, the canned corn, and drank the coffee that Brick had prepared. Then, with water from the little spring, the dishes were washed and the men relaxed. Brick and Thad were side by side upon Brick's bed. Curly was at the fire and Silk but a short distance from him.

"Another week will see us where we want to go," Brick announced, stretching lazily and taking from his mouth the cigarette that Thad had rolled for him. "That right, Silk?"

Silk looked at Brick and then at Curly. It was Curly who answered Brick.

"We're far enough now," Curly announced bluntly.

Brick sat up. He was unarmed, having placed his belt and gun on his saddle while he cooked supper. Thad's belt gun too was on his saddle. He did not move but stayed on the bed, one leg doubled under him, the other stretched out as he sat.

"What do you mean?" Brick demanded, looking keenly at Curly.

"We've come far enough," Curly repeated. "Silk an' me have."

"But we're goin' to Gato," Brick expostulated. "We ain't . . ."

"You ain't goin' to Gato," Silk announced, his voice hoarse and a little strained. "None of us are. It would take an army to get that payroll."

"Then why . . . ?" Brick began. He did not finish the sentence but stopped, his mouth opened and his eyes wide. Silk was sitting cross legged close by the fire, his gun drawn and its muzzle trained squarely on Brick. Curly, balancing on widespread legs, had also drawn his gun and was covering Thad where he sat upon the bed.

"Yo're fixin' to kill us?" Brick demanded, incredulity in his voice.

"That's right," Silk glanced toward Curly and then looked back to Brick again. "That's right, Brick."

"But why?"

Silk grinned mirthlessly. His eyes were thin slots in his face and his lips were as thin as the eyes. "I figure to make a little money on you," he answered levelly.

"Kettleman?" Brick was staring straight at Silk. On the bed Thad sat numb, incapable of any movement.

Silk shook his head. "This is another deal, Brick. We'd of let you in on it but yo're so damned stuck on yore dogie kid you wouldn't of listened. A fello' named Ben Prince is payin' us for this. We collect on you an' the kid."

Ben Prince! Thad straightened. Some of the shock was leaving him, his mind was functioning normally once more. Ben Prince was Krespin's foreman. Thad looked at Brick, moving his eyes without turning his head. Brick had straightened until he sat erect. Brick's saddle and his belted gun were eight feet away. Thad could see beads of sweat forming on Brick's forehead.

"You see," Silk drawled, and incredibly there seemed to be amusement in his voice, "the kid has got a claim on an estate that Prince is interested in. It's worth a thousand dollars to Prince an' Krespin to have the kid dead."

Brick's voice was low and hoarse. "Then you tolled us up here to kill us?" he said. "That was all a lie about the payroll?"

Silk's smile broadened. "Sure," he agreed cheerfully. "We got you up here where we could show you to Prince, an' collect. We had to have proof."

"Let Brick go." Thad did not realize for an instant that he had spoken, did not recognize his own voice, it was so hoarse and strained. "It's me that you want, not Brick."

"An' have Brick come back at us?" Silk queried gently, not shifting his eyes. "Not much, kid. It'll be both of you."

"Get on with it then," Curly rasped. "You goin' to talk all night? Get on with it, Silk."

"There's no hurry," Silk purred. "I want this red-headed bum to know what's comin'. You damned fool!" He seemed to throw the words at Brick now. "You thought that we'd come to you because you had brains! You thought we needed you to pull a little job. I ain't forgot the way you lorded it around after we went back to Las Flores. I ain't forgot how you called us cowards an' made us go back an' get that damned kid out of jail. Now by hell, you'll find out! I'm goin' to shoot you in the guts an' watch you kick!" The unrestrained ferocity in Silk's voice made Thad flinch and as he moved the little stingy gun, forgotten until that moment, nudged him in the belly with its butt.

"Why don't you beg?" Silk snarled. "Why don't you crawl, Brick? Mebbe we'd let you off an' just take the kid if you begged. You damned . . . !"

"Cut it out, Silk!" Curly rasped. "Get done with it."

"You gettin' yellow, Curly?" Silk snarled. "If you are . . ."

Silk's gun was coming up; Thad could see the slow movement. Brick had tensed. Brick's single hand was pushed against the ground and Thad could see Brick's muscles bunch. Brick was going to make a try for it! Brick was going to throw himself toward the holstered gun that lay across his saddle, and go out fighting.

Thad did not realize that he moved. The long, rawhide muscles of his body tensed and snapped into action, seemingly without volition. Curly, momentarily diverted by Silk's savagery, was not ready for that movement. For an infinitesimal part of a second Curly's body and mind were separated and in that fraction of time Thad Breathea threw himself back on the bedding and his hand snatched the stingy gun, the little .32 Smith & Wesson lemon squeezer from his waistband.

The roar of Curly's laggard shot and the smack of the bullet through the air above Thad's prone body, drowned out the spiteful crack of the .32. Thad fired straight down the length of his body toward the head of the seated man, fired across his boot toes as he lay prone, and Silk Gerald, his gun half lifted, paused and then dropped the weapon from his hand; for Thad had not tried for Curly, had disregarded the gun and the man that had menaced his own life, and had shot at Silk. On Silk's face there was an expression of blank incredulity and then, still cross-legged, he bent forward, and as he fell Thad could see that just between Silk's eyes, squarely centered, there was a small black hole.

For an instant Thad did not move. Then he rolled, coming up as he completed the movement, thrusting himself from the bed so that his body was lifted. Brick, almost in motion as Thad fired, sprawled along the ground, his hand snatching at the heavy gun on his saddle. Thad snapped a shot at Curly but missed, and Curly, all his mind fixed upon Thad, confused by the suddenness, the swiftness of the action, fired at Thad, the shot narrowly missing its target. It was Brick Mahoney, red face a snarling mask, who accounted for Curly Winters. Brick Mahoney, sprawled on the hard earth, his big Colt in his hand, thumbed hammer and fingered trigger twice, so swiftly that the two shots blended into one crashing roar. Curly, hard hit above the belt buckle and in the chest, went down as though struck on the head with an ax.

Thad scrambled up. Brick too gained his feet. For perhaps a full second they stood, each man swaying, and then Brick ran toward Thad and still holding the big Colt, threw his arm about the lad's shoulders.

"Kid," he said, his voice choked, "Kid! Are you all right?"

Very slowly Thad answered, his voice low. "I'm all right, Brick. Did you . . . did they . . . ?"

Brick turned from Thad, freeing him. The snarl, the mask of hatred was still upon his red face, redder now because of the firelight. "Damn them," Brick snarled. "Damn them!"

Once more his arm lifted. His tense thumb held back the hammer of the Colt as he swung toward Curly. Thad caught the extended arm. "No, Brick!" he commanded. Slowly Brick's arm came down.

For a time he stood so, panting as though from some overwhelming exertion. Thad too found that his breath was short, his heart pounding suffocatingly, almost in his throat. Then Brick moved, crossing to where Silk Gerald lay toppled forward over his crossed legs, his position as grotesque as that of a floppy rag doll. Brick touched Silk with his boot toe and Silk toppled down, falling over upon his back so that his lifeless eyes peered up at the black sky. Brick looked at Silk for a long minute and then, turning abruptly, moved toward Curly, and as he moved Curly stirred. Instantly Brick's gun came up and then as he looked down at the man he lowered the weapon again.

Thad had followed Brick, not of his own volition but unconsciously emulating his companion's actions. Together Brick and Thad knelt down beside the wounded man.

Curly's agonized eyes were fixed intently upon Brick's face and his lips moved in awful grimaces as he tried to speak. The two men bent closer until they could distinguish Curly's words.

"Silk . . . had to . . . talk," Curly gasped. "Just . . . had to . . . talk. We'd of . . . killed . . ." The gasping words choked off. Brick lifted his eyes until they met Thad's own. Both knew what Curly was trying to say. If Silk had not talked, if Silk had not tried to play cat and mouse, Curly Winters would not be dying.

"He . . . had a girl . . . in Flores," Curly said haltingly. "Pearl . . . We . . . was . . . goin' to . . . bleed Krespin. . . . Ahhh!" The voice died away. Curly's legs stiffened as though he would push himself up, and then relaxed. His head rolled limply toward the right and his mouth sagged open. Brick continued to kneel by Curly's side. Thad stared down at the distorted face and suddenly looked away. He was sick, sick with a retching nausea that would not down. Reaction had set in.

Brick scrambled to his feet. "Why," said Brick, his voice low, filled with amazement, "I slept with them fellows. I shared my blankets with 'em. I . . . For God's sake, kid! Let's get out of here! Let's shift camp an' go!"

CHAPTER SEVENTEEN

A Rendezvous with Justice

AT nine o'clock Charlie Farrel came home. A wifeless man, he lived in a small adobe house close by the edge of Las Flores.

There was a stable behind the house where Farrel kept a horse, and there were two rooms in the adobe, a kitchen and a bedroom. He preferred to live so rather than to keep a room at a hotel or boarding house and stable his horse in the livery barn. It gave him a certain measure of privacy.

Farrel turned the key in his door and, pushing it open, went into the house. He had had a hard day. Things were piling up on Charlie Farrel and he could not see an immediate end to them. He was tempted to resign and let someone else have the grief; but if he resigned, what else would he do? A man of fifty who has been an officer for thirty years might have a hard time changing his ways. Farrel scaled his hat across the dark room to where he knew the bed was placed, and proceeding through the darkness, struck a match, located the lamp on the table and lighted the wick. Replacing the chimney, he turned, intending to sit down in the chair beside the table, pull off his boots and relax awhile before he went to bed. Having turned around he changed his plan. A man was sitting on the bed, Farrel's hat beside him. The man was red-headed and had but one arm. Between his knees the redhead's hand loosely dangled a big Colt.

"Well, Charlie?" said the man on the bed.

"What did you come in for, Brick?" Farrel asked quietly, holding himself very stiff and still. "You want to give yourself up?"

Brick Mahoney frowned, not a scowl of hatred or of fear, but rather one of concentration. "I need some help," he said. "I come in to you to get it."

"Help?"

"Yeah." The dangling gun made a little gesture. "Sit down, Charlie."

Farrel seated himself. His own gun was in a shoulder holster under his left arm. He could reach it and, perhaps, get it, but he did not. Brick was studying the officer with worried blue eyes. "Yo're the only man I know that can help me out," Brick said. "You see it's the kid, Charlie."

Farrel forgot all about the gun under his arm. He leaned forward in his eagerness. "You mean Thad Breathea?"

Brick nodded soberly. "He's made up his mind to kill Dale Krespin an' a man named Prince," Brick announced, his voice worried. "An' I can't talk him out of it."

"To kill Krespin an' Prince?"

"That's right. He found out that they rigged a deal on him. Krespin lied about the kid when he said he'd never saw him. Then me an' the boys come back an' took the kid out of jail, an' that made him an outlaw as far as the sheriff's office was concerned. Now then the kid knows what happened an' he's gone plumb bronc on me." Brick's voice carried a complaint. "I can't talk him out of it, neither."

Some of the tightness had left Charlie Farrel's face and he leaned back in his chair. "Brick," he drawled, "I'm all dressed up. I'd like to get some clothes off an' rest awhile. I've had a hard day an' you an' me want to talk a little. How about it?"

Brick's eyes were wary. "I guess so," he agreed. "Only be careful, Charlie."

Farrel stood up. Deliberately he removed his coat and hung it over the back of his chair. The shoulder holster and the butt of its gun jutted out from beneath his arm. Farrel pulled the elastic loop of the holster from his right shoulder, let the leather loop slip down from his left shoulder and, holding the holster by the leather, carried it across the room and hung it on a nail. His eyes were twinkling as he came back to the chair beside the table. "Now we can talk confortable," he said.

Brick grinned as he put his gun back into its sheath and relaxed upon the bed. "Yeah," he agreed.

Farrel put one leg on the table, tilting his chair back and looking at his visitor through narrowed, calculating eyes. "So the kid wants to kill Krespin an' Prince?" he said.

"Uhhuh." Brick was gloomy. "I had a hell of a time with him too. You see, Charlie, them two hired Silk Gerald an' Curly Winters to hunt up me an' the kid an' kill us. Silk and Curly found us in Franklin an' told us a big cock an' bull story about a payroll in Gato. The kid an' me was plannin' on South America an' I wanted to make a stake so I listened to what they had to say, an' it looked pretty good. We come up across the Pecos an' got clear past the Red River, an' then Silk an' Curly tried to get the job done.

"Silk got to talkin'. He wanted to rub it into me an' he said that Krespin an' Prince had hired them to kill us because the kid had a claim on Krespin's ranch. The kid took a chance and got Silk with a stingy gun that he'd been holdin' out; an' Curly run into some tough luck about that time." Brick broke off. His eyes were on Farrel but the officer could see that Brick was not looking at him. Brick's mind was far away.

"So then?" Farrel prompted.

Brick took a long breath. "So then we moved camp," he said. "We pulled out of there. I had hell with the kid then an' I've been havin' hell with him ever since. First off he was all stirred up because he'd killed a man, an' then when I got him calmed down over that he got this other idea in his head. The kid's had some pretty tough times an' he lays it all on Krespin. He ain't wrong neither. He's made up his mind he's goin' to walk in on them two an' tell them what they done, an' then kill 'em. There ain't no use of tryin' to tell him it wouldn't work. I told him that we could lay out with a rifle and get the job done, but he wouldn't hear to it. He's bound to give those skunks a chance."

Brick stopped. He had freed his mind of what was in it, and now he waited for the other man to speak.

Farrel carefully fitted his fingers together and locked them in place. He stared at the fingers for a long moment then asked a question. "Where is the kid?"

Brick grinned. "We got a camp," he explained. "I talked the kid into waiting awhile. I told him we'd have to scout the country an' stake out some horses so we could get away, an' we needed some grub. He wanted to get a friend of ours to get it but he can't talk Spanish an' so I got him to hold down the camp while I come to town."

"To see me?" Farrel asked.

Brick shook his head. "I went up to Krespin's," he admitted. "I didn't blame the kid none an' I thought mebbe I'd take it off his hands. The kid ain't cut out for the business I'm in. He stays awake too much at night worryin'. But before I got to Krespin's place I got to thinkin'. The kid's got a claim on that place and I'd like to see him get it. I don't want him to lose out on what he's got comin'. I thought mebbe you could help me out, Charlie. The kid isn't bad. That time at the bank, Hoyt Lowell gave him those horses to hold an' we made a mistake comin' back and takin' him away from you. He was goin' to give himself up one time an' Krespin was with the posse an' taken a couple of shots at him. The kid ain't really been in nothin' bad."

There was a plea in Brick's blue eyes. Charlie Farrel unlocked his fingers and reaching out, took a cigar from a box. He tossed the cigar to Brick and reached for another for himself.

"No," he agreed thoughtfully, "the kid ain't bad at all. It's all been a mistake an' Krespin's to blame for it. I know some things too."

"Do you?" Brick paused in the act of lighting the cigar. "You believe me when I tell you that the kid's all right? That he really ain't mixed up in anything?"

Farrel nodded. "I know he hasn't been," he said quietly. "I know that Krespin lied when he said that he'd never seen the kid an' I know that Krespin wants the kid out of the way. There's already been one murder over this thing, Brick. I'm glad that you come in."

The match burned Brick's fingers and he flipped it away. Farrel struck a match, lighted his own cigar and then got up and gave Brick a light. Returning to his chair he puffed comfortably, blew the smoke away and looked at Brick.

"You see, there was a fellow named Ten High Croates that found a letter the kid lost," Farrel said. "Ten High an' Lulu Black tried to blackmail Krespin. Prince killed Croates but I can't prove it. There's a whole brandin' crew ready to swear that Prince wasn't away from camp but just long enough to go to the ranch an' back. But I know that Prince killed Croates. I'd like to prove it on him, an' I'd like to prove that Krespin was behind it. This business of hirin' Silk Gerald an' Curly Winters is kind of serious too."

"That's what I thought." Brick voiced his satisfaction.

"Krespin has got plenty to worry about," Farrel announced. "So has Prince. They know I've been askin' a few questions an' there's a lawyer down here from Wyoming that's started suit against Krespin for the Breathea kid. This lawyer's named Althen, Wade Althen. He's red hot to find the kid an' get what's comin' to the boy out of Krespin. You know . . ." Farrel broke off.

"Yeah?" Brick encouraged.

"I'd like to get Althen down here," Farrel said. "The three of us . . ." He looked questioningly at Brick.

"Go get him, then," Brick said.

Farrel got up and slipped into his coat and vest. He smiled at Brick Mahoney. "I'll be back in thirty minutes," he promised. "Althen is just down at the hotel but I might have to wait for him to dress."

"I'll wait for you," Brick said, rising and following Farrel to the door. "I'll lock up behind you, Charlie. Somebody might come in an' it wouldn't look good for you if they found me here."

Farrel nodded, said: "I'll be right back," and went out. Brick turned the key, went to the table and thoughtfully lowered the lamp wick; then, proceeding to the bed again, he sat down and relaxed.

There was no compact between Brick Mahoney, outlaw, and Charlie Farrel, officer. Given another set of circumstances, Brick would run and Farrel follow, intent on capture, living by a certain code. Enemies, diametrically opposed to each other, still now they had laid aside the opposition, laid aside lawlessness and lawfulness, and joined together to do what was right. Brick puffed on the cigar and tried vainly to blow a perfect smoke ring.

The cigar was a stub when Farrel returned. Brick heard the footsteps coming, heard Farrel's gentle knock and his low voice announcing his identity. Brick unlocked the door and opened it, and Farrel, following another man, came in.

The man with Farrel was short and pudgy. When he removed his hat he exposed a bald head surrounded by a ring of gray hair, and beneath the plump round face the bones were strong and firm, making a stubborn bulldog jaw.

"Make you acquainted with Wade Althen, Mr. Mahoney," Farrel said. "Yo're both friends of Breathea's."

Brick and the lawyer shook hands and sat down. Farrel leaned against the table. "Tell Althen what you been tellin' me," he ordered Brick.

Brick began. Tersely he recovered the ground, retelling the story he had outlined to Farrel. Althen listened, nodding from time to time and, when Brick paused, spoke. "You say that the boy has decided to kill Krespin and Prince?" he asked.

"Yeah," Brick agreed. "He's got it figured that he'll walk right up to them an' accuse them of what they done to him. I'd be with him, of course, but even at that we wouldn't get too far. They know they're guilty as hell an' before the kid ever got a word out they'd cut down on him. An' either the kid or me would get hurt even if we did settle them two. I've tried to tell the kid what would happen but he won't listen. He's got his mind made up."

"It won't do," Althen said crisply. "If he killed them it would be murder."

"Murder," Brick drawled, "ain't so bad. There's skunks that need killin'; but I don't want the kid hurt."

Althen disregarded the remark. "It seems simple enough," he commented. "If you and Thad were to appear before a court and testify as to this story you've told me, I have no doubt but that the court would order the arrest of Krespin and Prince. I believe that's the solution."

"It might be," Brick agreed, "but there's a catch in it. If I got up in front of a judge he'd sentence me to ninety-nine years in the pen an' a hangin' too. It wouldn't be healthy for me, would it, Charlie?"

Farrel cleared his throat. "Brick is wanted, Mr. Althen," he said. "He's kind of in some other trouble besides this. He just come in because he's a friend of the kid's."

Althen looked from one man to the other, his eye shrewd. "I'd say he was a very good friend of Thad's," the lawyer commented dryly. "I'd like to shake hands with you again, Mr. Mahoney."

Brick flushed and, awkwardly, extended his hand.

"And I want to congratulate you, Farrel," Althen said when he had released Brick's hand. "There aren't many officers . . ."

"Everybody trusts Charlie," Brick interrupted. "We know he's square."

Althen sat down. "We've got to make some sort of a plan," he announced. "We have possession of a number of facts but owing to the circumstances we can't use them. It's a difficult situation."

There was a pause in the talk. Charlie Farrel's little bedroom was quiet. Brick shifted restlessly. "I could go over by myself an' kind of talk to Krespin an' this fellow Prince," he suggested. "I started to do that anyhow but I got to thinkin' that maybe it would be blamed on the kid, an' he wouldn't be in the clear. Them two need killin' if a man ever did."

Farrel remained silent but Althen shook his head. "I'm afraid that won't do," he said. "No, there's got to be another way. I think . . ."

"I've kind of got an idea," Farrel drawled. "Brick talkin' to Krespin an' Prince wouldn't be so bad at that. Providin', of course, that he just talked. Brick knows where the kid is. Suppose Brick offered to trade the kid for some cash?"

"Why, damn you, Charlie!" Brick came to his feet, his face red, his hand reaching back to his holstered gun. "You know I wouldn't do that!! You know . . ."

"Easy, Brick," Farrel interrupted. "Of course you wouldn't trade the kid off. But if you did that an' me an' the judge an' some other fellow we could trust was there listenin', we'd likely get an earful. How about that, Judge?"

Slowly Althen nodded his bald head. "It has possibilities," he agreed.

"An' what do I do with the kid?" Brick complained. "I'm havin' hell holdin' him in right now. I'll have to take him along. An' who would we get that we could trust? I don't know anybody."

"Morgan Vermillion," Farrel said promptly. "He likes the kid an' wants to help him. He told me so."

There was astonishment on Brick's face. "But the kid told me that Vermillion sent to town to turn him in to the law! The kid . . ."

"The kid left an' didn't know what Morgan was doin'," Farrel snapped. "Morgan fired Walt James for stickin' his nose into business that wasn't his. Morgan likes the kid."

"Huh!" Brick's astonishment came in one grunt.

"Let's work this thing out," Farrel said. "We got an idea. It ought to be all right. Now Brick, you could write Krespin a letter tellin' him you knew where the kid is, offerin' a trade an' makin' a meetin' place. Vermillion an' me would be there the night you showed up to make yore talk. An' we'd . . ."

In that small smoke-filled adobe room the talk went on and on. Brick, seated at the table, scratched with pen upon paper, Althen looking over his shoulder, making suggestions, Farrel looking on and occasionally adding a word. The night whiled itself away. Charlie Farrel's box of cigars was depleted. The first gray of morning tinged the east.

"I guess that's it," Brick Mahoney said finally. "Thanks, Charlie."

"It ought to work," Althen said.

"I've got to get some grub and go back," Brick's voice was moody again. "It ain't so bad for you fellows: all you got to do is wait for Vermillion to come over an' Krespin to get that letter; but I've got the kid on my hands an' I've got to stall him off an' string him along. He's an obstinate little devil."

"You can do it," Farrel said. "We'll be there, right on time."

Brick grunted.

"Where you goin' to get your grub?" Farrel asked, "an' how you goin' to leave town?"

Brick grinned broadly. "I kind of helped myself in your kitchen, Charlie," he answered. "There's a sack out there, ready to go, an' I put my horse in yore shed an' fed him a little grain."

"You had your nerve with you!"

Althen laughed. "And I'm very glad you did," he said. "You'd better leave now, Mr. Mahoney, before it's daylight."

"Well . . ." Farrel said, "all right then. I'll even get yore stolen grub for you."

He stepped to the kitchen. Althen walked across to Brick. For a moment he talked, low-voiced. Brick shook his head. Althen spoke again, insistently. Brick nodded reluctantly and Althen said: "Thad would want it that way."

"Well, all right," Brick commented.

Riding out of town through the thin morning light, a sack of provisions on his saddle and his horse fresh and strong under him, Brick Mahoney's spirits were higher than they had been for many a day. It was a full day's ride back to the camp where he had left Thad. That was a point in his favor. The day was one gained. But there were other days coming and at thought of them Brick lost all his elation. It was not going to be an easy task to hold Thad down. Staying with a thin-eyed, square-jawed, silent young fellow who had but one idea, who thought and brooded and planned along only one line—and that line killing —was no bargain. Brick wished that he did not have to go back to camp at once, but he knew he must. He had sold Thad the idea of this trip alone, he had Thad's promise that for the time Brick was gone Thad would remain in hiding; but Brick knew that if he did not return soon Thad would start looking for him and that was the last thing Brick wanted.

"Got to get there tonight," Brick Mahoney muttered to himself. "If I don't he'll start out an' hunt me. I've already been gone two nights an' a day. I got to get back." He considered his horse's head. Brick was riding a big, full-barreled bay that was all life and run. The horse worked his ears constantly, now forward, now back, now pointing one and now the other. "Yeah," Brick growled. "Work yore damned ears. You don't know nothin' about it. You don't know just how tough this thing is."

Before evening came Brick was south of Las Flores and far enough east to be coming into the cedar breaks above the rim. Three times during the day's ride he had seen other riders. Two of these he had passed without being seen. The third man had come toward him and Brick had got down from the bay and waved his hat around his head in a slow circle. The rider had taken the hint and moved off. Few men in that time and country disregarded the wave-around. The bay horse was tired but he still worked his ears.

When the sun went down Brick was descending a canyon, following a little-used road to get below the rim. Under the rim, evening dusk had already come though there was still sunlight on top. Brick rode out of the canyon the road followed, angling north and working along the bottom bench of the rim, coming presently to another indenture. Now following up that crack in the rim's massiveness, he whistled a long low note, imitating the call of the California quail. An old quail, followed by her young brood, ran from beneath his horse even as he whistled. Back down the canyon came the answering call, and Brick rode toward it. He rounded a point, followed up a brief side-canyon where the grass was lush, and then stopped. Thad Breathea came around a big rock and stood looking up at his friend.

"I was just about ready to start after you," Thad announced. "You get the grub?"

"Yeah," Brick said.

"We could have done without it," Thad announced. "Did you see Alfredo?"

"How do you suppose I got the grub?" Brick equivocated. "How you been, kid?"

"All right. I stayed in camp most of the time. I went out awhile last night."

"Where?"

"Toward Krespin's."

Brick got down from his horse. "I got some canned stuff an' some coffee an' salt pork," he said. "I'll put my horse with the others."

"They're above camp." Thad was untying the sack from Brick's saddle. "What did you find out, Brick?"

"Not much," Brick answered.

"The crew is in at Krespin's headquarters," Thad announced morosely.

"You went clear up there?" Alarm was in Brick's voice.

"Far enough so that I could see," Thad answered. "Brick . . ."

"Yeah?"

"I've waited long enough."

Brick walked ahead, leading his horse. Thad followed, carrying the sack of groceries. The camp was just beyond the rock. Reaching it, Brick stopped and began to unsaddle. "You don't just walk in an' kill a man, kid," he announced. "There's things to do first. We've got some time to wait."

"Why?" Thad put down the sack of groceries.

"Because I'm not a damned fool," Brick snapped, pulling off his saddle and dropping it to the ground. "Because I'm goin' to have it fixed so that you an' me will come out of this with our hides whole. First we're goin' to rest these horses for two days anyhow. We're goin' to have fresh horses when we leave here. An' we're going to take two horses down to that little placita below the river an' leave them there with the storekeeper. When this thing comes off we'll leave in a hurry if we leave at all. There'll be men after us an' I'm goin' to put a lot of country between me an' here. An' that's the size of it, kid."

Here was an unanswerable. Thad knew that Brick was entirely right. The horses did need rest; and two fresh horses, thirty miles along their line of flight, grain fed and strong, would be of inestimable value.

"Yeah," Thad agreed reluctantly. "I guess you're right, Brick."

"Yo're damned right, I'm right!" Brick echoed. "Let's get some supper."

CHAPTER EIGHTEEN

A Man to Take Along

BRICK, having outlined a program, carried it through. Between them he and Thad had seven horses: their own mounts, the horses that Curly and Silk had ridden, the two bed horses and the pack horse. These were in the canyon above the camp. There was water up the canyon and plenty of grass, and the steep rock sidewalls and the sheer drop at the upper end made a natural corral of some eight or ten acres. The horses were doing well, but they needed rest for they had been pushed fairly hard for two weeks.

There was another thing in favor of the camp besides the pasture: there were no cattle on the range and Thad and Brick surmised that the locality of their camp was used by some ranchman atop the mesa as a winter country. They were therefore fairly safe from molestation. Cowhands in the summer time do not go into their winter pasture unless for a reason. Sometimes they work the country for strays, sometimes there are horses on the winter pasture; there are a number of reasons for men to ride winter country in the summer time, but it is not an ordinary procedure. With the precautions they were taking, concerning fires in the daytime that would send up telltale smoke, and confining their activities outside the canyon to late evening or very early morning, Thad and Brick were safe.

For a day after Brick came back they rested their horses. Early the following morning they left the camp, taking the bed horses with them. There was not a sorry horse in their little remuda; men in the profession that Brick followed cannot afford to have a poor horse—and the bed horses were good saddle horses. By noon Thad and Brick had covered the thirty miles to the little

placita below the river and then Thad stayed out of sight while
Brick took the two spare horses in and made arrangements to
have them cared for. He came back after the noon hour, licking
his lips and with four tamales wrapped in an old paper, for
Thad. The tamales were hot enough to set fire to an ice cake and
Thad, after downing them, drank a great deal of water and held
his mouth open to cool it further.

Brick was pleased with the results of his trip to the little
village. The storekeeper, with a fenced pasture and a supply of
grain on hand, had promised that the horses would be fed and
kept up every night, and Brick had given him five dollars with
the promise of five more.

"We'll need them at night or of a morning," Brick explained
to Thad, "an' that way he'll have 'em up."

The two men did not start back to camp immediately but
waited for the cool of the evening. It was six o'clock before they
recrossed the Red River and they rode into camp when dark had
come. Thad went up the canyon to turn the horses they had ridden in with the others, while Brick cooked supper.

Now came the hard part of the task for Brick. The activities
of moving the two horses and staking them out with the storekeeper had been something to do and had kept Thad's mind
occupied; but to stay around camp, only going to look after the
horses, eating, cooking when night came, loafing the rest of the
time, worked on the younger man. Thad was impatient, fidgeted, fretted and strained at the leash. Brick did what he could
to make things easier but was adamant concerning their moving.

"We'll wait till these horses have rested an' put on a little
fat," he stated positively. "That's all there is to it."

On the fourth day the two quarreled bitterly. Thad, impatient,
accused Brick of over-caution. Brick's temper was badly frayed.
One word led to another and finally Thad accused Brick of
cowardice. Brick's flare of temper was instantaneous and it was
not until Thad started up the canyon with the avowed purpose
of catching a horse and going to the Lazy 5 at once that Brick
was recalled to his senses. Then he used the oldest of wiles to

effect a reconciliation. He announced in an injured tone that Thad did not want to take him along; that a cripple with only one arm would not be of any use and that he would only hamper Thad. Thad immediately came back, contrite and sorry, and spent the remainder of the day placating Brick and assuring him of his, Thad Breathea's, regard for his red-haired friend. Brick could hardly restrain a grin, albeit Thad's hot words still rankled irritatingly in his mind.

By noon of the fifth day there was no restraining Thad. All morning Brick had used every method at his command to keep his friend occupied; then while the two munched their cold food, Brick made sudden announcement.

"I think we can go tonight," he stated abruptly. "I think tonight's the time. The horses are rested an' we're as ready now as we'll ever be."

Thad could scarcely believe what he heard. He sat bolt upright beside the rock against which he leaned, and looked wonderingly at Brick.

Brick nodded. "An' I've been thinkin'," he continued. "I've got a kind of plan worked out."

"What is it?" Thad asked eagerly.

"The thing I haven't liked about this is your idea of just walkin' in on Krespin an' Prince," Brick said slowly. "I've told you that, and I've told you why I didn't like it. I don't think you'd get by with it an' I been wondering why you wanted to do it. The way I've got things figured out, yo're not just sure, is that it?"

Thad could not give a definite answer to the question. He knew—there was no doubt in his mind—that Krespin was the underlying cause of his troubles. He was certain that Prince, with Krespin's backing, had hired Silk Gerald and Curly Winters to kill himself and Brick. And yet there was an undefinable something in Thad that would not let him kill in cold blood, no matter how guilty the man he killed. He could not express that thing in words and so, accepting Brick's explanation of his feeling, he nodded.

"Well, then," Brick drawled, "we'll make sure an' at the same time we'll give ourselves a break. Now here's what I've thought we could do: We'll go up there an' reach the place after dark. The crew will be in the bunkhouse an' Krespin an' Prince will likely be together right after supper. We'll hide our horses where we can get them easy, an' we'll go on afoot. Then I'll go in alone . . ."

"Oh no you won't!" Thad refuted. "You won't do that!"

"Now wait a minute!" Brick snapped. "Let me talk. I've got as big a stake in this as you have. Curly an' Silk tried for me just as hard as they tried for you. You keep still an' let me finish!"

Under that short sharp tirade Thad subsided. After a moment Brick continued. "I'll go up alone an' call Krespin an' Prince out on the porch. Then I'll proposition 'em. I'll tell them about Curly an' Silk fallin' down on the job an' that I know where you are; then I'll ask 'em how much yo're worth to 'em. They're goin' to answer that an' you'll have a chance to hear just what kind of people they are. You'll learn a lot more than if you just went in, accused them two an' went to shootin'. And when they've talked enough you'll come up an' we'll settle with 'em, one way or another. Now that's my scheme."

"I don't like it," Thad objected. "I don't like your going alone. Suppose they aren't together? Then what?"

Brick snorted scornfully. "That's the way to get 'em together. If Krespin is alone he'll call Prince so that they can both talk to me."

That was true. Thad knew it.

"An' yo're goin' to hear the whole thing," Brick held out the idea tantalizingly, knowing that it was sure bait. "Yo're goin' to hear it all."

Slowly Thad nodded his head. He had taken the bait that Brick offered.

"All right," Brick said briskly, "this afternoon we'll cache this stuff. We can't take it with us but there's no use just letting it scatter. Something might slip an' we'll want to come back here. There might be too many folks at the place an' we'd have to put it off. We'll eat plenty tonight before we start an' we'll take some cold grub on our saddles an' we'll fill that canteen with coffee. When we leave here we'll be goin' a long ways an' we'll be goin' fast an' not stoppin' to cook. Let's get fixed up, kid."

And so, that afternoon, Brick's plan was carried out. The beds were rolled and put into the fork of a tree. The food was placed in a sack and hung from a limb so that it would be safe from pack-rats or other marauders. Everything about the camp was made ship-shape and late in the day Brick cooked salt pork for sandwiches and boiled the coffee. At five o'clock they ate, Thad with no appetite and forcing down the food, and by five thirty they were saddling the two best horses of the five that were left.

The three horses that remained they turned loose. It had been easy enough to keep the horses together. The pack horse was the boss of the remuda and him they kept hobbled. The others stayed close by the pack horse. Now they removed the hobbles from that animal and freed him. He would stay in the canyon for a time, they knew, and the other two horses would stay with him. Their saddles in place and with everything done, the two men mounted. Brick took a last look around the camp.

"If we have to come back it'll be here," he said. "If we don't, some rider is goin' to find a lot of stuff he can use when they move the cattle in here come Fall. Let's go." He started down the canyon and Thad followed.

They took an easy pace for they had plenty of time. Riding north they twice crossed water, taking advantage of the creek banks to stay below the skyline. As dusk descended they came to a pasture fence and knew that they had reached the horse pasture of the Lazy 5. Here they paused and Brick, grinning at Thad, let down perhaps a hundred feet of wire, kicking the strands loose from the posts and placing a rock on them.

"If they haven't got horses up they ain't goin' to have so easy a time catchin' mounts to chase us," he explained, returning to

Thad. "Mebbe their horses will drift through here. It's a good idea, anyhow."

Thad said nothing. Brick seemed to take it for granted that they would be pursued. Indeed he seemed to take this whole thing for granted, the slow ride north, the purpose of the ride, everything. Not so, Thad. Resolved as he was, he had found that carrying out his idea, even these first harmless steps, was not nearly so easy as thinking about it. *Planning* to confront a man with his wickedness, and kill him, and the actual accomplishing of those acts were two entirely different and separate things, and Thad was finding it so. He was tense and nervous, tight as a fiddle string. Two things fought in him: his resolve and hatred and the injustices that had been done him strove against an innate long-cultured respect for law and the sanctity of human life. There was a mighty internal dissension going on inside young Thad Breathea. He did not understand, could not believe, that Brick could be so calm and matter of fact. Brick was taking this as though it were all part of a day's work, a familiar day's work.

"We'll cut across the pasture an' let down some wire on the other side," Brick said easily. "We got plenty of time an' we don't want to come in through the horse pasture anyhow. We want to come down from the west so we can look the layout over."

Thad said nothing and Brick struck toward the west.

Within a few minutes they again came to the fence. Here once more Brick repeated his process of kicking down wire and holding it down with a rock; then, leaving the level country, they struck up toward the rim and, finding the low first bench, followed along it, winding in and out among the cedars that grew profusely. Twenty minutes more they rode and then Brick reined in and Thad stopped beside him.

"There's the layout," Brick said, pointing.

Looking past the cedar behind which they had stopped, and in the direction that Brick pointed, Thad could see the buildings of the Lazy 5 lying under the blue haze of descending dusk.

There were lights dotting the house and the bunkhouse, and the barn and corrals were a darkly sprawling blotch close by.

"We can come in from the south," Brick said, "an' leave our horses in that draw behind the corrals. That way they'll be right where we want 'em when we leave."

Thad gulped down something in his throat. When they left! When they left there would be bodies sprawling on the porch or in the house down there. When they left they would be running, guns hot in their hands, pursuit on their heels. Thad could see Silk Gerald's boots lying in the light from the campfire. He could hear Curly's rasping breathing. He could see . . .

"Why," Brick said in a pleased voice, "the light in the bunkhouse is out. It looks like the boys might be goin' to town. It surely does."

Once more Thad gulped.

"They'd be sittin' around inside playin' pitch or somethin'," Brick continued. "Surely they ain't gone to bed this early."

"Brick," Thad's voice was irresolute, "do you think . . . ?"

"I think it's goin' to be as easy as rollin' off a log," Brick encouraged cheerfully. "Let's ride down off the hill, kid. I don't want to be ridin' over a lot of loose rock an' boulders in the dark. We can get down an' then wait till it's dark."

"All right," Thad answered, the words clogging in his throat. Brick, apparently, did not notice the strangeness in his companion's voice. He set his horse at the slope from the bench and they began their hazardous descent.

It was darker at the bottom than it had been on the bench. Thad found himself following Brick, his horse's nose crowding the tail of Brick's horse. They wound smoothly in and out through the rocks at the bottom of the bench, and then when the rocks gave way to broken, grassy country, Brick dropped down into a draw and followed along it. Presently he stopped and, dismounting, looped a rein around a clump of bear grass and made it fast. Thad, too, dismounted and tied his horse a little distance away from Brick's. He joined his companion to find Brick searching his pockets.

"Where'd I put my chewin'?" Brick muttered. "I . . . oh, here it is." He produced his plug, methodically bit off a portion, tearing the tough tobacco with his strong white teeth, and restored the plug to his pocket. His jaws moved rhythmically and presently he spat. Thad, taking a few steps up the slope, looked over the top toward the buildings. They were dark. Dimly through the fallen night he saw the outlines of barn, bunkhouse, and outsheds.

"Well," Brick was cheerful but he kept his voice low, "let's go, kid. You stop when I tell you."

Brick moved ahead, Thad following him. They came out of the draw and walked across the sodden grass toward the house. The barn shadow was deep and Brick avoided it and kept to the open, Thad following close on his heels.

Along the side of the house opposite the barn they walked and then, reaching the corner, Brick gripped Thad's arm and Thad stopped. He was to stay here, he knew. Brick took two more steps and his boot scraped on hard earth, and on the porch above Thad a voice said:

"Who's there?"

From the night Brick answered evenly. "It's Mahoney."

Up on the porch Krespin spoke. "Come up, then," and a rocker creaked as a man moved.

"No," Brick answered. "I'll stay here. You got word from me?"

Thad could not believe his ears. Brick was asking Krespin if word had come to him. It was preposterous and unbelievable.

"There's just Ben an' me here," Krespin answered. "I've sent the men off like you wanted."

"That's good," Brick's voice was a level drawl. "We can talk business."

Ben Prince said: "You wrote you knew where the Breathea kid is an' that you could deliver him. Where is he?"

Hot anger flooded Thad's whole body. Brick had betrayed him! Brick, of all men! Brick, whom he had trusted, who had brought him here. Who . . . Thad's hand closed around the butt of his holstered gun. Brick was there in front of him not three steps away. Brick . . .

"He's safe," Brick drawled.

On the gun butt Thad's fingers relaxed. He could wait awhile. He would listen.

"You made a mistake sendin' Silk an' Curly after us," Brick continued after a moment's quiet. "You sent boys to do a man's work. They didn't get the job done but Curly an' Silk told me all about it before it was over with."

On the porch a man gasped. That would be Krespin for Prince's voice came immediately, smooth and unflurried. "So they didn't get the job done," he said. "Well, Mahoney, let's do business."

"All right," Brick agreed. "Let's do business. I can deliver the goods. What's yore price?"

"What's your price?" Prince countered.

"Five thousand dollars."

Again from the porch came a sharp intake of breath.

Prince laughed. "Too much money," he stated. "Young Breathea ain't worth it."

"I think he is," Brick drawled. "He's got a claim on this place. He's blood kin to old Jake an' Krespin is a step-son. There's already a suit filed against Krespin on the kid's account, an' you already killed one man over it, Prince. He's worth five thousand, all right."

Thad was bent forward, listening intently. He could not realize that men could bargain so coldly in life. He could not believe what he had heard. Surely this was not so. Surely . . . Why, they were bargaining over him. Out there Brick Mahoney was carrying out a plan that he had told Thad about, and Prince and Krespin were responding as perfectly as though they were reading the written lines of a play.

"You know a lot about it," Prince said.

"I get around," Brick answered with assurance.

"I'm a little curious," Prince announced. "How did you know I killed Croates, Mahoney?"

"I've got friends that tell me things," Brick answered. "Anyhow you killed him."

"He tried to blackmail us!" Krespin was speaking now. "Ben killed him . . ."

"Just like I'd kill you, Mahoney, if you tried to double-cross us," Prince interrupted smoothly. "Is five thousand your last word?"

"It's my last word," Brick said. "We ain't tradin' horses, you know. I've got one price an' I don't come back for more. How about it?"

There was a waiting silence and then Prince said: "How about it, Dale?"

Krespin seemed to choke over his answer. "Five thousand dollars," he said. "It's a lot of money."

"But the job is worth it," Brick reminded.

"I . . ." Krespin hesitated. "I . . . all right; five thousand it is."

Thad had heard enough. He came from his place at the corner of the porch, walking erect, head held rigid, anger seething in him, all his qualms forgotten. Up on the porch Prince said: "Who's that?" sharply, and Brick's voice was a wail as he moved toward Thad.

"Kid! Stay back! Stay *back!*"

Through his anger Thad heard a man call loudly, the voice coming from the opposite end of the porch. "Yo're under arrest. This is Farrel. Prince . . ."

The call was broken by a burst of gunfire. Up on the porch red flame boomed and explosions beat against the night. Thad felt Brick catch his arm and he tore free from the grasp. Past the porch now, Thad looked to his right. The shots from the porch were being answered. Not ten seconds had elapsed since Thad had taken his first step, and yet it seemed as though time stood still and was endless. He caught at his gun, pulled it out and had it halfway raised, the hammer back under his thumb, finger tense on the trigger. Back of him Brick was yelling something, words that Thad did not hear and did not heed. He took another step, the gun fully lifted now, and then the black sky crashed down, engulfing him, blotting out the shots and the round rings of flame that burst at the ends of the gun barrels.

Thad's head was aching with a steady thumping when he opened his eyes. He was looking directly into a lantern and he closed his eyes hastily against the light. The pain in his head momentarily reached out until it seemed that he was all ache, and then subsiding gradually, thumped and stopped and thumped and stopped. Thad risked opening his eyes again, slowly this time, and saw Morgan Vermillion looking down at him, a grin splitting his face below the black mustache. Behind Vermillion was another familiar face, one that Thad had seen often: Wade Althen's face. Thad rolled his head and it hurt, and he was looking at Charlie Farrel. With a start he pushed himself up from the boards on which he lay, panic coming into his eyes.

Charlie Farrel spoke gravely, erasing that panic with his voice. "Take your time, son. You got a pretty hard bump."

Wade Althen, moving from behind Vermillion, put his arms under Thad's shoulders and lifted, and Thad got slowly to his feet.

Vermillion bent down and picked up the lantern and put it on a table beside the lamp, and Thad saw that he was in a room. His shirt clung wetly to his chest and he reached up and pulled it free, looking down at it curiously.

"We doused you with water," Vermillion said conversationally. "Mahoney must have given you a pretty hard lick."

"Brick . . ." Thad said. "He . . . ?"

"Brick," Wade Althen interrupted gravely, "isn't here, Thad. He's gone."

Thad stared about him. Brick had pulled out! Brick . . .

"You see," Althen explained, "he wanted to go to South America, and there were some people that didn't want him to leave. He finished his job here and he's gone." The lawyer stopped and looked defiantly at Charlie Farrel. "And I gave him the money to go on," he announced with gusto.

Farrel grinned. "I'd figured that out," he said.

"Brick an' me," Thad was still in a daze, the sound of his words seeming to come from some distant source and yet he was perfectly sure of what he said, "came here to . . ."

"Brick told us," Althen interrupted. "We know what you intended doing, Thad. But you had friends and they made other plans for you. Prince and Krespin are dead."

"I don't . . ." Thad began, and wavered on his feet.

Vermillion pushed a chair under him and Althen, taking a stand in front of the boy, stood with feet widespread and looked down.

"You don't understand and you don't know what has happened," he said. "I'll tell you, Thad.

"Brick Mahoney left you in camp. He said that he was going to town to get food but really he came to Las Flores to see Mr. Farrel. Brick Mahoney is your friend and he knew what you intended to do. He did not want you to do the thing you planned. He knew that it would be murder and although it might have been justifiable in the light of what had been done to you, still the law would not have seen it that way. Brick did not want you to be killed and he did not want you to lose the heritage that rightfully belongs to you. So he came to Mr. Farrel and Mr. Farrel called me in and we made a plan. With what Gerald and Winters had told Mahoney, and what we already knew, we believed . . ."

"But . . ." Thad's eyes were wild as he interrupted, "Brick didn't . . ."

"Mahoney assured us that he killed both those men in self defense," Althen said sternly. "He said that you could vouch for the fact. Now please listen to me, Thad. We believed that Prince had killed a man named Croates. We could not prove it because Prince had an alibi, but Croates had attempted to blackmail Krespin with the lost letter your father had written. Mr. Farrel was anxious to prove that murder, so Mahoney offered to come here and bargain with Krespin and Prince for your life. Mr. Farrel and Mr. Vermillion and myself were to be hidden near by and listen to the conversation. Our scheme was carried out just as we had planned, but you almost spoiled it. You started out from where you were hidden and Mahoney had to stop you. I heard him call to you but you kept right on, so he knocked you out with the barrel of his gun. Prince resisted arrest when Mr. Farrel called to him, and was killed. Dale Krespin died sitting in his chair and there is no mark on him. Apparently his heart was bad." The pudgy little lawyer stopped. He had been lecturing Thad exactly as a didactic teacher might lecture a pupil.

Thad's gaze was centered upon the floor as he tried to put things in order, tried to comprehend what Judge Althen had told him.

"An' everything's all right, son," Morgan Vermillion rumbled. "You aren't wanted by the law any more. You've got a clean bill of health. Ain't that right, Charlie?"

"That's right," Farrel agreed. "You're in the clear, son."

"Brick's gone?" Thad asked. He could not quite realize that Brick Mahoney was not with him. It did not seem possible that Brick was not there.

Althen seemed to read some implied criticism in the question. "Brick Mahoney is the best friend you ever had or ever will have!" he snapped testily. "He stayed until this thing was finished. He put his own head into a noose to keep you from committing murder or being killed. He's gone. And I'm glad he's free and that he got away!"

Farrel's lips twitched into a tight smile as he looked at the lawyer. "You ain't the only one," he drawled. "An' . . . Judge . . ."

"Yes?" Althen snapped.

"I didn't want Mahoney very bad," Farrel concluded softly. "There's a lot of things to do around here before this mess is cleaned up. We've got to go to town as soon as it's light enough to travel. Can you fellows give me a hand?" He included Althen and Vermillion in his glance.

Vermillion nodded, but Althen turned toward Thad Breathea. "How about . . .?" he began.

"Come on, Judge," Farrel ordered, nodding his head toward the door. "I'll need you, too." He walked out, Vermillion and Althen following him.

Wise old Charlie Farrel. He knew that there were times when a man needed to be alone to think things out, to digest what he has learned, to recover from shock and clear his dazed mind and return to normal thinking once more. The footsteps of the three echoed in the hall as Thad Breathea sat stock still and stared blankly at the wall. Gradually the thoughts began to order themselves in his mind.

He was free! No more running away, no more pursuit, no more stealing through the night, no more riding the rims and the pinnacles. Free and clear!

Thad Breathea lifted his head and in the light of the lamp that Farrel had left on the table, his eyes were very bright and very clear.

CHAPTER NINETEEN

Snow on the Plaza

THERE was snow in the plaza of Las Flores and the cottonwood trees that made a pleasant shade in summer were gaunt skeletons of themselves. Thad Breathea, coming up from the courthouse, stopped on the corner and looked across the square. There, opposite where he now stood, beyond the snow-covered grass, a kid had held three horses short months ago. Out of the brick bank men had come running and mounting those horses had galloped out of town amidst a burst of gun fire. Just a short time ago, just a little while.

As Thad stood there on the corner, remembering, Shorty Coventry came from the post office and, perceiving Thad, made bowlegged progress toward his friend. As administrator of the estate of Jake Breathea, deceased, Morgan Vermillion had placed Shorty at the Lazy 5. Everyone knew Morgan Vermillion,

everyone trusted him, everyone believed in him. Morgan Vermillion had that valued thing, power. Not the power of wealth
or of great possessions but the power that comes from the confidence of many people. Thad remembered how the judge had
smiled as he said: "I appoint you Administrator, Mr. Vermillion. I have no doubt but that you can straighten out all this
affair."

Shorty strode up to Thad, stopped, and from the pocket of
his sheepskin, produced two letters. He handed them to Thad.

"I got the mail," he said. "I had a letter from Morgan. They
want us to come over for Christmas."

Thad took the letters and nodded.

"Does that mean we'll go?" Shorty asked.

"Yeah," Thad agreed, "you just bet we'll go! Charlie is going
to have supper with us tonight, Shorty, and we'll stay over at his
place. We'll go back down to the ranch tomorrow."

Shorty grinned. "Charlie is kind of celebratin'," he announced. "I heard that Lon Popples had been let out as city
marshal by the town council. That kind of suits Charlie."

Thad, answering Shorty's smile with one of his own, inserted
a forefinger under the flap of an envelope and ripped it open.
The letter was from Wade Althen and after a brief discussion
of certain business connected with the estate, concluded with
an invitation to spend Christmas with him at Fort Blocker. If
Thad could not come, then Althen would take the train to Las
Flores and spend Christmas with Thad. Thad's smile broadened.
He would write to the Judge and tell him to come up to Las
Flores. They would all go to the Flying V Bar for Christmas.

"That other letter has got some kind of a foreign stamp on it,
Thad," Shorty said. "Save it for me, will you?"

Thad nodded as he ripped open the other envelope. Unfold-
ing the letter he read the scrawled page, and now he smiled in
earnest for this was the final touch to his happiness. As he read,
two women, one big and still retaining a blowsy sort of beauty,
the other smaller and henna-haired, entered the square and
walked toward him. Lulu and Pearl! They passed behind Thad

without his seeing them, but Shorty Coventry favored the pair with a long, bold stare.

"That's him," Lulu said, after they had passed. "That's young Breathea."

"He's sure good lookin'," Pearl announced admiringly. "Do you think . . .?"

"He'll never come to my place," Lulu snapped. "The lucky stiff! He's got all the friends in the world. Why, do you know what happened? The Colonel came down and told me I had to tell Farrel all about Ten High, that's what he did! and it was on account of that kid there, too. Farrel made the Colonel do it. He knows that the Colonel owns my place. Why . . ."

Pearl had stopped and was shamelessly looking back. Lulu, returning a short step, took her companion's arm. "You weren't listenin' to me at all," Lulu charged. "You didn't hear what I said."

"Gee," Pearl murmured, "he's good lookin'."

Thad read the letter through. "Dear Kid:" it began, the letters of the words big and round as though formed by a child. "I got here all right. I come down on a boat that hauled some registered bulls and we was both seasick. I am sorry I had to hit you on the head but you would of run out and gotten yourself shot so I put my handkerchief around my gun and hit you. I am going to hook up with a big outfit down here to run their pure-bred herd of shorthorns. They don't think my one arm is a handycap and they treat me fine. If you want to write me my address is 55 Calle Laguna Hermosa care of Sr. Cristobal M y D Benevides, Buenos Aires, Argentina, S. A. That is some address. I wish now we had done like we planned in Franklin and come here together we would of had a lot of fun. Some day you and me will get together again. No hard feelings about the head. Your friend, Brick."

"Who's it from?" Shorty asked.

"Brick," Thad answered, a far-away look in his eyes.

"Oh," said Shorty.

Up the street two women entered a store.

Across the plaza the wind picked up a bit of snow and whipped it, scurrying away. The sky was lead and heavy where the clouds hung low and the wind was biting. Thad did not feel the sting of the wind. He was gazing into distance, not at the sky, nor the snow nor the white expanse of the plaza; but back through time, back to a green, frightened, hunted kid and a red-haired man who stood sturdily by that boy's side.

"Some day you and me will get together again." Some day! The day would never come. Vaguely Thad realized that, but it was good to know that Brick was living, that Brick, like Thad Breathea, no longer ran before the law. It was good to know that somewhere in the world there was a man like Brick, a man who stood up, who went with you and who when you looked was always by your side.

"Let's go," Thad Breathea said to Shorty Coventry. "Charlie will be waiting at the restaurant."

Bennett Foster was born in Omaha, Nebraska, and came to live in New Mexico in 1916 to attend the State Agricultural College and remained there the rest of his life. He served in the U.S. Navy during the Great War and was stationed in the Far East during the Second World War, where he attained the rank of captain in the U.S. Air Corps. He was working as the principal of the high school in Springer, New Mexico, when he sold his first short story, *Brockleface,* to *West Magazine* in 1930 and proceeded to produce hundreds of short stories and short novels for pulp magazines as well as *The Country Gentleman* and *Cosmopolitan* over the next three decades. In the 1950s his stories regularly appeared in *Collier's.* In the late 1930s and early 1940s Foster wrote a consistently fine and critically praised series of Western novels, serialized in *Argosy* and Street & Smith's *Western Story Magazine*, that were subsequently issued in hardcover book editions by William Morrow and Company and Doubleday, Doran and Company in the Double D series. It is worth noting that Foster's early Double D Westerns were published under the pseudonym John Trace, although some time later these same titles, such as *Trigger Vengeance* and *Range of Golden Hoofs*, appeared in the British market under his own name. Foster knew the terrain and people of the West first-hand from a lifetime of living there. His stories are invariably authentic in detail and color, from the region of fabulous mesas, jagged peaks, and sun-scorched deserts. Among the most outstanding of his sixteen published Western novels are *Badlands* (1938), *Rider of the Rifle Rock* (1939), and *Winter Quarters* (1942), this last a murder mystery within the setting of a Wild West Show touring the western United States. As a storyteller he was always a master of suspenseful and unusual narratives.